Susan Castillo Street

CU00828304

Casket Girls

To Sue,
with love and admiration.

Susan

24 July 2019

PaPer
Swans
Press

Paper Swans Press

77 Cambrian Road

Tunbridge Wells, TN4 9HJ

Original text © Susan Castillo Street

Cover design by Susan Castillo Street

First published by Paper Swans Press 2019

ISBN 978-1-9160529-0-1

Printed and bound by 4edge Limited

www.paperswans.co.uk

For David

and for my grandchildren

I have learned, over the course of an eventful academic career, that the best work is a combination of careful archival research and passion for our subject. *Casket Girls* builds on research I have carried out as a scholar, but it also reflects some of my own passions: the possibility and desirability of genuine friendship between women of different ethnic, racial and social backgrounds; the importance of economic independence for women; and a commitment to social justice.

When I decided to write a novel and was casting around for a subject, it occurred to me that the Casket Girls would offer the opportunity to explore these concepts and flesh them out. The title of *Casket Girls* refers to the *filles a la cassette:* young women of good birth but without family or financial resources, who were sent by King Louis XV of France in 1728 to New Orleans under the auspices of the Ursuline nuns as prospective brides for the unruly colonists (even then, New Orleans had a reputation for licentiousness). The cassette or casket refers to the little trunks they were given to carry their trousseau to Louisiana. One of the conditions under which the Ursulines were allowed to found a Convent was that they would be required to educate, not just gently reared young women in the colony, but also Native Americans, prostitutes, and enslaved women.

I felt that it would be interesting in *Casket Girls* to explore the interaction between these young Frenchwomen and other young women with a very different backstory. The novel tells about of four of them: Sidonie, a bookish young Frenchwoman who wants to be a teacher; her friend Joelle, also a Casket Girl, who dreams of marriage to a wealthy planter; Immaculata, a deranged nun; and Palmyre, an enslaved woman. They are faced with Convent life and its limitations, sexual violence, and the horrors of slavery.

Writing about these subjects does pose challenges of its own. One of which I am very aware is the danger of what is described as 'wetting one's pen in the blood of others.' Many of the events depicted in *Casket Girls* are based on actual eyewitness accounts of historical events. In episodes dealing with the violence lying beneath the surface of Southern history and the beauty of the Southern landscape, I am aware of the danger of descriptions of violence which could be seen as unpleasantly voyeuristic or titillating. At the same time, however, I have deliberately avoided depicting a South of moonlight, magnolias and happy slaves strumming banjos, which would distort historical reality. When we look at what actually happened, we quickly reach the following conclusion: you really could *not* make it up.

Susan Castillo Street

Part One

New Orleans 1728

Chapter 1

Sister Immaculata

It is hard to believe that these foolish girls are nearly my own age. All they think about are adventures, men, and trying to look pretty. I gave up on that long ago, even before I became a postulant. I was sallow, scrawny, graceless, cursed with a wart on my left nostril that made it look as though a drop of black snot was hanging there. My mother looked at me when I was small and sighed. 'Good looks aren't everything, Zezette,' she said. 'Pretty is as pretty does.' But I have to confess that I used to look wistfully at the images of Our Lady in the village church. I wanted with all my heart to resemble her, to be pink and blonde and untouchable.

But I wasn't. Every day I worked hard on my family's farm near Rouen along with my cousin Jacques. There I fed the pigs and cleaned the stables like a man. Not that anyone ever gave me any thanks. My father died of apoplexy one evening. He was sitting in his usual place at the head of the dinner table, and fell over face first into the *cassoulet*. I knew that he had been worried about money, because the last three harvests had been meagre. After his death we learned that he had borrowed heavily from the local *Casse d'Epargne*, and that we would lose the farmhouse and our lands. My mother followed him soon after.

On the advice of the local priest, I went to the Ursuline convent near Rouen. There was nowhere else. I did my best to impress the Sisters with my piety. I mortified the flesh, wore my shoes on the wrong feet, bound my breasts tight with sackcloth, fasted until I became even scrawnier than before. Mother Jerome, the Mother Superior of the Convent, was touched by what she thought was my fervour, but told me that excessive piety and self-denial ran the risk of toppling over into Pride, which was one of the Seven Deadly Sins. Of course, I told this to the Jesuit who was our confessor. He yawned and prescribed ten Hail Marys. But I continued in the solitude of my cell to rip my fingernails down to the quick, to flagellate my legs with a leather belt. I was convinced that in this way I would imitate the sufferings of Our Lord and travel further down the road to godly perfection and sainthood. I always knew that I was different from the rest, was destined for heroic things if I could tame the weaknesses of my mortal flesh and purge every vestige of sin.

Finally, the Sisters decided to admit me as a Postulant. We were allowed to suggest three names, since we were beginning a new life and becoming a new person. Some of the nuns had chosen names of male saints, like Mother Jerome. Others opted for names embodying Christian virtues and Christian faith, like Sister Fidelis. But there was only one name that held appeal for me.

'Immaculata,' I said. 'I want to be like Our Lady, a virgin, apart from men and all their filthy habits.' Mother

Jerome sighed, but in the end she gave in. She saw that once my mind was made up, I could be stubborn as a Breton mule.

Brittany seemed a world away now. I looked out at the ship that was rounding a bend in the channel, drawing closer to our little flotilla. It looked like a ghostly apparition. The swamp landscape of Louisiana, with its wisps of mist and moss, its strange animal sounds and furtive splashes, was unfamiliar and sinister. It felt as though the trees were listening. I felt a prickling at the back of my neck.

When the other ship, called the *Bon Espoir*, drew abreast, I was staggered by the hideous stench that came from its hold. It reminded me of the fumes emanating from the slaughterhouse at the edge of my village back home in France, a noxious mixture of the ferrous reek of blood and the more pungent one of *merde*. There followed a brief exchange between our captain and the captain of the other vessel. I didn't understand much of what was said, but gathered from the little I could overhear that it was mostly about the depth and navigability of the channel. I shivered as the *Bon Espoir* floated off into a side channel and was lost in the mist.

One of the sailors, a young man with a pink boyish face, saw me standing at the rail. 'A blackbirder. Pray for them, Sister,' he said. 'They're going to jettison some of the cargo before they reach New Orleans.'

'What's a blackbirder? And what cargo do you mean?' I asked.

'A slave ship,' he said. 'About half of the slaves are dead.'

Sidonie

Joelle and I looked out at the banks slipping by as our boat sailed upriver toward New Orleans. The land was flat, and at times it seemed that the water was melting into the sky. Gradually we moved into a cavern of trees in what I knew must be a swamp. I had never seen a swamp before, though I had read about them in our geography classes back in France, and hardly knew what to think. It was a dim space, with moss hanging down from cypress trees, and in the distance I could hear the cries of strange birds. It had an eerie beauty.

Joelle sighed. 'Sidonie, what do you think will happen when we arrive? Will we be auctioned off like cattle? What will the men in New Orleans be like?'

I patted her hand. 'I just don't know,' I admitted. 'I cannot believe that the Sisters would force us to accept someone against our will. And, of course, if all else fails there's the choice to become nuns ourselves.'

Joelle burst out laughing. 'Me, a nun? Joelle had been in the convent for six years, since she was eleven years old. She was blonde, red-lipped, with a throaty laugh that made the nuns frown. Most of Joelle's family had died in a typhoid outbreak in Marseilles, and she knew that she could not go to live with her sister Claude. There was only one uncle, with a large family of his own, who was unable to take her in. He was adamant, however, that his niece should find a refuge that would safeguard her virtue; he was all too aware of what might happen on the streets of Marseilles to a pretty young girl with no visible means of support. So off she went to the Ursulines.

'Well, no,' I admitted. 'But you do realise that we will be forced to choose between marrying or finding work of some sort, either as servants or maybe as teachers, if the Sisters found a school as they say they will.'

'Perhaps,' she said, pouting. 'But I will not worry about that until the time comes. And what about you, Miss Know-It-All? Which of these things would you choose?'

I shrugged. 'Perhaps teaching,' I replied. I could see myself with a classroom of Indian girls, teaching them to read stories of the saints. The Sisters had told us that one of the main purposes of building a school would be to provide instruction for the Heathen and bring them to Christ. While I was not particularly pious, I loved the vision of myself in a teacher's pinafore, hair pulled back, hands dusty with chalk. So far, the few men I had encountered had not shown much inclination to pursue a deeper acquaintance with a young woman with a passion for reading and for speaking her mind. I was tall and lanky, and I had no illusions that throngs of beaux would be vying for my hand. I looked out into the mist. "Joelle,' I asked, 'suppose that we could be anything we wanted, anything at all. What do you really want to be? '

Joelle thought for a minute. 'I'd want to be a lady with beautiful gowns and a handsome husband and several children. What about you, Sidonie?'

'I want to be a hero,' I said without hesitation. The nuns did not approve of novels, but I had read *Don Quixote* in a copy one of the younger nuns had smuggled into the convent. 'I want to right wrongs and slay dragons. And I want to have adventures.'

As the banks flowed by, I recalled the long voyage from France. I am not a good sailor, and after so many weeks at sea I was longing to reach Louisiana. Mother Jerome and the other nuns had brought me water, given me food, chided me when I could not keep it down. I touched my own mother's silver crucifix, now hanging between my breasts, remembering how I had prayed that Our Lady would bring us safe across the water.

I could hardly remember my mother. She, my father, and my two brothers had died in a cholera epidemic when I was only four. I do not know what would have become of me if Mother Jerome and the Ursulines had not taken me in. I thought now with longing of the convent near Rouen, of the calm of the cloisters, the symmetry of the gardens. It seemed so far away.

It took us nearly five months to reach Louisiana. We sailed from Lorient in February on the *Gironde*, and only reached the mouth of the Mississippi in August. We girls and the nuns had occupied a space apart from the other passengers, between decks, about eighteen feet long and seven feet wide, with one small porthole the size of a man's hand. When we opened it to get some air, sea water poured in and our bunks were soaked. There were eighteen of us, with six beds on each side, three bunks stacked one over the other. The nuns spoke to us of the beautiful land where we were heading, the handsome men we would marry, the wonderful families we would create. This, when we were retching into buckets, sounded like a distant fairytale.

I had overheard some of the older nuns talking in the convent back in France. For the last several months, our meals had become even more austere, and I knew that the Sisters were feeling pinched financially. Perhaps that's why the Order had proposed the establishment of a convent in New Orleans, this new settlement on the Mississippi River. Wily Mother Jerome had managed to gain financial support for this undertaking by pointing out to the Bishop that it would be to France's advantage to provide stability and decency to what was rapidly gaining a reputation as its most unruly and licentious colony. She added that the nuns of her Order had experience in tending the sick, and that they could found a Hospital and a school as well.

The Ursulines believed in educating girls like us. Mother Jerome had told us of the colony's strategic importance for France, since its location at the mouth of a great river that penetrated to the heart of the American continent was ideal for trade. I had always loved our geography classes, and this to me made good sense. We had learned about trade centres and

15

markets in the convent back in France. What made less sense to me was Mother Jerome's argument that the turbulent character of New Orleans, whose settlers were mostly male, would be transformed by the arrival of marriageable young women of good character. I knew that for the Ursulines, who had given refuge to vulnerable young women and many orphans like myself, it was an ideal solution: it would alleviate their financial difficulties while allowing them to salve their consciences and assure themselves that they were doing the right thing for us by getting us off their hands. Each of us was given a small trunk, a *cassette,* containing the linens and clothing that would become our dowry. This is how we became known as the Casket Girls, the *filles á la cassette.*

At the mouth of the Mississippi, they transferred us to a shallop and two pirogues, since the deep-bottomed vessel we crossed the Atlantic on could not reach New Orleans. Ten of us, including my friend Joelle and myself, went in the pirogues along with two of the younger nuns, Sister Marie-Joseph and Sister Immaculata. The heat descended on our shoulders like a thick wool cloak, dripping water. The air was so warm and humid that it felt as though I could drink it. I could see that the blue of the Gulf now contained streaks of muddy brown clouds. 'Why is the water like that?' I asked Sister Marie-Joseph. She smiled. 'It's the river, *Cherie.* The great river that comes from the heart of the continent. It's because of this river that New Orleans, *la Nouvelle Orleans*, exists.'

I wondered what to expect there. I was seventeen years old, and for the last three years it had been made increasingly clear to me that the Sisters expected me to think about marrying and forming a family. I had no surviving relatives. While I had nothing against marriage, and while I sometimes thought wistfully of having a family of my own, I loved my studies of history and languages, and reading and writing were a source of great joy. But I was aware that, in the world outside the convent, there weren't many opportunities for women to enjoy books and writing.

The alternatives did not seem very appealing to me. Some of the older orphans had whispered about men and the things they did. Joelle, who was my best friend, told me about her sister Claude, who had married ten years ago at the age of sixteen, and who already had six children. Her husband was a farmer who had been affected by droughts, and he shouted at her and the children and drank more than he should. Claude, who had been a beautiful and spirited girl, now often appeared with bruises around her eyes and neck, her shoulders stooped. This is not what I wanted for myself. I knew that I had no religious vocation; indeed, I often felt guilty about how impatient I felt with the nuns and their droning litanies. But they had taken me in, and I felt a certain fondness for some of the older Sisters.

Suddenly, one of the sailors called out. In the narrow channel, amid the cypress trees, another ship came into view. Sister Immaculata looked back toward Joelle and me. In her black habit, belted in with a leather girdle, and her black wimple and veil, she resembled a bedraggled carrion crow. 'Enough nonsense, girls,' she hissed, in a tone that brooked no argument.

Chapter 2

Sidonie

I still remember our first sight of New Orleans. It was early morning, and mist was rising like steam from the river. Everything here seemed moist and dense: the heat, the air, the light. There was a central square, flanked by churches and low brick houses, and in the distance a line of thick dark forest. Despite the hour, the sun was already pouring down like honey. I felt my pulse quicken.

The trip upriver was arduous. It took us three days and two nights to reach our destination. Our captain had decided to send some of us ahead in two pirogues, since they were faster vessels, in order to announce the arrival of the sloop with the remaining passengers. We embarked with four girls in each boat, accompanied by a nun, with a sailor to navigate. The boat rocked as I jumped in, and when we pulled away from the *Gironde* it felt as though we were leaving the last tangible link to France. We camped on the riverbanks at night, since the darkness was so warm and thick that we could not see to navigate. At first, this appealed to my sense of adventure. Soon, however, we were attacked by clouds of mosquitoes. I felt a guilty sense of relief that the mosquitoes seemed to prefer Joelle's pale fair skin to my own. Since the trees and undergrowth were so dense, we were forced to camp right on the riverbank. On the last night, there was a thunderstorm, and we were all drenched to the bone.

Now, as we drew close to the quay, I could make out the figure of a tall black-robed Jesuit. Even from a distance, I could sense that he radiated an air of command: he walked tall, with his head held high, and I could see that the people around him listened to what he had to say. He had dark hair and pale skin. I was suddenly aware of my bedraggled, mud-spattered state.

Sister Marie-Joseph was the first to alight. The priest extended his hand to assist her. 'Sisters,' he said, 'we feared that you had been lost at sea, and prayed that Our Saviour would bring you safely here. It is good to welcome you to New Orleans at last.'

Sister Marie-Joseph blushed to the roots of her hair. She lowered her head and bobbed in something between a curtsy and a genuflexion. 'We are grateful for His protection, Reverend Father and for your prayers. I presume that you are Reverend Father Luc Beaubois, *n'est-ce pas?*'

'Indeed I am, Sister. And you are?'

'Sister Marie-Joseph, of the Ursuline order. We have come to announce the arrival of another pirogue and a sloop with passengers.' She glanced back at us. 'As you can see, we were caught in the storm.'

'Ah yes,' said Father Beaubois. I'd heard the older nuns speak about him at the convent back in Rouen. He was said to be charismatic, at times abrasive, a man who said what he was thinking. 'And these are the *filles á la cassette*? *Pauvres petites.*' I knew that our faces and clothing were filthy, but I did not like one bit being called a poor little thing. 'Your quarters are still under construction, so for now you will have to stay in the building where I am housed. Please follow me.'

The building where we would be living until the Convent was constructed was built in the *columbage*, half-timbered style, over two floors, with a small bell tower at one end. On the ground floor were a small chapel, a kitchen, and several rooms, which, we were informed, would provide provisional space for the Ursuline school. There were some small cells for the cloistered choir nuns, and a few spartan rooms for the Casket Girls and converse nuns. We would be sharing five to a room. Our rooms were narrow and austere, with white walls, rough wooden floors, iron beds with straw mattresses, and a slop jar for our nightly needs. I noticed that the windows had no glass, but were covered with light muslin cloth, which would let in a bit of light and, I hoped, keep the local mosquitoes from feasting on our blood. Across the courtyard was a small wing where Father Beaubois, who would be administering to our spiritual needs, lived.

I drew the cloth back and sunlight flooded in. When I stood on tiptoe and looked out, I could see a courtyard, backed by an unruly garden and three wild trees of enormous height and girth, and a profusion of flowers I didn't recognise. I imagined the courtyard filled with flowerpots: geraniums, bougainvillea, roses, and thought with longing of the Convent garden back in Rouen. There we had mostly cultivated vegetables: potatoes, onions, garlic, cabbages, carrots. I had finally convinced Mother Jerome to allow me to plant flowers by suggesting that we could use them to adorn the Chapel altar. Sister Immaculata had commented that flowers were a concession to vanity and sensuality, and indeed there was something lush and carnal about my camellias and my lilies. But I loved my flowers and stroked their petals with the tip of my finger when I was unobserved.

Sister Joseph clapped her hands. 'Girls,' she said, 'today we will begin by giving a thorough clean to our new home, and to our persons. Remember: cleanliness is next to godliness! There are pails and soap by the fountain in the courtyard. If I am satisfied with your efforts, we may take a walk to look at the building that will be our convent one day.'

I was glad to discover that I'd be sharing a room with Joelle, along with two other Casket Girls, Berthe and Josiane, but less pleased to learn that Sister Immaculata would occupy one of the beds. Back in Rouen I had found Immaculata's relentless negativity wearing, and there was something about her that made my skin crawl. She smelled of unwashed flesh. I chided myself for this unchristian attitude, and began to put away my few things, placing my little trunk under the bed. Joelle hummed as she put away her clothes and began to sweep the floor, and Berthe bustled about with a feather duster. Josiane sat in a corner, looking dully into space. I knew she missed home and was finding the summer heat oppressive.

Sister Immaculata began to mop the floor, muttering under her breath. I'd chosen the bed furthest from hers. In the Louisiana heat a coppery odour of sweat emanated from her in waves that made me want to retch. Again, I felt remorse for my lack of tolerance.

Later that afternoon, when it was a bit cooler, we walked down the street in an orderly line, two by two, modestly dressed, eyes cast down. Sister Fidelis walked at the head with Reverend Father Beaubois, while Sister Immaculata brought up the rear. Father Beaubois set off at a brisk pace. He turned down the Rue Bienville toward the river. When we reached the quay, we could see fishing trawlers hawking their wares: oysters, mussels, perch, and a large fish I'd never seen before. There was a small market with women selling vegetables of different sorts. Some of them were darker-skinned and I asked myself if I was seeing my first Indians. Behind me, Sister Immaculata tutted. *'Sauvagesses '*, she said. One was burning sage, and I breathed in its smoky unfamiliar scent. I turned to Joelle. 'Do you think the Indian women and their children will come to our School?' Joelle shrugged. 'Perhaps. It doesn't matter to me if they do or they don't, because by the time the school is up and running, I shall be a married woman. All you think about is boring school, school, school.'

'And all you think about is marriage,' I retorted. As we walked along the riverbank, we came across a shocking spectacle. A woman with jet-black hair was bent over a wooden horse, stripped to the waist. To the right, a group of soldiers was queueing to give her lashes. She was near my own age, and the sight of what was happening filled me with horror. 'Why is she being punished, Sister?' I cried to Sister Immaculata. 'What has she done?'

'Look away,' hissed Immaculata. 'She is a *putain*. New Orleans is full of them. The Governor has decreed that they are to be whipped by all the soldiers of the regiment. And quite right too.' In the Convent in Rouen, we had heard of such women, but I had never seen a *putain* in the flesh. I cringed as I heard her cries and the rough laughter of the soldiers. I felt Joelle shudder at the sight of the red welts on the woman's back.

Further along, we turned inland to walk along the Rue Saint-Adrien. Most of the houses were low, made of brick, with courtyards in back. I breathed in the heady scent of roses and orange blossoms. I could hear in the distance a sound of hammering and the cries of street vendors. Father Beaubois indicated that we should follow him down the Rue de Chartres. He pointed to a plot of land partly covered by weeds and brambles. In the centre, we could see that the process of clearing the land had begun. 'Sisters, *mademoiselles*, here is where the Ursuline Convent will be.'

'Can you tell us what it will be like, Father,' said Sister Fidelis, looking up through her eyelashes at Father Beaubois. He shrugged. 'It will be much larger than the quarters where you are housed. It will be made of brick, half-timbered, with a bell tower in the middle. There will be spaces for a small infirmary, and for the School.'

'Reverend Father,' I asked, 'what sort of students do you think will come to the School?' He seemed taken aback that a mere girl like me had dared to ask a question and looked at me as though he only now had noticed my existence. But then he answered, 'Many sorts. There will be young women from the surrounding farms. Before, they had to be sent to France, but now they can remain here for their education. Your Superior has also agreed to offer classes for the *sauvagesses* and the *negresses*, and for some of the women of irregular conduct here in New Orleans.'

Behind me, I felt Sister Immaculata recoil. 'Reverend Father Beaubois,' she exclaimed, 'surely our Superior cannot have agreed to expose our young women of good character to the lascivious customs of these creatures.'

Father Beaubois looked at her, and I was struck by the directness of his gaze. 'Sister, remember the story of St. Mary Magdalene, who was the first to discover that Our Lord had risen from the dead. And remember Christ's teaching: cast not the first stone.'

Immaculata lowered her head, but I sensed her fury and revulsion.

Sister Immaculata

When we reached our quarters in New Orleans, I dropped my bundle on the cot and looked down at my hands.

25

They were big and square. They were calloused from all the farm work I had done, with black river mud under my fingernails. I knew that I stank. However, vanity is a sin, so I resolved to begin by mopping the wooden floor of my room, turning the mattress, scrubbing the walls. I left washing myself for last. We had been given some rough linen sheets, and I scrubbed my hands and forearms before making the bed. I didn't want to stain the whiteness of the sheets. I felt jealous of the cloister nuns, who had their own cells. I, however, was forced to share with three silly girls. This was not fair, and it rankled.

Later, Father Beaubois presided over a mass of thanksgiving for our safe arrival in a small chapel next to the Refectory. When it was over, we went out to the courtyard. Sister Fidelis clapped her hands. 'Girls,' she said, 'Reverend Father Beaubois has agreed to take us on a walk to see our future Convent.' A murmur of excitement arose. She went on, 'I wish, however, for you to remember to avert your eyes if you see things that are not meant for young ladies. There is much sinfulness in this city, and New Orleans is truly the Devil's Empire!' She pursed her lips. 'There are many women of a certain sort.'

In the previous days, as we headed upriver, Sister Joseph had said as much to me. She confided that she had heard rumours that most of the women in New Orleans had come from brothels and houses of correction, sent there by the Company of the Indies. I shuddered. It would be a challenge not to allow ourselves and our young charges to be seduced by the vice and debauchery we would see all around.

The idea of an empire ruled by the Devil was very real to me. For whatever reason, it made me think of my younger cousin Jacques, of the clumsy way in which he had touched me in the darkness of my father's barn. Jacques was not a devil, but a rough insignificant farm boy. I, on the other hand, knew that there was a Devil inside me. I had to constantly be on guard against the lure of his dark power. I remembered how the Devil would take me over and enter my body when Jacques and I tumbled amid the straw. One night, when the moon was high, I took him to the hayloft, threw him onto the straw. At first, he struggled, but I held his wrists and straddled him. 'I don't want...' he whimpered, but I slapped him hard. 'You don't know what you want, fool!' In the dark, I howled and laughed and bucked and rode him like a broomstick, made him want me in the end. When it was over, I saw the he was crying, took him in my arms, and crooned a lullaby under my breath. Jacques looked at me in the shadows He pulled away in horror and crossed himself. 'What are you, Zezette?' he cried. After that he avoided me and refused to do the milking if I was around.

In the convent back in France, the choir nuns used to look down their noses at girls like me. They were the daughters of landowners, rich bourgeois tradesmen, even nobles. Sister Fidelis and I were both converse nuns from farming stock, with worn hands and rough skin. I had always envied the choir nuns and felt resentful about my status as a converse nun. Now, as we prepared to go out into the streets of New Orleans, I realised that my converse status could have its advantages. The choir nuns would be expected to do all the teaching, to remain cloistered and not venture out into the wider world. Converse nuns like me, however, would be able to venture outside the convent walls to deal with tradesmen and the like. I repressed a smile of anticipation. Back on the farm, I'd always wanted to do heroic things like men did in the wider world. When I saw that wasn't going to happen, I'd thought the convent would help me become a hero of a different kind. But now I'd be able to go out and barter and explore the real world on my own. I had always dreamed of having my own shop, and it would be interesting to see what sort of shops there were in this backward colonial outpost.

The first weeks in New Orleans passed in a haze. Though I was used to hard work on the farm, I was worn out at the end of the day. It was all very well for Mother Jerome and Sister Marie-Joseph to sit and pray as rosaries dripped through their long white fingers, while I scrubbed floors and moved chairs to prepare for our first students.

The schoolroom had white walls, pine floors, and some rough low tables which would serve as desks. Mother Jerome called me in one morning. 'Immaculata, we shall need to prepare out classroom. There will be around 25 students. We are going to receive our first students in only three days, so we shall need to ensure that the classroom is spotlessly clean.' I reflected that this 'we' was of the royal sort, since Mother

Jerome was not going to lift a finger, and expected me to sweep and mop the floors, move the desks, wash the walls. 'Yes, Mother Jerome,' I said. She must have detected a shade of insolence in my tone, because she looked at me through hooded eyes, but said nothing. For her, I was an insect, a creature beneath her notice.

Sister Fidelis had been placed in charge of cooking, and I was expected to help there as well. This morning we were making *calas,* or rice *beignets.* Sister Fidelis had soaked the rice in water and yeast. She had promised to teach me to cook. 'Immaculata, bring me five eggs,' she said. 'Now, break them into this bowl. Then beat them and add this to the rice mixture.'

I did as she said. There was something deeply satisfying about rapping the eggs against the counter, then gently pulling apart the shell. The sun was pouring through the window and, in the distance, I could hear the barking of a dog. 'Sister Fidelis,' I asked, 'what made you decide to join the Ursulines?'

Fidelis sighed. She was a pretty girl, on the plump side, with dimples in her cheeks. 'I wanted to dedicate my life to the Lord,' she said. I knew that she was being evasive.

'Well so do we all,' I retorted. 'But there must have been some other reason.'

She began to drop spoonfuls of dough into hot oil, and the kitchen was filled with the scent of nutmeg and vanilla. 'I was engaged to be married,' she said, 'to the son of a neighbour. He died.' Her eyes filled. 'Now it's your turn. Drop the *calas* into the oil, and when they turn golden, remove them and place them here on this plate.'

Sister Fidelis, if truth be told, was the only person I'd ever encountered who bothered to be kind to me.

Chapter 3

Sidonie

Shortly after our arrival to New Orleans, Mother Jerome ordered the preparation of a room as infirmary, since part of the agreement allowing the Ursulines to settle in New Orleans involved caring for the sick. I had overheard her talking to Sister Marie-Joseph about the complicated negotiations she had undergone with the Jesuits back in France and admired her shrewdness. She knew the population of the colony was largely male, and the colonists' reputation for brawling and general bad conduct had become notorious. What was uppermost in the mind of Mother Jerome and the Ursulines was the conversion of the Indians, but she knew that in order for them to be allowed to carry out their missionary activities, she would have to offer the colonial authorities and the Jesuits some trade-offs—which turned out to be the commitment to found a school and a hospital. Our current quarters were cramped, so finding a place that could be used as a sickroom was a challenge. The solution was to use the attic, which had many disadvantages. It was dark and stiflingly hot.

A week before our school was due to open, two of the Sisters came down with a fever. The climate of New Orleans, the tropical heat and the stagnant river air, were a breeding ground for fevers, and I had heard the sailors on the *Gironde* talk about previous epidemics of Yellow Jack, a deadly fever

31

that some said was spread by mosquitoes. The elder of the two nuns recovered, but the younger nun, Sister Henriette, began to vomit blood. Her skin took on a greenish-yellow tinge. Since we were short-handed, I helped with the nursing, although there wasn't much I could do to alleviate her suffering.

Sister Henriette's eyes were sunken, and her fingers picked aimlessly at the counterpane. In the background, I could hear the buzzing of a fly. I dipped a cloth in water, wrung it out, wiped her forehead. 'You're going to get better, Sister,' I lied. 'Just think of the wonderful School we're going to create, of all the students whose lives you can change.' She murmured something. I leaned close. 'Pierre,' she whispered. I had no idea whether Pierre was a brother, an uncle, an unlucky suitor, or indeed St. Peter, founder of the Church.

I remembered that she had told me she was from Annecy. 'Remember Annecy, Sister Henriette,' I said gently. 'Remember the sun on the cobblestones, the children playing in the square.' I had never been to Annecy, but supposed that most small French towns were pretty much alike. But this seemed to calm her for a while. Later, however, she grew agitated once more and began to gaze in terror at the flickering shadows cast by the candlelight.

My friend Joelle tapped at the door, came in. She looked at Sister Henriette and sighed. '*Pauvre petite*,' she said, although she was a few years younger than the little nun. 'Let me sing to you.' She held Sister Henriette's hand and began to sing a children's song about cathedrals in France, a gentle round in a minor key: 'Orleans. Beaugency. Notre Dame de Paris. Vendome, Vendome.'

Suddenly Sister Henriette started and sat upright. She looked out into the darkness, cried out. 'There's a devil in the shadows.' Joelle tried to soothe her, and held a cup with water to her lips, held her when she began shaking with chills until her teeth rattled.

When Sister Henriette fell into a restless sleep, Joelle and I whispered in the corner. 'Is she going to die, do you think?' I asked. Joelle leaned her head against the wall. She shrugged, and her eyes filled with tears. 'if she does, what a lonely death, far from those she loves, and so far from her home in Annecy. Sometimes I wonder why on earth we have come here.' She knew, and I knew, that we were here because we had no other choice.

This state of things continued for two days, but on the evening of the second day Sister Henriette's condition worsened. We called Father Beaubois to administer the last rites. Just as dawn was breaking, she heaved a sigh, convulsed, and died.

I loved my friend, but I had often thought Joelle was a light-hearted, featherbrained coquette. I was wrong. She had shown an unexpected strength and compassion with the sick, speaking to them in her low melodious voice, singing to them, and also taking on less glamorous tasks such as washing them and helping me change their bedding. Sister Immaculata was also helpful, but there was something about her demeanour that I found disconcerting when Sister Henriette was dying. Her eyes were in shadow, but I sensed a fierce alertness, like a vulture waiting to swoop down upon its prey.

When it was time to prepare Sister Henriette's body for burial, Sister Immaculata shooed us out. With feigned kindness, she said, 'You two are impressionable young girls, but I've done this before. Go and rest, and prepare for the funeral mass.' We were exhausted, so went to our room. When I walked out, I glanced back and saw the enormous shadow Immaculata cast in the candlelight, watched her flickering blackness leaning over Henriette's inert body.

Sister Immaculata

I love the dead. They do not shout at me. They don't talk back or condescend to me. They lie there waiting for me to prepare them to meet Eternity. When I shut the door after Sidonie and Joelle, I closed Sister Henriette's eyes, placing a gentle finger on her lids and shutting them like a window shade. I took a pair of scissors and cut off the bloody nightgown she was wearing, and thrust the scraps in a corner to be burned later. I held a cloth and washed her gently, tenderly, as though she were my very own doll. Back in France, I never had a doll of my own. When her head rolled back, I saw that there was a locket around her neck. When I pressed a spring on the side of it, it sprang open, revealing the image of man around my own age, about twenty, lean, swarthy, with a long aquiline nose. I removed the locket and placed in the pocket of my habit. 'You

34

pretended to be a Bride of Christ, Henriette,' I whispered, 'but you were no better than you should have been under that pale pious surface...' Her limbs were beginning to stiffen imperceptibly, so I wrapped her in a white linen shroud and finished laying her out for burial.

To the tolling of bells, we buried her in the courtyard after a mass for her eternal rest. The heat was so intense that we did not want to wait; in Louisiana's climate, we knew it was important to get them in the ground fast.

Sidonie

When Mother Jerome called me in to her study, I knew something was afoot. "Sit down, Sidonie,' she said, motioning toward a chair. She took her seat behind her desk. 'The nuns have told me how helpful you've been in the infirmary. And, of course, we remember you as one of our brightest students in Rouen.'

I smiled. I was not going to be drawn in to any exchange because I had an inkling of where this might be going. Mother Jerome seemed tired, I thought. It was summer, and the heat in New Orleans was like nothing we had ever experienced in France; it rose in waves from the ground, and the air was so suffocating and humid that we were constantly drenched in our own perspiration. Mother Jerome's forehead was beaded with sweat, and there were dark circles under her eyes. She had drawn the blinds to keep out the heat of the sun, and her study was full of shadows.

35

She cleared her throat. 'As you know, our students will be arriving tomorrow. We had planned to take only fifteen, but it seems that there will be around twenty-five. However, with the loss of Sister Henriette, we are short-handed.' She paused. 'I was wondering if you would be willing to teach a small group. Sister Marie-Joseph will take the main group, which is made up mostly of the daughters of planters and of shop owners here in New Orleans. Since she is a choir nun, however, we must be mindful of her religious needs.'

In recent weeks, I had learned thing or two by observing Mother Jerome's negotiations with the Jesuits and with the city authorities of New Orleans. A year ago, I would have cried out in glee that I was honoured and delighted, that I had always dreamed of being a teacher. But now I had learned from the nuns that it is always best not to reveal our hand in advance. 'I see, Reverend Mother,' I said. 'Sister Henriette's death was indeed a great loss.' Mother Jerome knew that I had helped nurse her, that I had been genuinely fond of her. 'What will the second group of students be like?'

Mother Jerome sighed. 'It will be an unusual group. We will have one *sauvagesse,* one slave, and two local women. You will be expected to teach them to read and write, and to tell them stories of the saints.' She continued, 'The advantage, of course, is that it will be a smaller group than the first one. The students, even the Indian, all speak French. And, of course, this would only be a temporary measure, until you find a husband.'

I was not entirely naïve. I knew that, although the number of students was indeed smaller, teaching such a diverse group would have challenges of its own. And Mother Jerome had reminded me very subtly that I was there on sufferance until a husband could take me off the Ursulines' hands. But I knew as well that I too held a few cards. Of all the Casket Girls, I was the only one with academic inclinations. Besides, time was of the essence, with the students arriving tomorrow. And it was clear that, while the Ursulines had agreed to accept these students, they would prefer to keep them apart from the pampered daughters of the landowners.

I lowered my eyes. 'Mother Jerome,' I said demurely, 'I am pleased to be of service. Would you like for me to begin tomorrow?'

On the first day of class I woke up in a strange state of anticipation and terror. I put on my grey pinafore, pulled my hair back into a bun at the nape of my neck. Although I did not have the least idea of how to teach, I had been pretty much left to my own devices, under the tacit understanding that I would keep my students separate from the other more conventional young women. Clearly, I would have to improvise and make it up as I went along. I wasn't sure whether they could read and write, so I hit upon the idea of asking them to draw. I realised that I looked far too young and wondered how on earth I would be able to impose my authority on my students. I stood tall, squared, my shoulders, and walked into the classroom.

My students rose when I entered. I motioned to them to be seated. 'Good morning, mademoiselles,' I said. 'I am Sidonie Lemaire, your teacher.' I handed out pieces of paper and a pencil to each student. 'I would like for you to draw a picture that tells me something about your life, so that I can learn a bit about you.'

They looked at one another, then began to make marks with their pencils. While they did so, I looked at them. One was a tall woman who was, I guessed, about my own age. Her skin was the colour of strong tea, and her features were strong and disturbingly beautiful, like some African masks I had seen in the Convent back in Rouen where nuns had brought them back from the missions. There were also two French women. One had brassy egg-yolk yellow hair and had rouged spots on her cheeks that made her look like a fairground doll. I estimated her age as about twenty-five. The other was small, like a frightened little bird, with frizzy hair and freckles, maybe fourteen years old. The *sauvagesse* was slender, with dark hair neatly pulled back in a braid down her back.

Our classes were supposed to last until lunchtime, and I wasn't quite sure how to fill the time, so I let them sketch for a while. When I saw that they had all finished, I rapped on the desk. 'Very well. Let's see what you have done. Please tell me your name, and tell me and the others about your drawing.'

They all looked down at their desks. Finally, the brassy blonde spoke up. 'I am Nanette,' she said. She held up her drawing. It showed a city, and a boat. 'Tell us about your drawing, Nanette,' I encouraged. She replied, pointing at the crudely drawn buildings, 'This is Paris.' I could hear the longing in her voice. 'And this is the boat that brought us here.' She looked at her younger companion, who went beet red. I turned to her.

'And you, Mademoiselle?' I asked. The girl went even redder. I pointed at her drawing, which also depicted a boat. 'Did you come on the same boat as Nanette? And what is your name?'

'Clotilde,' she muttered, and nodded.

'Did you live in Paris too,' I asked. She looked down at her hands. 'Yes,' she stammered. I could sense that she was painfully shy. I turned my attention to the Indian girl. 'And your name, Mademoiselle?'

'I am Coahoma,' she replied. Her French was accentless. She had drawn the river, and what looked like a rounded hill. I asked her to tell us about her drawing.

She pointed at the river. 'This is the great river,' she said. 'And this is a mound that is sacred to my people.'

'Who are your people, Coahoma?'

'The Natchez,' she replied. Her voice was filled with pride. 'My name means 'panther'.'

I looked at the slave woman, 'Your name, Madame?'

'Palmyre,' she replied. She had made not one but two drawings. I blinked when she held them up; clearly she had talent, and her figures radiated strength and individuality. One drawing was of a big house, with many little houses in the back.

She had sketched stick figures working in the fields surrounding the house, a dog, and a man on a horse.

'Tell me about this drawing,' I said. She pointed at the big house. 'This is the plantation, where I used to live. And behind it are the cabins, for us, the slaves.'

'Do you no longer live there?'

'No.'

'And this second drawing?' I asked. 'It looks like a boat. Can you tell us more?'

She looked down. 'The boat was dark. We were chained and packed below decks. No air, little food and water.' I could see a tear began to stream down her cheek. 'My baby died,' she said.

I did not know what to say. The Ursulines themselves owned slaves here, to work in the kitchens and in our gardens, but I had never spoken to a slave before, never been brought up hard against the reality. I looked at Palmyre. 'I am so sorry for your loss,' I stammered. I knew that our class was supposed to last two hours, but decided that enough was enough. 'Very well,' I said. 'That will be all for today. Tomorrow I will ask you to tell us a story.'

'What kind of story?' asked Nanette, looking at her fingernails.

'Whatever kind you like,' I said. 'It can be a made-up story, or a story about yourselves. And then we will start to learn the letters.'

Later, I sat in the courtyard with Joelle, under the orange trees. 'How did your first lesson go?' she asked.

'It was...strange,' I said. 'I thought that teaching would be easy. It isn't. The students are so different to us, and yet there's so much in common.'

'How do you mean?' Joelle frowned. 'How can we have anything in common with slaves and Indians and prostitutes?'

I struggled to find words for what I was feeling. 'We've always been taught that prostitutes are living in a state of mortal sin. And the nuns have told us that Indians are as well, until they are converted.' The convent in Rouen was all I had ever known from the age of three, and until sailing for Louisiana I had only travelled in my reading. It had never occurred to me to question the authority of the nuns. My love of books, though, had brought me into contact with different ways of looking at the world, and I felt confused. I went on, 'Like us, they don't have control over their lives. You and I and the other Casket Girls are expected to find husbands here. The ladies of the night depend on men too. The Indians' territory is being conquered by the French. And the slaves...Joelle, my student Palmyre described the slave ship. I thought our crossing on the *Gironde* was hard, but this must have been like hell, chained below decks in the dark. And her baby died in her arms. Now, if her owners take a dislike to her, she can be sold to anyone who makes an offer. It's hard for me to understand how that can be the Lord's will.'

Joelle sighed. 'It's the way of the world, Sidonie, and there's nothing we can do to change it. You and I are supposed to be free, but when it comes down to it, the most we can hope for is to find a man who is kind, and who has enough money to give us a comfortable life.' She looked down at her hands. 'To lose a baby must be the very worst thing. One day I want to have one of my own. Like a doll I can play with and love and protect.'

Sister Immaculata

Back in France, I always enjoyed going to market. My father was a silent man, but he did say on one occasion that I had a good head for figures. This was an advantage, because I could calculate the correct change in my head, and the stall-keepers found it hard to cheat me on weights. Maybe that is why Mother Jerome entrusted me with shopping for food. I knew that she did not like me. She was always elaborately courteous and never said anything unkind, but I sensed instinctively that she found my appearance repulsive. However, I had a strong back and an aptitude for hard bargaining. She called me in one morning and gave me a list. 'Immaculata, try not to waste time, and ask for receipts for everything.'

Food in the convent was simple, both because of the nuns' belief in mortifying the flesh and because there wasn't a great deal of money. But I had known what real hunger was, so tended to eat as much as I could whenever I could. This led to reprimands and reminders, which I ignored, that Gluttony was one of the Seven Deadly Sins. The soil in Louisiana was unbelievably fertile, and there were many different fruits and vegetables in the market. I walked down by the river where the stalls were.

One Indian woman was selling peaches and watermelons. After haggling a bit, I added several peaches and a small watermelon to my basket, then went on to buy potatoes and rice, and then more vegetables. The tomatoes were red and fleshy, ripe with scent. I held them up, looked at them carefully, discarded those that were bruised or overripe. I wandered down by the river among the stalls selling persimmon cakes, where slave women were brushing off clouds of flies. The river was like a python, a big grey-brown snake coiling through the city, and I was mesmerised by its ripples and eddies. Dragging myself away, I headed for the butcher's. They were only open two days a week in summer, because the heat made it impossible to preserve meat. When I walked through the door, the butcher was standing behind the counter. He was tall, with black hair and a barrel chest, and wore a white bloodstained apron. From the ceiling hung quivering carcasses. '*Bonjour*,' I said.

'*Bonjour*,' he replied. 'What will it be today?' I could tell from his accent that he was also a Breton, and this for whatever reason pleased me. 'Two pounds of *flanchet,* please.' It was good stew meat, and was cheap. 'But cut it properly, if you please, against the grain,' I added.

He grinned. 'Are you a good cook, Sister?' I blushed to the roots of my hair, which was concealed under my wimple. 'Better than most of the cooks in this filthy colonial city,' I snapped. This was a lie. I had watched my mother cook and shop for meat, but I had never made a stew myself.

'And a Bretonne, from what I hear in your voice.' It almost seemed as though he was flirting with me, but I knew that men never gave me a second glance. I drew myself up, stared directly into his eyes. 'I am an Ursuline nun, from the convent near Rouen,' I said, thinking that this would silence him. 'How much?'

'Two sols,' he replied. I counted out the money and put it in his outstretched hand. I noticed that the blood under his fingernails had turned brown, and saw the black hair on the back of his hands and the calluses on his fingers. I snatched my hand back, turned to leave.

'Au revoir, *petite Soeur*,' he said. I noted a tone of mockery. I decided that, whatever Sister Fidelis said, we would be eating fish from now on.

I used to wish that I was pretty, but one of the advantages of being like me is that I can make myself invisible. It must be the nun's habit. People do not see me as a woman. And it's also because I am plain, which is a polite word for ugly. But I no longer care: this gives me a freedom that the pretty ones will never have. I can come and go, roam the streets unhindered, explore all the hidden corners. Mercifully, there was a tinge of autumn in the air, so the heat wasn't as suffocating as usual.

It took a while to learn my way around New Orleans, but now I know the streets, know the best places to buy good bread and delicate pastries and fish. This morning down near the river I happened upon a slave auction. A fresh cargo had arrived the day before, and the slaves were being auctioned one by one. I remembered the stench of the slave boat we had encountered on our trip upriver from the Gulf and shuddered.

The first was an older woman, shackled. The auctioneer began his spiel: 'And here is a fine cook. She can make the best pastries, all the latest French delicacies.' The woman looked exhausted, but she stood straight and looked into the distance. After a few bids, she was sold to a fat man with a moustache and led off.

The next slaves to mount the block were a woman and a child. The mother was the colour of jet jewellery I had seen in shop windows back in France, but the child's skin was the colour of *café au lait*. A murmur went through the crowd, which was made up mostly of men: she was slender, tall, and I could see they found her beautiful. 'This is a rare opportunity,' said the auctioneer, 'to get two slaves for the price of one. The woman is a fine specimen, with experience as a ladies' maid. The child could serve as a page or be used for field work.' A man standing near me in the crowd muttered to someone standing near him, 'Lemoyne's wife must have decided to get rid of her husband's *putain* and illegitimate brat.' The auctioneer pointed at her breasts, leered. 'How much am I bid, *Messieurs*?' Two men began to bid against each other, and when I heard the winning bid, my mouth dropped open. It would have been enough to buy a small house in my village back in France.

Next up was a man, with heavy chains around his arms and legs. When he stood on the auction block, he gazed out at the crowd with eyes that were full of intelligence and scorn. He was tall, muscled, and the sight of his body aroused feelings in me that I knew I would have to confess later to Father Beaubois. 'A fine worker,' said the auctioneer,' but one who should go to a master who is a firm disciplinarian. He is strong and hard-working, but given to shows of insolence and resistance to authority. But nothing that a competent slave breaker could not deal with.' I had heard whispers that there were such persons, who dealt with difficult slaves. 'How much am I bid for this fine specimen?'

I heard a voice ring out from a man who was standing in the corner, regarding the proceedings with a sardonic air. The amount he mentioned caused the others to gasp. The man was wearing a linen suit and broad-brimmed hat. He was swarthy, tall, and looked as though he was used to giving orders. I was surprised that no one dared to bid against him. Standing by his side was a short man with a twisted arm and bristling ginger hair.

'Sold to Monsieur Armand Ardoin,' the auctioneer cried. A man standing behind me said to another, 'That's the owner of Les Chenes, the big land grant upriver. I've heard that his overseer can get work out of a stone.'

A scuffle broke out nearby. A boy had stolen a purse from a man's pocket and ran through the crowd attempting to escape. In the confusion, I was knocked to the ground. I felt myself being lifted by the armpits, set back on my feet. I heard a mocking voice I thought I'd never hear again. 'So, it's you again, Sister. What on earth are you doing here? This is no place for white women, and certainly no place for nuns.'

It was the black-haired butcher.

He brought me a glass of water and drew me over to a bench at the edge of the square. He could see that I was shaken, but I was determined not to show weakness. 'Why were you watching a slave auction, Sister?' he asked.

'One of the goals of my Order is to educate slaves,' I said, in tones designed to freeze him, make him go silent. He didn't. 'Why?' he asked.

'To save their souls,' I answered primly.

'Poor devils,' he said. 'They remind me of people like my family back France. '

My eyebrows shot up. 'How can slaves possibly remind you of a Breton family?'

He shrugged and leaned back against the bench. 'My family were peasants, attached to the land of a local Count. I had eight brothers and two sisters. My parents worked from sunrise to sunset, but there was never enough to eat, and we knew that we could be turned out of our cottage at any moment. Not too different from slaves.'

I was drawn into conversation despite myself. 'I too grew up on a farm, and I know that it is not an easy life. But slaves are black, the colour of sin, of night, while we are French and white.' I found the idea that we might actually have something in common with these creatures repulsive.

The butcher yawned. 'They will have taught you in the Convent about the Curse of Ham. This is nonsense. It's what the landowners do to make sure they have cheap labour.' He stretched out his hand. 'My name, by the way, is Pierre. Cormier.'

Instinctively I stretched out my own. 'Immaculata,' I said, and then snatched back my hand. There would be yet another sin to confess to Father Beaubois. Here I was, sitting on a bench with a man to whom I had never been introduced. I stood up, dusted myself off. 'I must continue with my errands for the convent. Thank you for your assistance, Monsieur Cormier, but I am quite capable of looking after myself.' This wasn't strictly true: in the past, I had occasionally had what I called my funny turns, but I knew how to recognise the signs and seek solitude.

I headed for the *patisserie* on the Rue Bienville. Sister Marie-Joseph had a secret sweet tooth and had given me money to buy fine French pastries for her. 'Don't tell anyone, Sister,' she said. Another hypocrite, I thought, who prattles about the sin of Gluttony and devours almond pralines alone in her cell. But I knew she would not protest if I kept the change on the transaction. I was hoping to build up a little nest egg. For what purpose, I still didn't know.

As I walked down the street, I pondered over what I had seen at the slave market. Then something struck me: the butcher had not found me invisible but had actually seen me. I realised that I did not find this idea distasteful. I knew that I would have to exercise even more control over the dark urges that Satan sent me from time to time.

I knew that Mother Jerome was eager to find suitable husbands for the Casket Girls. So far, the Ursulines had not had much success in doing so. One of the girls who shared my room, a plump loud girl called Berthe, had caught the eye of the local greengrocer, M. Clement, though where he had seen her was a mystery to me. It was not the most romantic of courtships. M. Clement had demanded an appointment with Mother Jerome and had asked to see Berthe and two other girls. He then pointed to Berthe and said, 'I'll take that one,' as though he was buying a bag of potatoes. I could tell that his attitude made Mother Jerome deeply uncomfortable. They were married by Father Beaubois three days later, and Berthe was now lording it over everyone behind the counter of M. Clement's establishment. Mother Jerome's quandary was to find husbands for the girls, but in a way that would not make her feel that she was selling them off to the highest bidder. This gave me an idea.

I entered her study. 'Reverend Mother,' I said, 'With respect, it seems to me that as long as the Casket Girls attend mass here in the Convent, it is not possible for them to see New Orleans, or for the gentlemen of New Orleans to see them. I know that it is difficult for cloistered nuns to venture beyond the Convent. But if a converse nun like me were to escort them to mass in the Place d'Armes, they might attract the attention of appropriate suitors.'

For the first time, I saw a flash of respect for me in Mother Jerome's eyes. Not, of course, that she would ever voice it. 'An interesting idea, Immaculata. I shall give it some thought.'

Of course, I had my reasons for offering this. I figured that if any of the Casket Girls were courted by rich men, I might be able to earn some money taking messages to and fro. And I was bored in the Convent, bored by the relentless piety and interminable masses.

Mother Jerome continued, 'If I do decide on this course of action, I shall rely on you to ensure that the girls' deportment is impeccable. We cannot allow even a whisper of scandal to affect them.'

Yes, I thought, because that would affect their market value. But I lowered my eyes. 'I am always pleased to be of service, Reverend Mother.' She looked sharply at me to detect whether there was a note of mockery, but my face revealed nothing.

Chapter 4

Sidonie

It was raining hard on the morning of my second class. When I walked into the classroom, I could see that my students had got soaked in the downpour. I knew that if they were drenched and chilled, it would be impossible for us to get anything done.

'Good morning, mademoiselles,' I said. 'Please make yourselves comfortable, and wait here for a moment. I'll be right back.'

I had managed to ingratiate myself with Sister Fidelis, who was in charge of the kitchen. Like me, she was from the countryside around Bordeaux, and would occasionally keep aside cakes and other tidbits for me. I popped my head around the corner of the kitchen door. 'Sister,' I asked, 'could I please put the kettle on to make some cups of mint tea?'

Sister Fidelis was a good-natured soul. 'Of course, Sidonie', she replied. 'Who are you making it for?"

'My students,' I confessed. 'They're wet and cold. I think they may be hungry as well.'

I heard a sniff from the corner. It was Sister Immaculata. 'For the *putains?*' she sneered.

Fidelis turned to her. 'Immaculata, have a little Christian charity.' She put the kettle on and assembled some cups on a tray, along with some small cakes. 'How are you finding your classes, Sidonie?'

'Not easy, but fascinating,' I confessed. 'There is so much I don't know.'

'A fine teacher you are!' said Immaculata. Sister Fidelis handed me the tray. 'I hope it goes well, *Cherie*,' she said. She frowned at Sister Immaculata.

I returned to the classroom and told my students to bring their chairs around the table rather than sitting in rows. Then I distributed the steaming cups of tea and the cakes. I was right: they were hungry indeed. For a while, the only sound was of chewing. In our first session, I had noted a certain reticence, but the tea and cakes seemed to make my students less withdrawn. 'Do you all live nearby?' I asked.

Once again, Nanette was the first to reply. 'Clotilde and I live two streets over, on the Rue St Louis. We used to live in a house that wasn't very nice, but Father Beaubois told us that if we left it and came to learn to read and write, he would arrange a place for us in the house of a widow. We do some light cleaning.'

'Good,' I said. Father Beaubois was rising in my esteem. 'And you? I said, turning to the Indian.

Coahoma replied that she was working as a laundress every afternoon on the rue Royale. 'The work is hard,' she said,' but I send the money to help my families. I go to see them every Sunday.'

'What about you, Palmyre?' I asked.

Palmyre's expression was impenetrable. 'I belong to the Ursulines, so I live here in one of the little houses at the end of the vegetable gardens. I work in the gardens, clean, and do their laundry.'

'Very well,' I said. 'Now that you've warmed up a bit, let us think about your stories. Who would like to go first? I expected Nanette to begin, but it was Coahoma who spoke first.

'My people tell a story about the stars,' she said. 'There once were seven brothers, who wanted to prophesy. First, they fasted for seven days, then for seven months. Then they decided to fast for a year. After all this, they were wild, and did not want to be near people. So, they lived in the woods, and decided to transform themselves into pine trees. At that time, there were no metal axes. But when the French came, they began to cut down the trees. When the brothers saw them destroying the pine trees, they decided to turn themselves into rocks, since all rocks do is lie there on the ground. But then the white men began to use the rocks for many things. Finally, the seven brothers realised that the only way to escape them was by rising into the air, and they became a constellation.'

'The Pleiades!' I exclaimed. I love stories, and was entranced by this one. 'I remember on the ship coming to Louisiana that we used to look up at the stars, and it made me happy to think that wherever we are, the stars are still the same.'

The other students smiled, and I could see by the wistful look in their eyes that they were remembering faraway places.

At the same time, Coahoma's story brought home to me the changes that had taken place in the lives of her people with the coming of the Europeans. 'Have things changed much for your people since the French arrived?'

She looked down. 'Many died,' she said in a matter-of-fact tone. 'The French brought a plague of boils. Many of my people had no resistance. I lost my parents and my older brother.' The plague of boils, I thought to myself, must have been smallpox. 'I am so sorry,' I said, but my words seemed inadequate.

'Who would like to go next? 'I asked.

Nanette's mouth twisted. Finally, with reluctance, she said, 'Once upon a time there was a beautiful princess,' she said. 'Her parents, the King and Queen, died, so she went to live in the house of an evil witch. The witch treated her like a servant, forced her to do the bidding of some dark devils who took on human form.'

'What happened to her?' I asked.

'After one of the devils hurt her until she nearly died, there came a ship. It had come to take her away to a new land where she could be happy.'

'And then?'

'Ah,' she sighed. 'We still don't know how this story will end.' I noticed that she looked tired.

The following day we kept on with the stories. I decided to continue as well with the seating arrangements, since it seemed so much more pleasant to sit around a table over a cup of tea rather than facing students seated in rigid rows. I was aware that I could get in trouble for this and knew that the nuns would not be pleased. I hoped that Sister Fidelis would not get in trouble for giving us cakes.

'Good morning, ladies,' I said. I turned to Palmyre. 'Palmyre,' I asked, 'what story can you tell us?'

Palmyre thought for a moment. 'I will tell you a traditional story about why we women have long hair.' She raised her eyebrows. 'Once, two women got angry with each other. One of them went late at night and dug a deep hole in the path leading from the other woman's house to the village well. The next morning, when her enemy was going to fetch water from the well, she fell into the hole and shouted for help. Her friends ran to her and grabbed her by the hair to pull her out of the hole. But the hair stretched and stretched, and when they managed to pull her out, her hair was as long as a man's arm. At first, she was ashamed, and went to hide herself. But then she realised that long hair was beautiful and walked about with pride. All her friends were jealous and wanted long hair for themselves. So, they jumped into the pit, and when they were pulled out by the hair, their hair was long as well. And women have had long hair ever since. And it is beautiful.'

'What a lovely story,' I exclaimed. I had always taken my own long brown hair for granted. Palmyre's hair reminded me of a lion's mane; it had an exuberant life of its own. I was fascinated by the way Palmyre held herself straight and tall and by her air of self-assurance, her ease in her own body. Her face came to life briefly while she was telling her story, but then her features returned to an expression of sadness. 'Coahoma's people are called the Natchez. Is there a name for your people?'

Palmyre gave me a haughty glance. 'We are the Yoruba. What is the name of *your* people, Mademoiselle Sidonie?'

'We are the French, of course,' I said. But then I added, 'I am a *Bordelaise* too, though I left my home when I was a baby, after my parents died.'

'What are the Bordelaise?' she asked.

'The people who live in or near Bordeaux, a beautiful city on the sea.' I replied.

Palmyre seemed unconvinced. 'If the city of Bordeaux is so beautiful, why do the French come to live here in New Orleans?' I could see Coahoma was listening to this discussion with considerable interest.

It was hard to know what to say. 'I love my country,' I replied. 'But there are many poor people there. Near the Convent in Rouen where I grew up, there were many peasants whose lives were very hard.'

'Why is that?' asked Palmyre.

'It's difficult to explain,' I said. 'Most of the land belongs to the King and to the nobles, who are very wealthy.'

'Are there many nobles?' she asked.

I felt it was important to be honest. 'No,' I said. 'There are relatively few nobles, and many poor. So, for the poor the idea of coming to Louisiana and making a new life for themselves is very attractive.'

Nanette sniffed. 'I encountered a few nobles in Paris. They were not very nice people, under all their fine clothes.'

Coahoma cocked her head to one side. 'Do the nobles in France ever marry commoners?'

'No,' I laughed. 'They usually marry other nobles. And royalty usually marries royalty. Our young king, Louis XV, for example, married a Polish princess three years ago.'

She giggled. 'If they are all cousins, their children will be weak and stupid. Our king is called the Great Sun, but he must marry a Stinkard.'

'What on earth is a Stinkard?' I asked.

She smiled. 'Stinkards are the lowest class of all.' She continued, 'Our nobles must marry Stinkards too.'

'Well it's certainly not done that way in France,' I said briskly. 'Very well. Tomorrow, I shall begin to teach you the letters.'

That evening, as I sat out in the courtyard with Joelle, I tried to make sense of it all. 'You would not believe some of the things my students tell me,' I said. 'Can you imagine a place in which Kings and Queens marry the lowest sorts of commoners?'

Joelle twirled a blonde ringlet around her index finger. 'Not really,' she said. But she went on, 'How lovely it would be if a prince took notice of me.'

The following morning, as we were going to breakfast, it was announced that Mass would be in the church by the Place d'Armes instead of in our own small Chapel. This was unexpected, but we thought it was excellent news. It was one of those golden October days that make one glad to be alive. Back in France, I knew people would be shivering against the cold, and tried not to feel smug about this. Sister Immaculata would be accompanying us, and I was less pleased about that. Still, what could we do.

Off we went, two by two, down the Rue Chartres toward the Place d'Armes. The church was not nearly so impressive as our cathedrals back in France. It was a squat and solid building made of brick and plaster, with a steeple on top, two side wings and a rose window over the door. I knew that there was talk of building a proper cathedral named for St. Louis. This also, conveniently, was the name of our King Louis XV. I had heard that the King had expressed impatience with the moral laxness of the colony.

But it was far too beautiful a morning to think about these things. Flowers were bursting into bloom on all sides, in colours ranging from salmon to pink to magenta. The air was woven thick with their scent. When we reached the Church, I could see the sunlight dancing on the river. It seemed almost a pity to go into the Church's gloomy interior, and I felt guilty for my lack of piety.

Under Sister Immaculata's stern gaze, we filed into the church and took our seats in a pew near the front. The church was overflowing. There were people of every sort: well-dressed ladies in silks and brocades, ruddy-faced shop-owners, wriggling children, heavily made up women in garish clothing, and seated at the rear, some with darker skin. The blend of aromas was overwhelming: incense, lilies from the side altars, cologne, a faint undertone of perspiration. At my side, Joelle was rapt. 'Look at that lady's sleeves!' she whispered. 'Like the sort they were wearing in Paris.' She was looking particularly pretty, and her blonde ringlets kept falling out from under her bonnet.

To the left of us, my attention was suddenly drawn to a tall man in a linen jacket. He was one of those men who would attract attention wherever he went, with the indefinable air of someone who is used to command. I noticed that Sister Immaculata was also staring at him, with an expression I could not decipher. He turned around, and his gaze fell on Joelle. There was something in the intensity of his look that gave me chills. Joelle must have felt it, because she looked up and returned his gaze, then turned bright pink and looked down into her missal.

When the mass came to an end, we emerged into the sunlight of the square. As we milled around, I noticed that the tall man was coming out way. He nodded to Joelle. '*Bonjour*, mademoiselle,' he said. 'My name is Armand Ardoin.' He bowed.

Joelle was left speechless, but then summoned her wits. '*Bonjour*, monsieur,' she said, dimpling. Her cheeks were rosy, and her curls were tousled by the breeze.

'And you are?' he asked.

'Joelle Lemoyne,' she stammered.

At that point, Sister Immaculata came bustling over. 'No shilly-shallying, girls. We must head back to the Convent for lunch.'

Armand Ardoin brushed her aside as though she were a particularly annoying fly. He gazed at Joelle. 'I shall call on you.'

The bells began to toll, and Sister Immaculata shepherded us away. We took the longer route home by the river. It rippled at the edge of the quay, eddied and swirled like a living thing. 'What do you think he wants, Sidonie?' Joelle asked me. She was trembling.

'I think you have just acquired a suitor, my friend,' I said with a smile. Joelle was so naïve about some things.

Chapter 5

Sister Immaculata

It was a lucky coincidence that I had to go to market the day after Mass. I was eager to find out more about this Armand Ardoin, the planter I saw in the slave auction, who had stared at Joelle in Mass. The only possible source of information I had was the butcher Pierre Cormier. I went into the kitchen and found Sister Fidelis peeling potatoes and leeks.

'Good morning, Sister,' I said. 'Lovely day, isn't it?"

Sister Fidelis raised her eyebrows. 'You're feeling bright this morning, Immaculata.' I found mornings hard, and when it was time to get up had to battle against the sin of Sloth. The warmth of my bed was such a delectable thing. But I knew that this was yet another proof of my sinful nature.

'What are you making for dinner?' I asked.

'Stew,' she replied. Stew was, of course, a cheap way to cook.

'Would you like for me to go get you a chicken? We could use whatever is left over to make croquettes,' I said.

'Yes, but don't dawdle. I shall need you here in the kitchen later.' She handed me some coins and a basket. Louisiana fowl were cheaper and fatter than chicken back in France, I noticed.

Off I went. It was a glorious morning, with flowers in bloom on every corner. I was used to the chilly springs of northern France and did not entirely trust the warm exuberance of Louisiana. It seemed somehow wrong and out of joint. At the same time though, when I felt the sun on my face, I felt for a moment like a flower myself, opening to the sun. Immediately I realised the absurdity of this. I know that I am not a flower, not a plant to be picked and cherished, but a weed. Perhaps a thistle. Still, I remembered from the days on my uncle's farm that weeds are tough. Even when they're torn out and discarded, they end up returning and flourishing where we least expect them to.

Shaking off these thoughts, I walked down the Rue Bourbon to the butcher's. It was early, and I saw through the window that Pierre Cormier was on his own. On the counter behind him were plucked scrawny chicken carcasses. 'Bonjour, M. Cormier,' I said.

'Bonjour,' he replied. 'What'll it be today, Sister?'

'I'd like a nice fat chicken, not one of those bony beasts.' I pointed at the chickens. 'Have you got others?'

He laughed. 'I'll have a look.' He went into a back room and came out holding a plump clucking hen by the claw. It beat its wings against the counter. 'Is this what you had in mind?'

I gauged its weight. 'Yes, if the price is right.' He quoted a price, and I sputtered.

'Think of your immortal soul, Mr. Butcher,' I said. 'And think of the virtue of Christian charity.'

He sighed. 'Very well, Sister.' I had hoped he would donate it to the Convent, but he would only go as far as reducing the price. Still, it was a start. 'Are you capable of killing it and plucking it yourselves?' he asked, with a wolfish grin.

I laughed in his face and took the bird by the neck. It fluttered its wings frantically, but in a neat pinwheel motion I wrung its neck. 'I'll pluck it back in the Convent,' I said. I handed over the coins and put the dead fowl in my basket. 'Have you ever thought of selling sausages?' I asked.

'Yes, I have,' Pierre Cormier replied. I could see a spark of interest in his eyes. 'The problem is finding the right pigs. Here in Louisiana, they do not know how to raise pigs. There are wild ones in the forest, so they have never bothered to raise them on farms.'

I turned to leave, then looked back. 'M. Cormier, who was that tall man at the auction? The one in the white linen jacket, standing in the corner left of the auction block, who bought the male slave? And there was a short ugly man with a twisted arm standing by his side.'

'Why on earth do you want to know, Sister?' he asked. But then he shrugged. 'That was Armand Ardoin. He has a big indigo plantation upriver called Les Chenes. The other man was his overseer. They are not the sort of people you would want to know.'

'Why do you say that, Monsieur?' I asked.

'Rumour has it that they carry their discipline of slaves a bit too far,' he said drily.

'In what way?

Pierre Cormier sighed. 'People say they beat one to death three weeks ago.'

'I must not detain you any longer, Monsieur,' I said. 'Au revoir.' As I walked back to our lodgings, I thought of the implications of this. Armand Adroin was wealthy. He wanted to pay his addresses to that featherbrained Joelle. This was a situation with huge potential.

Sidonie

As my classes continued, I realised that I had not spoken to my students about the lives of the saints. If the nuns found out about this, I knew I would be in trouble. We had been working hard on learning the letters, then on piecing them together to read. I had been impressed by the eagerness of my students. Palmyre and Coahoma had a quick restless intelligence and were avid to learn. Nanette was less clever, but I found her unabashed cynicism refreshing. Clotilde was good with numbers, but was painfully shy and found it hard to speak in class. So, I decided that our next class would be about the lives of the saints, their miracles, and their feats.

As had become our custom, we sat around the table. Light streamed in through the windows. Coahoma looked tired, I thought, and seemed on edge. Nanette's colour seemed healthier, and her vivacity had become a little less brittle. Clotilde, however, was as timid and jumpy as ever. Palmyre arrived later than the others, came in, and took her seat.

'Good morning, girls,' I said. 'Today we are going to learn about Saint Catherine of Alexandria. She was the beautiful daughter of the Governor of Alexandria, in Egypt.'

'Where's Egypt?' asked Nanette.

I drew a crude map depicting the continents and placed an X where I thought Alexandria was. 'She was a girl who loved to study, and decided to become a Christian. When the Emperor began to persecute Christians and have them killed, she rebuked him for his cruelty.'

'What is 'rebuke'?' Nanette asked.

I thought for a minute. 'It's to tell someone that they have done something wrong, or that their opinions are wrong.'

Coahoma's eyes were bright with curiosity. 'What happened then?'

I went on. 'She was made to defend Christianity in a debate with learned philosophers.'

'What is a debate?' interjected Palmyre. 'And what are philosophers?'

'Debates are when we present out opinions and try to win someone over with our arguments. And philosophers are wise men.'

'So, what happened?' asked Palmyre.

'She won the debate. Several of her adversaries were converted to Christianity by her reasoning.'

'What happened to her?' asked Nanette. 'Nothing good can come of besting a man in an argument.'

65

I sighed. 'So it proved. They tortured her to make her recant, but she refused. Then they tried to break her on the wheel, but when she pointed at it, it fell apart. In the end, they chopped off her head.'

The girls were silent for a while. 'What a sad story,' Palmyre said. 'What is it supposed to teach us?'

'It teaches us that we must always defend our faith,' I replied.

'To me it seems as though it teaches us that if we argue with men, we will come to a bad end,' Nanette said with a sniff.

Palmyre looked me in the eye. 'Teacher, would you like to hear about *our* religion?'

I was taken aback. I had always heard from the nuns that Indians and Africans were savages, and that their beliefs were devilish superstitions. It would never have occurred to me to describe them as religions. But I was curious. 'Go ahead, Palmyre.'

She leaned back in her chair. 'The Yoruba believe in Fate, which we call Ayanmo. What each of us does and thinks in this life has an impact on others and on the Earth, and on ourselves. We must try always to grow in spirit, so that we can become one in spirit with Olodumare, the source of all our energy.'

I was fascinated. 'Odumare sounds like your equivalent of our God.'

Coahoma then raised her hand. 'May I tell about the Natchez God?' I nodded.

'Our Supreme Being lives in the sky, and is called the Great Sun,' she said. 'Long ago his son came to us and gave us our laws, our customs, and our rituals. He also helped us to conquer our neighbours. Even today, our Chief is known as the Great Sun.'

I mulled this over for a minute. 'Our God lives in Heaven too. He also sent his Son to earth, to die on the Cross for our sins.'

Palmyre snorted. 'Your God seems to value suffering. St. Catherine was a clever woman, who dared to question men's opinions and was tortured and beheaded. Your God's son died a terrible death on the cross.'

'True,' I said, 'but His death gave us eternal life.'

'Of that, I am not convinced,' said Palmyre. She added, 'I would love to see my child and my husband once more, but I find it hard to believe I ever will.' Her eyes filled.

It was time to bring the class to a close. 'That, I think, is a matter of Faith.' I stood up. 'You've given me a great deal to think about, girls,' I said. 'Thank you for an excellent discussion.'

Coahoma grinned. 'Mademoiselle Sidonie, I think we have just had a debate.'

I smiled at them. In the beginning, I had thought I would be a lofty figure, the teacher imparting knowledge to her students. I never expected that they would end up teaching me.

Later I sat down by Joelle in the courtyard. 'I enjoyed my class today, Joelle,' I said. 'My students have such different ways of looking at the world.' Joelle, however, was not listening to me. She was twisting a curl around her index finger and gazing into the distance.

'Joelle,' I said. 'Is anything wrong?'

'No,' she said. 'Not at all.' She paused, fanned herself. 'Armand Ardoin came to the Convent today and spoke to Mother Jerome. He has asked permission to pay his addresses to me.' Her eyes were shining. 'Do you think he likes me?'

'I'm sure he does,' I replied. 'I saw the way he looked at you in Mass the other day.'

'He really is very handsome,' she said dreamily.

'Do you know anything about him? Where does he come from? Where does he live?'

'I don't,' she admitted. 'But I hope to find out in the coming days.'

Sister Immaculata

I knew that Armand Ardoin would not waste time. I had seen the look in his eyes when he gazed at Joelle, like a fox creeping closer to a ripe plump chicken. It was not a surprise when I saw his carriage in front of our lodgings, with a black coachman in livery and two white horses. I listened at the door when he spoke to Mother Jerome, but could not hear what they were saying.

Sure enough, there he was the following day in the front parlour. Mother Jerome had asked me and that silly Sidonie to be present while he spoke to Joelle. I thought this

68

was a bit much: surely one chaperone would have been enough. But Mother Jerome was taking no chances.

Armand Ardoin had brought Joelle pink roses and some almond pralines and persimmon cakes. He was a smooth talker, I'll give him that. Mother Jerome ushered him in to the parlour and invited him to sit down. She then nodded to me to summon Joelle and Sidonie, and I brought them in.

Joelle had taken pains to trick herself up. She was wearing a grey dress which brought out the colour in her eyes. I thought she had pinched her cheeks to make them look rosy. Sidonie was also dressed in grey, with her dark hair tied back in a knot. Plain and lanky as a plank, despite the airs she gives herself. What she and those heathens and blacks and tarts get up to, who is to know. Nothing good will come of it.

Both girls were tongue-tied at first. To see a man like Ardoin in a convent is not a common thing. The chairs in the parlour were stiff and uncomfortable, and martyred female saints frowned down from the walls. One, St. Lucy, held out her breasts on a platter, as though they were two fried eggs. Ardoin had polish, and he seemed to know how to put silly young women at ease. He asked them about their homes in France, their passage here on the *Gironde*, their impressions of New Orleans. I could see how Joelle was relaxing and letting her guard down in his presence. Sidonie was harder to read: she's deep, that one.

Joelle looked up at Armand Ardoin through her lashes. 'They tell me that you live upriver, Monsieur.'

'Yes,' he replied, 'on a plantation called Les Chenes. It is named for the oak trees that line the alley leading up to the house.'

'It must be beautiful,' Joelle sighed.

'Not as much as it will be one day,' he said. 'I am building a plantation house that will be the finest in Louisiana, with columns and balconies and a *garçonnière*. I will bring the best furniture from France, put glittering crystal chandeliers in the entrance, fill the walls with paintings.'

'How much land have you got, and what crops are you planting?' asked Sidonie. I thought this was a bit forward, and tutted. But Ardoin took it in his stride.

'Indigo, mademoiselle,' he said. 'Are you interested in agriculture?'

Sidonie blushed. 'I know nothing about it, monsieur. I know that in some of the English colonies the cultivation of tobacco is very successful.'

Ardoin brushed this aside. 'Tobacco is not an appropriate crop for this climate. It would never survive our summers. There is some talk among planters about cotton, or sugar. I have a plantation in St. Domingue, and there I have grown sugar successfully. But these are not matters to trouble two pretty young ladies like you and mademoiselle Joelle. I would be honoured if you came to visit my house one day.'

I stepped forward. 'I'm afraid that will not be possible.' If Ardoin thought he could invite one or even two Casket Girls to his house, unsupervised, he could think again.

Ardoin turned to me. 'Of course, they would need to be chaperoned,' he said. His tone was dismissive, with a hint of mockery that was not lost on me. He rose to leave, and bent over Joelle's hand a bit longer than was necessary. I cleared my throat and glared. He turned on his heel. 'Au revoir,' he said, and left.

Sidonie

I hardly knew what to think of Armand Ardoin's visit. Joelle was bowled over, that's for sure.

'Isn't he distinguished, Sidonie?' she asked me dreamily.

'He certainly seems so,' I said. I thought of the elegant cut of his jacket, his carefully trimmed beard, his general air of aplomb. His features were angular and aquiline, and his lips were thin. There was something about him that made my skin crawl, though I could not put my finger on what it was. Still, I wanted to be fair, and it seems unfair to judge the gentleman on just one encounter. 'I'd proceed carefully, Joelle,' I said to my friend. 'Meet with him, get to know him better, but try not to rush into anything.'

'This was not what she wanted to hear. 'You're just jealous because he didn't look at you,' she said, tossing her head. 'If you're not careful, Sidonie, you'll become a dried-up old schoolmarm. I think he's lovely.'

I knew that Joelle was so infatuated that it would be useless to reason with her. 'I just don't want you to be hurt,' I said. 'It isn't as though, once we choose a husband, we can change our minds. Catholic marriage is indissoluble, as you very well know. It's a really big decision. We're talking about the rest of our lives.'

She rolled her eyes. 'Or perhaps you will become a nun like Sister Immaculata, listening at keyholes and confessing sins she wishes she had committed.' But then she turned serious.

'Of course, I know that choosing a husband is a big decision,' she said. 'But you heard what he said. He has a large plantation and is building a beautiful house. When he spoke about crops, he seemed to know what he was doing. He would be able to support me in luxury. And on top of that, he is very handsome and *distingué*.' She grasped my hands and looked into my eyes. 'Be glad for me, Sidonie,' she entreated. 'My sister is back in Marseilles, and is lost to me, so you are the only sister I've got.'

That, I have to say, moved me deeply. 'Of course, *Cherie*,' I told her. 'You know that you can count on me, come what may.' We embraced. Still, I was left with a sense of foreboding. Why, I did not know. I asked myself if I was indeed jealous of Joelle, of her beauty and of the courage and gallantry with which she was prepared to take a gamble on her future. I really did not think so, but resolved to be more generous to my friend.

'Of course, he may never return!' Joelle laughed. 'Did you see that dragon Immaculata? How she glared when he kissed my hand.' The two of us dissolved in giggles.

We went into the garden, where I had begun to establish a small flower garden. Toward the back wall, I saw the cabins of the slaves. Suddenly, Palmyre came into sight. I waved. For the first time since our classes had begun, she broke into a smile.

'Who's that?' asked Joelle.

'One of my students,' I said. Joelle drew herself up. 'Surely it isn't fitting for us to allow slaves to take liberties.'

'What on earth do you mean,' I asked.

'Well, you saw that one just now. Shameless. Waving back to you, grinning as though she was our equal...'

I stiffened. 'Joelle,' I said, 'this is the student I told you about. The one whose baby died in her arms. She is the most intelligent student in my class. She is also my friend.'

Joelle's eyes widened. 'I had no idea,' she said. 'Poor soul.' Joelle did have the softest of hearts. But then she added, 'Armand has slaves, I know, but I am sure that he treats them humanely. After all, despite being African, they too are God's children. I shall pray for her.'

In the following days, we saw nothing of Armand Ardoin. Joelle began to droop, and spent the time gazing through the window. Once, when I went into our shared room, I noted something furtive in her manner, and she hastened to put away a sheet of paper. I glanced at it, and saw in her round childish hand, 'Joelle Ardoin,' written over and over and underlined with a flourish. One afternoon, though, I heard Sister Immaculata call to her, and the two went out to the corridor, where I heard the indistinct sound of their voices. After this, Joelle perked up perceptibly. She came out to the courtyard garden when I was weeding my flowerbeds.

'How can you work in this heat, Sidonie? You are going to ruin your hands,' she said. She sat on the bench under the tree. I got up and went to see beside her. It was good to sit in the cool shade under the big oak.

'You're in a much better humour today, Joelle,' I said. 'Can it be that M. Ardoin is going to pay you a visit?'

'I think he really likes me, Sidonie,' she said.

'How do you know? 'I asked.

She refused to meet my eyes. 'Oh, a woman just knows these things.'

She had brought some needlepoint and sat there stitching while we talked. 'What are you making?' I asked.

'A cushion for a chair,' she replied. It depicted dragons on a blue background, in an intricate pattern. I could not help thinking of the alligators we had seen on the shores as we sailed upriver toward New Orleans. 'It looks like a coat of arms.' I said idly. Joelle turned pink, coughed, and got up to leave. 'My friend, there is so much I wish I could tell you.' As she walked through the kitchen door, something dropped from the folds of her dress. I thought nothing of it and went on working. A few minutes later, however, Sister Fidelis called me over. 'Sidonie,

Joelle seems to have dropped this. Could you please take it to her?'

'Of course, Sister,' I said. It was an envelope, addressed in a bold black scrawl to Mlle. Joelle Lemoyne. The flap was open. Reading the correspondence of others is wrong, I know, and I didn't on this occasion. But I could glimpse the words '*Ma Cherie*,' and knew it was from him. Suddenly the strange inaudible whisperings between Sister Immaculata and Joelle made sense: I realised that Sister Immaculata was acting as a go-between, relaying messages between Joelle and Armand Ardoin. In normal circumstances, Immaculata always looked as though she had swallowed a bitter lemon. Lately, however, her smug expression reminded me of a scrawny cat who had just eaten a particularly succulent mouse.

I was concerned for my friend. Joelle was a gentle soul, and I was convinced that she had no idea of what she might be getting into. I returned to my digging. Two rows over, I saw Palmyre in the potato patch. Now that the sun was lower in the sky, the heat was not so intense, but we were both dripping with perspiration, and exchanged desultory comments about the weather as we worked. Gardening alongside someone gives us some excellent insights into their character, I thought as I dug. Palmyre never complained, and worked uncomplainingly in the burning sun, though I sensed that her heart was not in her labours. But she was conscientious, and her plot was neat and free of the weeds that in the Louisiana climate seemed to push up from the ground overnight. She had planted sweet peas around the edges of the potato plot, and bees buzzed lazily in the hot sun. Near her cabin, she grew more flowers, that bloomed in purple drifts, and I thought fancifully that they resembled hooded monks, but she was curiously protective of them and never allowed me to go near her flowerbed. I noticed that she never ventured beyond the walls of the convent, and wondered why she was not tempted to explore the city, or why Sister Fidelis never sent her on errands.

I'd observed that information seemed to circulate soundlessly among the slaves, through means that remained a mystery to me. It occurred to me that she might know a bit about Armand Ardoin, since he owned land upriver and had more than two hundred slaves. I thought it was best to be frank. 'Palmyre,' I said, 'I am worried about my friend. She has a suitor about whom she knows nothing. Do you happen to know anything about a planter called Armand Ardoin? He lives upriver, on a land grant that his father was given by Governor Bienville'.

Palmyre stopped digging and remained silent. I looked up from my weeding and was taken aback. Her face was ashen, and her expression was unreadable: a strange mixture of contempt, terror, and what looked very much like pity. She remained silent.

'What's wrong, Palmyre?' I asked.

She shook her head. 'Nothing, Mademoiselle Sidonie,' she said.

I pulled out a particularly tenacious thistle. 'My friend always sees the best in people,' I said, 'and she is far too trusting for her own good.'

Palmyre sighed. 'Sidonie,' she said after a long silence, 'there are things it would be dangerous for me to speak about. All I will say is that you are right to be afraid for your friend.'

The following days were eventful, to say the very least. After Mass one morning, Mother Jerome announced that Joelle was formally betrothed to Armand Ardoin, and would marry him three days hence. 'I am aware that this may seem precipitate," she said, 'but M. Ardoin will be leaving for St. Domingue and for Paris in a fortnight, so the marriage will go ahead. Father Beaubois has very kindly agreed to dispense with the reading of banns so that the ceremony may be solemnised before they leave.'

The other girls clustered around Joelle to offer congratulations and kisses. Of course, I too went up to her and embraced my friend.

'I am so pleased for you, Joelle,' I said. 'I hope that you and M. Ardoin will be very happy.' Joelle was radiant. 'Thank you, Sidonie,' she said, enveloping me in a hug. 'After I am married, and after we return from Europe, you must come upriver to visit me.'

I loved Joelle, and sincerely wanted for her to be happy. I knew that it would be useless to tell her of my fears, when I really had only my own instincts and my brief conversation with Palmyre to substantiate them. Also, Joelle was wilful, and I knew that a warning from me would only make her even more determined to marry.

After dinner, as I was helping Sister Fidelis remove the plates, I overheard snippets of a conversation between Mother Jerome, Sister Marie-Joseph, and Father Beaubois. 'Monsieur Ardoin has been more than generous,' Mother Jerome said. 'He has made a very substantial donation to our Order, earmarked for this convent and for our mission.'

Sister Marie-Joseph smiled. 'Magnificent!' she exclaimed. 'Perhaps we will be able to begin work on our permanent Convent building sooner than we had anticipated.'

Mother Jerome nodded. 'Indeed,' she said. But then she added, 'There is only one thing that I can't quite understand.'

'And what is that?' said Sister Marie-Joseph.

'The amount he has donated is precisely the same as the one in our ledger,' Mother Jerome replied. 'That is to say, the sum mentioned in the estimate sent to me by the builder last week.'

I looked over to Sister Immaculata, who was standing in the corner near Sister Fidelis. She had gone beet red, and knelt down to tie her shoe.

Father Beaubois had remained silent, but he too had observed Immaculata's reaction. 'There is something distinctly odd about this affair,' he said with a frown. 'It feels like a commercial transaction. And moreover, like a transaction in which the bidder has been tipped off about how much to bid. I do not like it.'

Mother Jerome's eyebrows rose in alarm. She knew that the wedding ceremony would be performed by Father Beaubois, and that it was essential that he be in agreement. 'Reverend Father,' she said, 'I am sure that your suspicions are unfounded. There is no one in the Convent who would stoop to such a thing. If they have, I am sure they would have confessed to you.'

Father Beaubois shrugged. 'Reverend Mother,' he said, 'it is obvious that I cannot violate the secret of the confessional.' But then he went on, 'However, it is true that, generally speaking, I have heard no rumours of such a thing.' I could tell, though, that he was not convinced. 'I shall perform the wedding mass,' he said, 'but I shall keep an eye on Joelle and on M. Ardoin, and travel upriver from time to time. There are no priests there, and those at Les Chenes will have pastoral needs which must be attended to. In time, they will have children, who must be baptised. And, of course, it is very generous of M. Ardoin to make a donation which will enable us to finish building the Convent.' I could tell, though, that Father Beaubois's conscience was not tranquil. ''Nor should it be,' I thought. 'They have sold Joelle to the highest bidder.'

Mother Jerome beckoned to me. 'Sidonie, your friend Joelle is going to be married in our Chapel next Saturday. I know that you have been cultivating flowers in our garden, and I would like for you to adorn the Chapel. We cannot provide

Joelle with an ostentatious wedding, but we can make the Chapel beautiful. M. Ardoin's brother Jean has arrived from Paris, and will be attending the Mass. So we must show them that although they may think this is a colonial backwater, we too have taste and style.'

I could hardly believe my ears. The austere Mother Superior's cheeks were pink with excitement. I would not have expected her to show concern with worldly matters like taste and style. But I remembered rumours I'd heard that she was from a wealthy bourgeois family from Paris. 'Of course, Reverend Mother,' I answered. 'There are some white roses and white lilies, that we can use.'

Mother Jerome smiled. 'You're a good girl, Sidonie,' she said. 'I know that you and Joelle are good friends. She is far from home, and we must try to stand in for all she's left behind in France.'

I thought with a certain cynicism that what Joelle had left behind was a downtrodden sister and a brutish drunken brother-in-law. Still, they were her family, and they were far away. I remembered Joelle's soft voice singing 'Orleans. Beaugency. Notre Dame de Paris. Vendome, Vendome,' to the dying nun. I resolved to make the Chapel as beautiful as I could, and to try to watch over my friend. How I would manage to do that I did not have the faintest idea.

Three days later Joelle and Armand Ardoin were married in our little Chapel, with the nuns and the other Casket Girls in attendance; some of the slaves looked on from the courtyard. With the assistance of Sister Marie-Joseph, I had garlanded the windows with white flowers. On the altar were two large sprays of lilies, and the entire Chapel was bathed their sweet scent.

Joelle was glowing as though she was illuminated from within. She was dressed in white, in a simple dress made of silk with a wide flowing skirt. I had made a crown of white flowers and placed it on her blonde ringlets, and she carried a bouquet of white roses and ivy. Since she had no male relatives present, Mother Jerome and Sister Marie-Joseph accompanied her down the aisle, one on either side. Armand Ardoin's face lit up when he saw her in the candlelight, and for the first time I began to think that perhaps he really did love her, and that the marriage would be a happy one. Another man was standing by his side. He, like M. Ardoin, was tall and dark. I could not see his face, but presumed that this must be the Parisian brother.

Joelle's voice as she said her vows was hardly audible, but Armand Ardoin's could be heard clearly in the last pews. Father Beaubois pronounced them man and wife, and after the mass we all shared light refreshments. Some French wine had appeared from an unknown source, and I thought with nostalgia of the vineyards of my native Bordeaux. Soon a carriage appeared to take the bride and groom to the river, to the ship that would be sailing to France.

Joelle embraced me just before she left. 'Please don't forget to write, *Cherie*,' I said.

'Of course I won't, Sidonie,' she promised. 'And you must come to see me when we return from Paris and from St Domingue. Armand's brother will be there too,' she added, with a hint of mischief in her eyes. 'He's an intellectual like you. Perhaps you will find you have a lot in common.'

'We must leave, Joelle,' said Ardoin, taking her abruptly by the arm. He lifted her in to the carriage, and Joelle waved to us all until the carriage was out of sight.

1729

New Orleans, Les Chenes

Chapter 6

Sister Immaculata

Good riddance, if you ask me. I was glad to see the back of that flibbertigibbet Joelle. Though I did well out of her, it's true. Over the past weeks, I'd built up a nice little reserve with all the comings and goings of notes and information between M. Ardoin and the Convent. One thing's for sure: money is freedom from the Convent, from the sneering nuns and their endless rosaries. It was true that when my parents died, the Ursulines were my only escape. But here in Louisiana, although I was aware of my propensity to sin, it was becoming increasingly clear to me that I'd never had a genuine religious vocation. The question now was how I should invest the money I was accumulating. The obvious solution would be a shop of some kind.

Several months passed. One morning in August, I went into town to buy food. There was a slight wind that made the heat less stifling. The cobblestones were slippery after a short shower of rain and, in the distance, I could hear the cries of the fishwives selling perch and bream.

I walked into the butcher's. 'Good morning, M. Cormier,' I said.

Pierre Cormier looked tired. 'Bonjour, Sister,' he said. 'What can I do for you today?'

'I want some *flanchet,* as usual, if you please,' I replied. 'But be sure that it really is flank, not the tough stringy meat you gave me last time. Have you got any decent sausage? The nuns would like it for a cassoulet. And some good bones for stewing.'

Cormier trimmed the fat off and sliced it into cubes. I could see the sureness in his bloodstained hands: much as I hated to admit it, that man knew what he was doing. He turned to me. 'Sorry, Sister, but I have no sausage today. It is impossible to arrange a reliable supplier of pigs. '

An idea took form in my brain. 'M. Cormier, do you have your own land?'

He raised an eyebrow. 'Why do you ask?'

'Have you never thought of raising pigs yourself?'

He laughed out loud. 'Yes, with all the time left over from this shop. The carcasses are delivered just after dawn from the slaughterhouse, and then I cut them up and prepare the meat for sale. And after that I am at the counter until dark.' He shrugged. 'There is hardly time to eat, much less to raise pigs. Though I do have a bit of land on the edge of town'

I pressed my point. 'It just occurred to me that there would be customers who would buy sausages and hams and other items of *charcuterie.* In this climate, they'd keep much better than beef, particularly in the summer.'

'There are things you know nothing about, Sister,' he said. 'Some of the Indians have pigs, and I'd thought of trading with them. But recently they've been acting strange and unsettled.'

I had never paid much attention to the Indians. I knew that two of Sidonie's students were Indian, but they hardly seemed threatening. But I didn't like the idea of an Indian uprising. 'Do you think New Orleans is in danger, M. Cormier?' I asked.

'Not for now,' he said. 'But Fort Rosalie might be. Do you really think there would be demand for sausages?'

'Of course there would be,' I responded tartly. But the idea of an Indian attack on New Orleans left me shaken. I looked out to the river, where the sun was glancing off the ripples. Suddenly the room seemed to swim around me, and I heard voices.

'Sister, are you unwell?' Cormier asked. His face faded in and out. Behind him I could see dark shapes. They pressed in on all sides. 'Make them go away!' I shrieked.

Cormier looked at me. 'There's nobody else here.'

Of course, he couldn't see them. The dark devils know that I am one of their own. I could not make out their words, but I knew that they were laughing. They knew how worthless I am. The idea of my leaving the Convent behind and owning a *charcuterie* with Cormier was a stupid fantasy. I am an ugly worthless weed, not a delicate pure flower. They crowded closer, flapping their dark feathered wings, and I began to shriek and bat them away.

I woke up moments later stretched out on a bench. My right check was smarting. Pierre Cormier was fanning me and holding a beaker of water in his callused bloodstained hands. He seemed mortified. 'Sister, I'm very sorry I had to slap you to bring you back to your senses. You were having hallucinations. It must have been too much sun.'

I reached for the water and drank several sips. Pierre took a cloth, moistened it, and wiped my face. For such a big man, he was remarkably gentle. I let myself sink into the blissful coolness, then stood up.

'It is I who must apologise, M. Cormier. As you say, it must have been too much sun.'

Pierre Cormier went behind the counter and began to slice the meat into cubes. 'Are you sure that you are well enough to walk back to the Convent on your own?'

I thought of what the cloistered nuns would have to say if they saw me walk in leaning on a handsome bloodstained butcher. 'Quite sure, M. Cormier,' I said briskly. 'And be sure to give me a good price on that meat, which must be two days old.'

When I left, I walked down the Rue Royale. There was a shop on a side street that I wanted to visit on my way back to the Convent. The shop front was painted blue. The interior was dark, and the woman standing behind the counter was the colour of honey. She was dressed in white, with a full skirt, and her hair was concealed under a turban. A candle was burning in the corner, and there was a smell of incense.

'Good morning, Sister,' she said.

I wasted no time on preliminaries. 'I want the most powerful spell you've got,' I said, 'to protect me from the Devil.'

'What kind of devils do you want protection from, *ma soeur*?' she asked. Her voice was low and musical.

'Dark ones,' I said. 'The very darkest.' To my horror, my voice was trembling.

She took out a dried leaf from a drawer. I noticed that it was split into five different sections. 'This is Five Finger Grass,' she said. 'Hang it in your room, and it will ward off evil.'

I wrapped it in my handkerchief and placed it carefully in the pocket of my habit. 'Do you have one for love and happiness?'

The woman cocked her head to one side and smiled. 'Sister, are nuns supposed to look for love?'

'Christian love, of course,' I snapped. 'We should love our neighbours as ourselves.'

She grinned. 'But of course,' she said. She took out an amulet from a drawer and handed it to me. It was a carving of a monkey and a cockerel entwined. 'This charm will bring you love, luck, and riches.' She quoted a price that made me blink.

'I'll take it,' I said. I handed over the money, grabbed the carving, and walked out the door. I had heard the slaves talk about voudoun and its powers. I knew, of course, it was all the heathen nonsense of barbaric unchristian people. Still, one never knows.

When I reached the Convent, I went straight to my room. I placed the leaf on top of one of the arms of the Cross hanging over my bed and tied it there with thread so that it would not be blown away. Sidonie and Josiane, with whom I shared a room, never paid any attention to me, and would not notice. And after all, it was I who did the cleaning, so there was no reason for anyone to take the magic Five Finger Grass away. But I wore the cockerel and monkey charm under my habit, close to my heart.

Sidonie

After Joelle left, time seemed to drag, and the summer heat was oppressive. Two other Casket Girls had married in recent weeks. Adelie, a plump girl with pale skin and darting eyes, had married a fishmonger, and Lucie, who was petite and feisty, had been successfully courted by a lawyer. I knew that the nuns would like to get me off their hands as well, but there seemed to be something about me that men found daunting.

It was lonely without Joelle. Josiane, who along with Immaculata shared my room, grew more and more silent, and her face took on a strange pallor. I knew she missed home. One day we were sitting in the courtyard after Vespers when a tradesman entered to deliver bags of flour and rice to Sister Fidelis in the kitchen. As he passed in front of us, Josiane suffered an attack of coughing. She held a handkerchief to her lips, and it came away with stains of blood. The man blanched, made the sign of the Cross, and left.

'What on earth is the matter with him?' I asked. My friend's face was drained of colour. 'Sidonie, I really must lie down,' she said in her soft Parisian accent. She had never said what had brought her to Louisiana as a Casket Girl; her accent was refined, and her gestures graceful. I helped her back to our room so that she could rest. Over the following weeks, she seemed to become thinner and thinner, and I could see the bones in her arms and shoulders.

As I was so lonely, I threw myself into my teaching. Palmyre had made great progress in her reading and writing, as had Clotilde, the youngest of my students. Clotilde was like a little wild creature who trembled when I asked her questions. I noticed that she was particularly jumpy around men, and wondered about what her life in Paris had been like before she and Nanette came to Louisiana. One day, after class, I asked Nanette to stay behind, and we walked out into the courtyard. The trees were bare, and winter had arrived.

'Nanette,' I said, 'I'm concerned about Clotilde. She's a very clever girl. She's got a good head for figures, and her writing and reading have progressed very well indeed. But I've noticed that she's painfully shy. Do you know anything about what may have happened to cause this?'

Nanette sighed. She looked tired, I though, with dark circles under her eyes, and her hair was untidy, with curls escaping from her chignon. She looked at me, and there was a world of weariness and cynicism in her eyes.

'Mademoiselle Sidonie,' she said, 'you are a virgin, are you not?'

I blushed to the roots of my hair. 'Of course.'

Nanette looked down at her hands. 'Both Clotilde and I were in a house in Paris. It was not a good place. I went there when I came to Paris at the age of sixteen, looking for work as a serving-maid. I worked as a maid in a very grand house for several weeks, but then the master of the house made advances to me.'

'Advances?' I said in horror. 'What do you mean?'

Her eyes were full of pity. 'You may be very clever, and have book learning, but you are such a child, Sidonie,' she said. 'He began to touch me in places where he shouldn't, when the mistress wasn't looking. One night he came to my bed. After that, he came every night, until the mistress realised what was going on. She burst into the room screaming, ripped the blankets off, and threw me into the streets naked.'

I gasped. Nanette continued, 'I was taken in by a woman who seemed kindly, who offered to let me stay at her house overnight. This seemed too good to be true. But it was a house of ill repute. I knew that I could never get a job in service, since I had been dismissed without a reference. So I ended up staying there. It was better than the streets. Most of the customers were lonely men who were starved for affection, or what passed for affection. But some of them were not very nice.'

'What do you mean?' I stammered.

'Some of them liked to beat us. But they were only a few. The worst were those who liked young girls. Very young girls like Clotilde.'

I felt as though I was going to be sick. 'How old was Clotilde?

'She was ten years old,' said Nanette in a matter-of-fact way. 'I tried to protect her as best I could. In a way, it felt as though she was my own child. I can't have children, because of things that had been done to me. But when one of the customers who liked to hurt us began to notice her, I knew it was time for us to leave. I spoke to one of my regular clients, who had friends in the court of Louis XV, and he told me about Louisiana. So, Clotilde and I escaped, made our way to the port, and came to New Orleans. Here, we both worked in a similar establishment, but when we heard that the nuns were offering classes to women like us, we seized the opportunity. Father Beaubois found a place for us in the house of a widow, and we do her cleaning.'

I realised that tears were streaming down my face. I took Nanette's hand. 'I think you and Clotilde are incredibly brave,' I said.

'Thank you,' she said. I was touched by her dignity. 'Whether or not learning the letters and doing sums will do us any good remains to be seen. But we are grateful to you for this opportunity.'

I had noticed that Clotilde was particularly nervous around the few men we saw in the Convent. 'This explains why

Clotilde is so jumpy around Father Beaubois,' I mused. 'He is a good man, but every time Clotilde sees him, she flinches.'

'Father Beaubois was kind to us, it's true. He is a priest, but he is a man after all,' Nanette said.

'Surely he hasn't made advances toward you!' I exclaimed in horror.

'No,' she admitted. 'Not at all. But with men, one never knows. I would like to believe that there are some good ones out there somewhere.'

Another thing I'd found strange was that Clotilde always wore long sleeves, despite the heat. I asked Nanette the reason for this.

Nanette shrugged. 'It's because of the scars.'

'What scars?" I asked.

'The ones left when one of the men burned her with the lit tip of a cigar.'

That evening, I sat with Father Beaubois, Mother Jerome, and Sister Fidelis at dinner. I knew they had noticed how much I was missing Joelle, and they had invited me to join them at their dinner table after she left. Suddenly a man rushed in. He looked sweaty and unkempt. Men were not supposed to enter the Convent, and this provoked a stir and a few furtive giggles. He made a signal to Father Beaubois, who met him at the door, and the two went outside.

'Whatever can this be about?' Mother Jerome said in exasperation.

Ten minutes later, Father Beaubois returned. He seemed preoccupied.

Mother Jerome served him some more chicken. 'Not bad news, I hope?' she asked.

Father Beaubois shook his head. 'The Indians,' he said.

Sister Immaculata

One of the advantages of being invisible is that I overhear people's indiscretions. When I serve them dinner, they tend to forget that I am there.

I could tell that Father Beaubois was furious. 'There's been an uprising in Fort Rosalie,' he said. I knew that Fort Rosalie was a trading post upriver that was also a military outpost which was supposed to protect us, not just from the Indians, but from the British. Father Beaubois went on, 'Around a hundred and fifty Frenchmen were massacred.'

The nuns gasped, and I saw Sidonie go white. 'My student Coahoma!' she cried out. 'I knew something was wrong, and then she began missing class. I haven't seen her in the last fortnight, and wondered if she was ill.' She turned to Father Beaubois. 'Do you have any news of them?

'Not of them specifically,' he replied wearily. 'But according to the reports, women and children and African slaves were spared.'

'Is New Orleans in danger?' asked Mother Jerome.

'We don't know the extent of the revolt,' Father Beaubois replied. 'Whether other tribes will join in remains to be seen.'

Sidonie seemed relieved. I thought it was foolish of her to be concerned about those savages, who would just as soon murder us in our beds. She asked Father Beaubois, 'Reverend Father, what led the Natchez to revolt?'

The priest looked at her with a curious expression on his face. I could swear it was respect, mixed with a certain disconcerting tenderness. Well, well, well. What have we here? I asked myself.

Father Beaubois answered, 'To be frank, Sidonie, the remarkable stupidity of the French authorities.'

'What do you mean?' Sister Fidelis asked, bristling.

Father Beaubois sighed. 'We had hoped to establish a mission near Fort Rosalie to convert the Natchez. But the colonists were greedy, and expected the Indians to work for nothing. For a while, any differences were settled by negotiations between Governor Bienville and the Natchez chief Tattooed Serpent. There was one episode in which colonists were allegedly attacked by the Natchez, and Bienville ordered their village to be burned to the ground and its inhabitants enslaved. But later it was discovered that the Natchez had been falsely accused, and that the attack was a fabrication.'

Mother Jerome recoiled. 'Surely, Reverend Father, honourable Frenchmen would never behave in such a way.'

Father Beaubois let out a harsh laugh. 'The colonists at Fort Rosalie were anything but honourable. The Natchez chief, Tattooed Serpent, said that the French seemed to have two hearts, a good one today and tomorrow a bad one.' He sighed.

'What happened next?' asked Sidonie.

'Things went from bad to worse. The Governor appointed an imbecile, the Sieur de Chépart, as Commandant of the Fort. Chépart had powerful friends, and he was greedy, so continued encroaching on Natchez lands. The final straw was when he told the Natchez that he was going to seize the land where their ancestors were buried, and that he would build his own plantation there. Now, it seems, they've risen up against the French. The man who just came to give me the news says that Chépart was taken prisoner and beheaded.'

There were gasps around the table. Mother Jerome said to Sister Fidelis, 'We must ensure that there is enough food and lay in supplies. Also, it would be best to see that the Convent's doors and windows are fortified.'

Sidonie never knew when to keep her mouth shut. 'Reverend Father,
how can we hope to convert them to Christianity when "Christians" set such dreadful examples?' Her cheeks were flushed. 'My student Coahoma is a good person. She told us about their beliefs, which have so much in common with ours. I do not believe that we can gain their respect if we do not respect them in return.'

Mother Jerome recoiled in horror. 'The very idea!' she sputtered. 'Their beliefs are heathen superstitions which do not deserve to be talked about, much less respected. The idea that our religion might have something in common with their outlandish ideas is blasphemy. There is only one Way to salvation, as the Scriptures tell us, and that is through our Lord Jesus Christ. You are supposed to be teaching them to read and write, not spend time in idle chitchat about these matters.' A vein in her forehead twitched, and she suddenly looked very old.

Sidonie looked down at her hands. 'Yes, Reverend Mother.' I knew, though, that this submissive air was all a front. But she didn't deceive me. Under that bookish exterior, there lurked a rebellious sinful heart.

At that point, I could not resist speaking out. I said to Father Beaubois, 'The other day, when I went to the shops, a man said he had heard the Casket Girls were vampires. He saw blood on Josiane's handkerchief. Sidonie's students, those Indian savages, with their heathen beliefs, must have bewitched her.'

Father Beaubois turned toward me. I had never seen him so angry. 'Immaculata, be silent!' he said. He was trembling in fury. 'Josiane, poor child, is suffering from consumption. It is unlikely that she'll live through the winter. This has nothing to do with witchcraft or with vampires.'

Sidonie

After dinner, alone in my room, I was shaking in rage. I tried not to imagine the horrors my student Coahoma had witnessed and seethed with indignation at the unfairness with which her people had been treated. I also felt ashamed of the anger that Mother Jerome's lack of Christian charity made me feel. And Immaculata's outrageous accusation that Josiane was a vampire had left me speechless. I asked myself once more what on earth had made Immaculata so angry and twisted. But I saw at once that Father Beaubois was right, and that Josiane was not long for this world. The nuns had taken the decision to send her to a sanitarium on the edge of the city, which meant that now, after the departure of Berthe, Josiane and Joelle, Immaculata and I would be sharing a room. The prospect did not fill me with joy.

The talk with Nanette had been upsetting as well, and I tried hard not to think about Clotilde and her scars and the dreadful experiences that she and Nanette had endured. I was concerned for the two of them and their future. I knew that, given their past, they would never be able to find work as teachers or governesses. But if they did not find some means of supporting themselves, the most they could expect was menial work as servants, where it made little difference if they could read or write or do sums. I was determined to help them, and to prevent them from falling back into the grimness of their previous way of life.

The problem was to find a way for them to make a living. In New Orleans, not many professions were open to women other than teaching or domestic service, or perhaps shop-keeping. I asked myself what sort of shop they could have, or what sort of articles they could sell. It was certainly the case that for merchandise other than food, we often had had to wait long months for ships from France to arrive. But there was money in New Orleans, and I occasionally encountered the well-dressed women whose daughters came to the Convent school.

The following morning dawned bright, with mist rising from the river in silver clouds. After breakfast, I went to the kitchen and encountered Sister Fidelis teaching Sister Immaculata to make bread. Immaculata's habit was dusted with flour, and bits of dough clung to her hands and face and to her eyebrows. She looked mildly deranged, but was pounding away at the dough with gusto. 'Gently, gently,' chided Sister Fidelis. 'You must knead the dough, not beat the life out of it.'

'Sister, would you like for me to run any errands for you?' I asked. 'I need to go into town to buy paper and pencils for my students.'

'Yes please, Sidonie,' Sister Fidelis replied, with a harried air. It was clear that Sister Immaculata was not destined for culinary genius, and it looked as though a hurricane had hit the kitchen. 'Could you please bring me some fruit and vegetables? Oranges, blackberries, squash, and a small pumpkin? And two pounds of sugar.'

I grabbed a basket and set out. I walked down to the Place d'Armes, and turned down a side street, then headed toward the market. Two young ladies, modestly veiled and dressed in what even to my unsophisticated eye looked like the latest fashion, were standing in front of a haberdashery. One of them was tall, slender, with dark curly hair. The other was small and plump.

The first woman seemed agitated. 'It is so frustrating, Laure,' she exclaimed. 'I am going to be married in six months, and not a single establishment in New Orleans has embroidered bed linens of quality. I would order them from France, but they would never arrive in time for the wedding. I simply cannot marry Gustave without an appropriate trousseau! What on earth am I to do?'

Like all the Casket Girls, I had learned how to sew back in France with the Ursulines. The nuns had taught us how to make simple garments, and to embroider handkerchiefs and the like. My fingers were nimble enough, but I was far too impatient to be good at embroidery; it always felt as though the time I spent sewing was time taken away from my world of books. It occurred to me, however, that this might be the answer for Nanette and Clotilde, and for Coahoma if she ever returned. If they managed to build up a trade in embroidered household linens, they could have a steady income and perhaps one day even a home of their own. Palmyre, of course, was a slave, and whatever extra income she earned would go to her owners, that is to say, the Ursulines. Still, if she could also learn a useful skill, it would help to ensure that she could be a house slave and thus better treated, rather than being sent out to chop cane or indigo out in the fields.

As I rounded the corner, absorbed in my thoughts, I bumped into Father Beaubois, who was heading in the direction of the Convent. I knew that he went most mornings to walk down by the river. '*Pardonnez-moi*, Reverend Father,' I said when I got my breath back. 'I must learn to look where I am going.'

'It is nothing, Sidonie,' he said, falling into step alongside me. Away from the Convent, he somehow looked younger, more carefree. 'You seemed worlds away.'

Something about the priest invited trust. 'Reverend Father, I am concerned about the future of two of my students. I know that you arranged for Nanette and Clotilde to come to the Convent school to learn to read and write. It was a very kind thing for you to do.'

' 'The world is remarkably cruel, Sidonie,' he said.

Encouraged, I ploughed on. 'I've been wondering what will become of them. I know that it's unlikely that they will become teachers.'

Father Beaubois shrugged. 'Perhaps, but a knowledge of letters and sums is always useful.'

Undaunted, I went on. 'It occurred to me that one way for them to make an independent living would be to take up embroidery and learn to produce fine household linens. I could teach them this skill. But I'd need some cloth to practice on,

102

and some linen sheets and needles and embroidery thread. These things cost money, and I have none of my own. So, it is probably not be possible.'

We walked along in silence for a while. As we drew close to the Convent, Father Beaubois said, 'I know that Mother Jerome has very little spare cash. She takes the Ursuline vows of poverty very seriously.' I thought I could detect a note of irony.

'Joelle's husband seems to have money, 'I said. 'I wonder if we could ask M. Ardoin for a donation.'

'No!' Father Beaubois exclaimed. 'Do not go near that man, Sidonie. He is wealthy, but he is not a good person.' He thought for a minute. 'I have some private income of my own. If you like, I could contribute to this. Or I could arrange for a French relative to do so.'

I clapped my hands in delight. 'That would be wonderful.'

'Let me think about the best way to do this,' he said. 'For now, best not to mention it to anyone else.'

That night, as I lay bed, I thought about Father Beaubois. He looked around thirty years old, which to me was a great age. Gossip was rife in the Convent, of course. I'd heard the other Convent girls speculate about what had brought him to Louisiana. Some said it was disappointment in love that had led him to enter the priesthood. Others said that he came from a wealthy background and had quarrelled with his family. That last I could believe; there was something about him that revealed the kind of assurance that only comes with a conviction of one's own innate superiority. But he wore his confidence lightly. I had never known him to be unkind, though the nuns, bless them, would wear out the patience of a saint with their witterings. I knew that he loved the river, and wondered whether he'd grown up by a big river back home in France.

For the next two weeks, nothing happened, and I reached the conclusion that Father Beaubois had decided that the project I'd suggested was girlish nonsense. But then a ship from France docked at the port. A few days later, Mother Jerome called me into her study.

'Sidonie, I have some good news for you. A relative of Father Beaubois has very kindly donated a sum of money to the Convent to train students in needlework. Most of it will go, of course, to our regular students, but Father Beaubois has persuaded us that a small sum should be used to train your students in embroidery. I shall expect you to keep rigorous accounts of what is spent on cloth, needles, embroidery thread, and so forth.' She patted my hand, and continued, 'You're a good girl, Sidonie. But it's far better for all of you to be working with your needles, rather than wasting time in idle conversation about heathen superstitions and the like.'

I lowered my eyes demurely. 'I am honoured, Reverend Mother.'

Later, though, I wondered about this sudden development. I knew that it took ships nearly three months to arrive from France. My conversation with Father Beaubois had taken place only a fortnight ago.

The conclusion I reached was inescapable: he had paid for this out of his own pocket. Curiously, the subterfuge caused me no qualms of conscience. The Convent was a world awash in secrets and half-truths, of things left unsaid. I knew that a personal donation from Father Beaubois might cause a stir and prompt accusations of favouritism. One small white lie, in the service of what was undoubtedly a good cause, was surely justified. I thought of Nanette and Clotilde, and resolved then and there to do my very best to justify Father Beaubois's faith in me. After all, hadn't the prostitute Mary Magdalene been the first to see the risen Lord? There but for the grace of God...Who knows what might have happened to Joelle and me and the other Casket Girls if the nuns had not taken me in. I feared that Palmyre would be less enthusiastic about embroidery, since as slaves she would not receive the fruits of her own labour. Still, perhaps there might be ways around that.

Chapter 7

Sister Immaculata

It's been busy in the kitchen, as usual. Sister Fidelis, after the recent Indian alarm, has been trying to teach me to cook a few more dishes. What I like best is making bread and pounding the dough. I pretend that the soft white dough of the buns I make are the soft fat bellies of the cloister nuns. They are completely idle and useless. All they do is pray, pray, pray. If the Indians scalp them, as they did at Fort Rosalie, I'd laugh. I don't believe the nonsense they were talking about at dinner, that the Indians had spared women and children. The Indians are godless savages, and the only thing they understand is force and brute strength.

One thing's for sure: the Governor knows what's what. Fidelis sent me out to buy flour, because after the attack there was a shortage of grain in New Orleans. I overheard a man saying in the grocer's that Governor Perier had ordered his soldiers to retaliate, but against a different tribe. They wiped out an entire village and left no survivors. Quite right too. People didn't like this, but that was foolish: Indians are all alike. Vermin. If we left any alive, they'd murder us in our beds one night. Now they're saying that the king is going to order the Governor back to France in disgrace. But at least that Indian girl in Sidonie's class is gone, and it looks like she's gone for good. Good riddance is what I say. I never liked the look of her.

Treacherous, scheming heathens, one and all. They carry disease and devils, and probably made Josiane ill. Though now that she's gone, there's more space in the room I share with Sidonie. She's never said anything about my voudoun plant, and takes no notice of me at all. Which is just how I like it.

As if Indian massacres wasn't enough, Sidonie is trying to teach the tarts and slaves embroidery! The very idea. As if any decent woman would touch anything they had made. But at least she isn't running errands for Fidelis any more. Cooking isn't bad, but what I really enjoy is going out to the shops. That way I can find out what's happening in the wider world and feel the sun on my face. And Sidonie was getting above herself, when she's really just a poor orphan like the rest.

I moved to the table and began to remove the fat and bones from the pieces of cooked chicken. The nuns may pretend to be delicate and ladylike, but they eat like stevedores. We can use the broth for consommé and put the meat into rissoles. These are tiresome to make, but they do make the meat stretch a long way.

And with vegetables from the garden, it is possible to make a tasty meal. I love the tomatoes. Back in France, they had to be cultivated in glasshouses because of the chilly springs in Brittany, but in the Louisiana heat they're abundant. The scent of fresh tomatoes is something I love. Who needs perfume, when they can smell like fresh tomatoes, and maybe peaches. In the market, there was also a strange vegetable called okra, which the slaves had brought from Africa. They cooked it with chicken and tomato to make a soup called gumbo.

When the water came to a boil, I put the bones back in and began to stir. A curious sense of contentment stole over me. Even with the heat, it was good to be in the kitchen, with light streaming through the window. Then the door burst open, and Sidonie came in from the garden. She was carrying a basket of lemons. When she saw me, she gasped.

'What on earth is wrong with you?' I snapped.

'Nothing, Sister,' she said. 'I was just startled for a moment when I saw you in a cloud of smoke, stirring bones. It reminded me of a fairy tale I once read.'

I snorted and returned to stirring the cauldron. I knew she thought of me in the role of the Wicked Witch. 'Pride goeth before a fall, missy,' I thought. 'I've seen the way Father Beaubois looks at you, and the way you pretend not to see.'

Sidonie turned to me. 'Sister, do you know if the ship from France brought in any letters for me? '

'And who might you be expecting to get a letter from, pray tell?' I sneered. 'Your family?' I knew all her family were dead.

'No,' she said quietly. 'From my friend Joelle.' I knew, because I know everything that goes on here, that Joelle had promised to write. Since they didn't know where Joelle and her husband would be staying in Paris, it was not practical for Sidonie to write to her in return, but I knew that she was eager for news of her empty-headed friend. It had been nearly six months since Joelle had left.

One good thing, at least, was that what I'd come to call my funny turns weren't as frequent. I'd learned to recognise when they were coming on: things began to take on a halo of light and seemed far away. I knew then to go to the broom closet under the stairs before my limbs began to shake and thrash. One thing that seemed to bring them on was flickering light: candles in the breeze, sunlight rippling on the river. I did not want for Sister Fidelis and the others to know about the black feathered shadows. If they did, I might never be able to escape the Convent, or even worse, I might be sent to the local lunatic asylum. I had heard rumours about the sort of place it was, where people were chained and left in the dark.

I untied the strings of my apron and prepared to go out in search of flour and rice. Sister Fidelis said that if New Orleans was surrounded and under siege, these staples would last. I thought she was overreacting. Now that the Indians had been properly dealt with, the rebellion seemed to have petered out. We'd had several days of rain, and the streets were full of mud. Louisiana rain was so different from the gentle rain of the North of France. Here the water fell in sheets from the sky and filled the gutters, until the streets flowed like rivers.

First, I went to the grocer's. We produced most of our own vegetables, but Sister Marie-Paul had a secret fondness for persimmon cakes, a local delicacy which, for a fee, I would smuggle into the convent. Stocks of grain and rice were running low, but I managed to get several bags and was very pleased with myself. I put them in a burlap bag, heaved it over my shoulder, and began to trudge back. Even after the rain stopped for a moment, the steam was rising from the cobblestones. I noticed that the clouds were long thin streaks in the sky.

I went into the butcher's. My black habit was soaked, and I was trailing water in my wake. 'You're heavily laden today, Sister,' said Pierre Cormier. He seemed formal, a bit distant. It occurred to me that he was probably terrified that I'd have another of my strange turns.

'Not at all, M. Cormier,' I said briskly. I noticed that his shop seemed empty, both of customers and of merchandise. 'Have the Indian troubles affected your business?'

'I used to get most of my beef from the farms upriver. They've been cut off. Things will return to normal, I think, before too long, if the idiot of the Governor is recalled, and if whoever replaces him treats the Indians decently.'   I sniffed. 'I suppose that means that all you have are those two scrawny chickens.'

'For now, that is so,' he said. He quoted a price for the chickens that made me blink. 'That is outrageous, Monsieur,' I cried. 'They are for the Convent. Think of your immortal soul.'

Cormier laughed. 'That is the way of these things, Sister,' he said. 'The fewer the chickens, the higher the price. If the Convent doesn't want them, others will. And my soul can take care of itself.'

I scowled and handed over the money. Cormier grinned. 'I know it would be hard for you to return empty-handed to a convent full of hungry nuns, Sister.'

'You have no idea, Monsieur Cormier,' I replied tartly. 'The sin of gluttony is rampant among us.'

He handed me some stew bones, and some bay leaves. 'For *lagniappe*,' he said.

'What's *lagniappe*?' I asked.

'It's a New Orleans word. It means a little extra. Like when the baker gives a thirteenth cake free when someone buys a dozen.'

'Thank you, Monsieur,' I told him. 'But the next time, deduct the *lagniappe* from the price.' He laughed. 'You should have been a shop-keeper, Sister.'

I sighed. 'That would have been my dream. But to have a shop, one needs money, and my family were poor. So, the Convent was my only choice. Either that or go into service, which was even worse.'

'What's wrong with domestic service?' he asked. 'My sister back in France was a lady's maid, and she married a farmer.'

'Good for her,' I said drily. The idea of myself, with my big awkward hands and clumsy feet, as a lady's maid, was ridiculous, I knew. 'I always wanted to be my own mistress, to come and go as I pleased and answer to nobody but myself.'

'That I can understand,' Cormier said. He looked out at the rain. 'Sister, I trust that in the Convent the nuns will be preparing for the storm.'

'What storm?' I asked.

'The hurricane,' I replied.

'What on earth is a hurricane?' I asked in exasperation. I did not like being made to feel ignorant, with all these unfamiliar words.

'It is a storm like none you have ever seen in France,' he said. 'They come from the tropics, with high whirling winds and torrential rain. I know that one is coming because of the clouds.'

I looked out of the window. The clouds were stretched tight across the sky, like grey silk ribbons frayed to the point of tearing. I did not like this one single bit.

'I must be off, Monsieur,' I said. 'I shall keep you in my prayers.' It was, of course, possible that Cormier was teasing me by making up stories about monster storms. Still, the air felt heavy and leaden. When I returned to the Convent, I knocked at Mother Jerome's door.

'Yes, Immaculata?' she said.

'Reverend Mother, the butcher told me that a big storm is on its way.'

She looked sceptical, but raised her eyebrows. 'Very well, Immaculata. Perhaps we should ensure that everything is tied down and secure, just in case.'   I went to the back of the courtyard and told the slaves to put their chickens inside. If

Sidonie wanted to stow the heavy flowerpots under the stairs, she could do it herself.

Sidonie

When I knocked on Mother Jerome's door, I bumped into Sister Immaculata. She pushed past me without a word, and I asked myself once more why she was always so unpleasant to me. Mother Jerome beckoned me in. There was a stack of papers on her desk, and I could see that she was busy.

'Reverend Mother,' I asked, 'is there any post for me?'

'As a matter of fact, there is,' she said. She handed me three letters, all of which had arrived on the same ship. I could see my name on the envelope, written in Joelle's round childish hand. She had left on her honeymoon in November, and it was now June. I was delighted at the prospect of news from my friend.

I went back to my room and settled down to read. Outside, the rain was falling, and the wind had begun to rise.

Paris, 3 March 1729

Dearest Sidonie,

I am writing this from the beautiful house Armand has rented for us in Paris, after a long voyage across the Atlantic. Paris is cold! I had forgotten just how cold it is here. But the streets are full of light, and the shops are wonderful. Armand has said that my New Orleans dresses are old-fashioned and dowdy, and he has taken me to a modiste to

113

have some new clothing made. He says I will need to have beautiful clothes as mistress of Les Chenes.

The seamstress seems to know him well. She said to me that she had made clothes for some of Armand's friends. I asked him who these friends were, thinking that it would be nice to have some female friends in Paris. This made him cross, and he turned away and wouldn't speak to me for the rest of the afternoon. That evening, though, he was wonderfully kind and loving.

The dresses are beautiful. One is made of rose-coloured satin, edged in black velvet ribbon. Another is white, with lace trimmings. Yet another is yellow, the colour of my hair Armand says. He is so wonderfully generous. I have little shoes, and fans to go with each dress.

I am so happy, Joelle. Armand is everything I dreamed of, so handsome and distinguished. When I walk with him down by the Seine, in the sunlight, I really feel that it would be impossible to be happier, and I know how lucky I am. How are you? How are your classes going? Are there any prospective suitors in sight? I think of you often, my friend.

Love,
Joelle

Paris, 30 March 1729

Dearest Sidonie,

Paris in the springtime is absolutely enchanting. From my window I can see children playing in the park. I long for a baby of my own, my friend. The last weeks have been a bit strange...Armand has been away several times, to tend to business affairs, he says, and when he returns his mood is dark. Last night I asked him when we were going to visit his mother in the South of France, and he turned on me and said some very hurtful things that I won't repeat here. At times he is very loving, but then it changes. Once, when he returned, he smelled of a perfume I didn't recognise, a heady scent of gardenias. I am praying that when we have a child, it will bring us closer.

How are you, and how are things in New Orleans? We have heard news of an Indian uprising...I do hope that you and the Sisters have not been affected. I worry about you, my friend, with that strange Indian student of yours.

I wish it were possible for you to write to me. Armand is now saying that we will return to Louisiana at the end of summer! We embark at the end of August, first for St. Domingue, then for New Orleans. How good it will be to see you, my friend. I am a little lonely here.

Love,
Joelle

10 June 1729

Dearest Sidonie,

I have the most wonderful news! I am going to have a baby. This will change everything. Armand now could not be more attentive, more generous and kind. He is doing everything he possibly can to ensure that the plantation house at Les Chenes is ready for the baby and me, but of course it is difficult at such a distance. We spend a good deal of time looking at furnishings for the house: fine crystal chandeliers, mahogany furniture., good linens, silver tableware. He says it is going to be the finest plantation house in the Mississippi valley.

How lives can change, Sidonie. To think that two years ago you and I were two orphans, living on the charity of the Ursulines and fearful of what the future might bring to us in Louisiana. Now I shall be the chatelaine of a beautiful plantation. I am determined to find a nice husband for you! If, of course, you haven't been snapped up by then.

I am a little frightened of actually giving birth. My dear friend: will you promise to be with me when it happens? Armand refuses to let me visit Claude and her family, and you are the only family I've got. I do miss you, and cannot wait to see you and hear of your doings.

All my love,
Joelle

I put Joelle's letters away carefully, in the little trunk where I kept my few possessions. Her words evoked her presence so vividly, as did the faint scent of lily of the valley that emanated from the pages. My friend seemed happy, but there was an undercurrent of something else that I couldn't quite identify. At times, I felt a certain frustration with my own lack of experience of the world. I had learned a great deal about humanity and about the complexities of human behaviour from my books, but there was so much I found baffling because I hadn't lived it. I hated feeling childish and ignorant of the ways of the world. Now Joelle was a married woman, and from what she was saying she was contented and loved her husband. I had no earthly idea what married life must be like. Still, life after marriage, it seemed, had facets that didn't quite fit in with the happily-ever-after endings of the novels and fairytales I loved. One thing was certain, though: if my friend needed me when the baby was born, I'd be there. Though the idea of being present at the actual birth, if truth be told, filled me with terror.

That night I could hardly sleep because of the howling of the wind. But the thought that my friend would be arriving in the autumn gladdened my heart.

Chapter 8

Sister Immaculata

Pierre Cormier knew what he was talking about. The winds rose in the night, and rain fell in sheets. We had had big storms before here in New Orleans, and they were nothing like the milder thunderstorms in France. This, however, was something else altogether.

At dawn, Father Beaubois and Mother Jerome summoned us all into the chapel. The older nuns huddled together, blinking like newborns. I saw that the Casket Girls who still hadn't found husbands, and the slaves, were there too. The dim light filtering in through the windows had a strange reddish tinge.

Father Beaubois looked drawn and tense. 'Sisters, mademoiselles, we must take precautions against the rising storm. I have spoken to the Commandant of the Port of New Orleans, and he has said that, since the Chapel and the provisional Convent are among the few brick buildings in town, we may be asked to allow people to take refuge here. At this moment, the Commandant has ordered his men to place sandbags into position to support the levees.'

'Are we in any danger here, Reverend Father?' asked Sister Fidelis. Her voice trembled.

'I would hope not, Sister,' Father Beaubois replied. 'However, when I was in S. Domingue, I experienced this sort of storm. It is called an *ouragan*, or hurricane. We should be prepared to evacuate to the upper floor if the river rises. If the levees break, God help us all.'

The nuns' faces were pale. They began droning a Rosary. I thought it would be far more practical to actually take precautions, and went with Sister Fidelis to the kitchen. There, we began to carry bags of staples—flour, sugar, chick-peas, beans—up the stairs. I called to the slaves and ordered them to help. One of them, called Palmyre, gave me an insolent look, but did as she was told.

Throughout the morning the winds continued to rise. The howling noise they made was like nothing I had ever heard. It sounded like the furious roars of a wounded creature a devil conjured up from the darkness of the swamps. By noon, some neighbours had taken refuge with us. Why they built their houses of wood, I do not know: stone is always the best, and failing that, good solid brick. I saw that Pierre Cormier had come in.

'You were right about the storm, M. Cormier,' I said to him. I motioned for him to sit on one of the benches propped against the Chapel wall.

'Yes,' he said curtly. His face was grim. His butcher shop was made of brick and clapboard, and I could tell that he was worried. I moved to make room for more arrivals, but at that point I saw water beginning to ooze in, rippling under the door. Father Beaubois saw it too.

'To the upper floor!' he shouted. The nuns shrieked and stampeded toward the stairs. So much for ladylike behaviour and Christian charity, I thought sardonically. Father Beaubois clapped his hands. 'Sisters, one by one. Let the older ones among you go first!'

Surprisingly, they obeyed. Most of the nuns were accustomed to doing whatever a man ordered them to do. We filed upstairs, followed by the Casket Girls and the slaves. I saw that Berthe, the fat Casket Girl who had married M. Clement the grocer, had come for shelter with us, along with about ten other people I'd never seen before. At the top of the stairs was a long room, with windows over the eaves, directly over the kitchen. It was there that I had stashed the food earlier and was small for so many people. There must have been forty of us. The tarts were there as well, along with the woman whose house they cleaned. I saw that the slave, Palmyre, had brought a large basket, from which clucking sounds emerged. Much as I hated to admit it, this was good thinking. If food supplies to the city were cut off, we would at least have eggs, and if we had to, we could eat the chickens. And there was fruit as well, though in this climate that would rot quickly. The sky had grown black, and the only light was from a large candle in an alcove.

We huddled together in the shadows. Outside, there was a crashing sound, and someone shrieked. I stood on tiptoe and peered through the window under the eaves.

Beneath was a sea of dark water. The shop across the street was flooded up to the first floor. I saw a large boat fly past. It felt strange to see it sail through the air. It was as though the worlds of air and water and land had become confused, and that birds would be swimming down below the sea. For the first time, I thought that I might die.

Pierre Cormier was seated on the floor in a corner. He was unshaven, and the flickering light played on his black hair and the shadows under his eyes. He smelled of sweat. Next to him was a woman with a baby and a small child. The baby was crying, but the child's eyes were round with delight. I sat down on Cormier's other side, in the corner and drew a blanket over our knees. 'Have you been through a storm like this before?' I asked.

He nodded. 'Yes, Sister, about five years ago. When I came here from France, I made a living trapping nutrias on Bayou Lafourche.'

'Do you ever miss France?' I asked. I really did not want to die here, far from home, from Brittany. Suddenly I felt his big rough hand take mine under the blanket. He began to stroke my wrist with his finger in gentle circular movements, and my breath began to come faster.

'Some things,' he said. 'I miss my mother's cooking. But here at last we're free to make a life for ourselves.' I noted a tinge of uncertainty in his voice.

Suddenly there was an eerie silence. The wind had stopped. 'May the Lord be praised!' exclaimed Mother Jerome. 'The storm has passed, and we are safe.'

'No, Sister' said Father Beaubois. 'This is the eye of the storm. In about half an hour, the winds will resume with even greater fury. Keep praying.'

I shall never forget that silence. We all sat there, waiting. Suddenly a sound broke the silence. A piteous miaow.

That fool Sidonie had rescued a cat.

Sidonie

I knew when we were called to the chapel at dawn that this wasn't a storm like the others. Strangely, I wasn't frightened, at least not at first. I tried to decide quickly what I wanted to save, and the only things that really mattered to me were a crucifix that had belonged to my mother, Joelle's letters, and my books. I didn't have many books, which is perhaps why they were doubly precious to me. I returned to our sleeping quarters and bundled them up carefully and headed back down the stairs. I glanced out into the courtyard and saw that my poor flowers had been battered by the wind; some of the flowerpots had been dashed against the wall and lay in fragments. I berated myself for not putting the flowerpots away yesterday and went out to the courtyard to see if anything could be salvaged.

Suddenly I saw a movement in a corner of the courtyard. I shrank back, fearing that it might be a snake. There were many snakes in New Orleans, because of the proximity of the swamps and the great river. But it wasn't a snake: it was a small, bedraggled kitten, a little tabby with green eyes. Its fur was soaked and matted, and it was shivering when I reached down to pick it up.

'*Pauvre petite minou*,' I crooned. Poor little kitty. It seemed to find my voice soothing. I dimly remembered a cat that had belonged to my parents, a rangy ginger tom. The only animals in the Convent were the chickens, which the slaves cared for, and a scrawny cow which provided us with milk. I loved cats, but we were not allowed to have pets. I could not bring myself to abandon the kitten, and tucked it under my cape and held it close when returned to the Chapel.

When water started lapping at the lower floor, we all took refuge upstairs. I sat in a corner with my students Palmyre, Nanette and Clotilde on one side and my friend Berthe on the other. Berthe was the jolly plump Casket Girl who had married a grocer. Although we'd shared a room before she met her husband, I did not know her well, since Joelle was my closest friend and I spent most of my free time talking and gossiping with her before her marriage to Armand, but I liked Berthe and found her practicality and good humour reassuring.

'What a storm, Sidonie!' she exclaimed. 'My husband is moving goods to our warehouse. I hope that he has the sense to take shelter, but you know what men are like.'`

Actually, I didn't know much about what men were like, but nodded vaguely. 'You seem happy, Berthe. I'm glad things are good for you, and glad that your shop is doing well.'

She shrugged. '*Bien*: I can't complain. Jacques works hard, and he does not beat me. We have plenty to eat, and I like working behind the counter. He says I'm good with the customers. And he keeps me warm at night.' She smiled and gave me a wink. 'What about you, Sidonie? '

'No suitors in sight, I'm afraid,' I said. 'But I enjoy my teaching very much. Some of my students are here now.' I nodded toward Palmyre, Nanette and Clotilde. I'd noticed that in such close quarters, some of the cloister nuns had shrunk away from contact with my students. Berthe, however, took their presence in her stride, and smiled at them. 'I hope that Sidonie doesn't make you work too hard.'

The roaring winds had gone silent. Suddenly I felt a movement under my cloak. A paw emerged, then a pair of ears, then a little face. The kitten let out a piteous miaow.

Somehow it broke the tension. The nuns clustered around me, reached out to stroke the little cat. Sister Immaculata, as ever, was a dissenting voice. 'The very last thing we need just now is a...cat. Filthy animals. Full of fleas and ticks.' She was sitting in the corner. Beside her was a black-haired man whom I thought I remembered seeing somewhere in town.

Father Beaubois's face had softened. 'You must admit, Immaculata, that this room is like an Ark surrounded by water. Perhaps this little creature will bring us luck.' He extended a hand. The kitten nuzzled his fingers and began to purr.

About half an hour later, the wind picked up again. We could not talk above the roaring. I heard a crash and peeked out the window. One of the big oaks in the courtyard had come down. I could see rooftops and treetops above the water, but not much else. I had thought about death before, on the boat coming here, and when the young nun died of yellow fever, but it always seemed to be something that happened to others. But now death suddenly felt real, and I felt angry at the prospect of dying so young with so much living left to do. I tried to remember the figures of my dead parents. All I could recall of my mother was the faint scent of lavender. Of my father, I remembered nothing. I thought of Joelle and wondered what it must be like to love a man and to carry a child within us. If we get through this, I thought, I am going to live and live and live.

The kitten nestled close, and it was good to feel another heartbeat. 'Try to sleep, Sidonie,' Palmyre said. She and Berthe covered me with an old blanket, and Clotilde gave the little cat a bit of bread. I knew that they were as frightened as I was. But the one thing that brought me much comfort was that if we were swallowed up by the waters, I would not die alone, but surrounded by the love of friends.

I was awakened the following morning by a ray of sunlight coming through the windows under the eaves. Mother Jerome and Father Beaubois were standing near the window, and their faces were grave. I tiptoed over and whispered, 'Is it over?'

'The storm has passed, thank the good Lord,' said Mother Jerome. 'The waters have receded, though there will be damage on the ground floor. Many of our neighbours' houses have been destroyed.'

The three of us stepped over the bodies of the sleeping nuns and descended the stairs. There was still about a foot of water in the kitchen, though it seemed to be draining away slowly. I looked out into the courtyard. The chicken coops were in ruins, and the slave cabins had splintered into jagged fragments. I wondered where Palmyre would sleep. The street outside was deep in mud and debris. A child's shoe was lodged at a strange angle on a windowsill. I tried not to think about what might have happened to its young owner.

Father Beaubois led us into the Chapel. There too the floor was covered in river mud, but the damage seemed less extensive. He turned to Mother Jerome. 'Reverend Mother, we must have a mass of thanksgiving for our deliverance from the storm. First, though, we must check to see if the well in the courtyard has been polluted and find out if we still have still fresh water.'

We waded into the courtyard. Father Beaubois lowered the rope and pulled out a bucket of water. He dipped into it with his hands and drank, then sighed in relief. 'It's brackish but drinkable. The Lord be praised. Dirty water is a source of disease.'

I was impressed by his knowledge. Presumably he had learned about hurricanes and their aftermath after his experience in S. Domingue. 'Were people ill after the hurricane in St. Domingue, Reverend Father?' I asked.

'Yes, Sidonie,' he replied. 'There were epidemics of yellow fever and cholera. At times it did seem that S. Domingue was under a curse.'

I knew very little about S. Domingue, except that it was a rich colony where sugar was produced. 'Why was that, Reverend Father?'

'The sugar plantations were visions of hell,' he said. 'Conditions there were so appalling that many of the slaves brought to work on them died.'

Mother Jerome interrupted. 'If we are going to have a mass of thanksgiving, there's no time for chitchat, Sidonie. We'll need to wash the pews and floors of the Chapel. Go fetch Sister Immaculata and Sister Fidelis, and of course the slave Palmyre.'

I did as I was told. The little cat had curled up with Berthe, who was still sound asleep.

Sister Immaculata

The morning after the storm, we looked out at the street. It was covered with more than a foot of mud. Many of the houses had been reduced to matchsticks. The Convent was forced to take in people who had lost everything, but since we didn't have much room to begin with, it soon became clear that more would have to be done. The Governor opened up some rooms of his Palace as temporary refuge, and the work of rebuilding began.

The smells were disgusting. Under the reek of river mud, there was a sweet scent of decay. I'd grown up on a farm, and knew what that meant: dead animals, dead people. Carts went around, and when bodies were unearthed from the mud, they were tossed into a cart to be taken outside the city and burned. The smell of smoke and burning flesh seemed to seep into our clothing. Flies buzzed everywhere. The mosquitoes had been ferocious before, but now when we went outdoors, they covered whatever was exposed: hands, face, ears.

The Convent itself was, of course, filthy, especially the ground floor. The cloister nuns and the students had to soil their dainty little hands and clean up muck just like the rest of us. It took us nearly a week just to remove the layers of mud and silt from the floor and walls. I worked until my hands bled. New Orleans was so humid that it seemed nothing would ever be dry and clean again.

It was an act of Our Lord's Divine Providence that the chickens had been saved, though their coop was destroyed. Just shows that even slaves can be an instrument of God if they are properly directed, because the slave Palmyre would never have thought to rescue them on her own. Pierre Cormier's shop had been damaged as well, but he knew a bit about carpentry, and he and Father Beaubois set about repairing damage to our rooms, to the kitchen, and to the slave quarters. First, however, they hammered together a coop for the chickens. Food was running short, and we needed those eggs.

One problem that arose was where to lodge the slaves. The idea of being under the same roof as those primitive creatures horrified me. But we needed them to do the work, so I bit my tongue when Mother Jerome allowed them to sleep on pallets on the kitchen floor. Mother Jerome had said, the day after the hurricane, that lodging would be found for them with some of our parishioners, and I couldn't help noticing Palmyre's reaction. I could see, even at a distance, that she was imploring Mother Jerome not to send her outside the Convent walls. Up to no good, if you ask me. One day we will all end up murdered in our beds.

As I scrubbed the stone floor, I could hear hammering outside in the courtyard. In the background, bells were tolling, and I thought, another one gone. There hadn't been much time for elaborate funerals: with the risk of disease, it was urgent to get them into the ground.

Amid it all, Pierre Cormier and Father Beaubois seemed to be getting along like a house afire. I heard the clang of a hammer falling to the ground, and a string of oaths, followed by a laugh. After rebuilding the coop, they were building wooden frames for the windows to put muslin cloth over them in order to keep out the mosquitoes. There wasn't much glass here in Louisiana. It had to be brought from France, and there was glass only in the houses of the richest people. After that strange interlude during the hurricane, Pierre Cormier and I had not spoken, but I could not get the memory of those moments in the dark, and the touch of his big warm hand, out of my mind.

That fool Sidonie had named her cat Ouragan, after the hurricane. Mother Jerome quite properly didn't let her keep him. It was hard enough to feed ourselves, let alone a cat. But Sidonie managed to persuade Berthe, the grocer's wife, to take him in. Very unsanitary for a grocer, if you ask me. The other day I went in to buy staples, and the cat was sleeping on the chick-peas in the sun. It licked its paw and looked up at me in disdain, turned over, and went back to sleep. I hate cats. Sidonie will come to no good: I saw how her eyes flashed when she was told to get rid of the cat. She should be grateful to the nuns for taking her in. What turned her head and gave her ideas above her station back in France were the classes with that young nun who taught the girls literature and geography and filled their heads with nonsense.

'Immaculata!' Sister Fidelis called. 'Stop scrubbing and come give me a hand here in the kitchen!' I stood up, threw a last bucket of soapy water into the street and went to help. We'd taken bags of dried beans to the attic and could boil those with potatoes to make soup.

Out in the garden, Sidonie was on her hands and knees alongside the slaves and the *putains*. 'That girl will never find a husband with those rough hands,' I thought, with unchristian satisfaction. What they find to laugh about, I do not know. Still, at least the root vegetables like onions and carrots and potatoes and garlic would keep us going. And in this climate, cabbages and greens grow fast.

Sidonie

The sun was beating down as Palmyre, Nanette, Clotilde and I dug in the garden, and there were clouds of mosquitoes buzzing around our faces and necks and hands. But I felt so glad to be alive. I think that my friends did as well.

'Have any of you ever learned to embroider? I asked.

Nanette wiped sweat from her face. 'Honestly, Sidonie. With the kind of life I've had, do you think there was time to learn?'

Palmyre sat back on her heels. 'I learned simple sewing. Once, in St. Domingue, I was the slave of a rich planter's wife, and was expected to do mending.'

'Excellent,' I said. 'That's a start.'

'A start of what?' she asked.

'I've had an idea,' I said. 'Maybe we could produce embroidered linens and sell them.'

Nanette snorted with laughter. 'Yes, for the planters' beds, where they can cavort with their ladies.' She assumed a falsetto voice: 'Come romp with me, *Cherie,* and pleasure my naked flesh amid the blue flowers!'

I blushed to the roots of my hair, but went on. 'It would give us some income of our own.'

Palmyre raised an eyebrow. 'Isn't money the root of all evil, according to you Catholics?' I knew she was teasing me.

'Perhaps it is, but it's also the root of all independence,' I replied.

Nanette looked thoughtful. 'That,' she said, 'is very true. But how on earth would we be able to buy the cloth and embroidery thread to start? And we would have to learn first how to do it.'

'Father Beaubois,' I said, 'has received a donation from a wealthy relative of his and has offered to help us. But first, you're right that you'd need to learn.'

'And when, pray tell, could we do that?' she asked tartly.

'I've been thinking about that,' I said. I decided to be frank. 'I don't think Mother Jerome approves of the way I've been teaching you. But in the Convent the Casket Girls all learned embroidery and sewing skills, so I could teach you those. I think that she would see this as something suitable for you to learn. She's a good woman, really.'

Palmyre spoke up. 'And would we receive the money from this? Or would it go to the Convent, or to the woman Nanette and Clotilde work for? And how would we sell what we produce?' Her eyes flashed. 'Somehow I don't think the fine ladies of New Orleans would want to buy fine linens from slaves and —' She broke off and glanced at Nanette and Clotilde.

'*Putains,*' said Nanette angrily. But she continued. 'Palmyre's right, you know. They're willing to let slaves tend their children, and they used to turn a blind eye to what their husbands and sons got up to with us. But to buy these things from us openly...' she trailed off. Her shoulders slumped. 'I just don't see it happening.'

'Well,' I said, 'I've been thinking about that too. My friend Berthe is a Casket Girl who married a grocer. She was one of the people who took refuge with us when the hurricane struck. She might be persuaded to sell them in her shop. But, of course, we would have to keep very quiet about it.'

Palmyre smiled. 'Sidonie, under that prissy exterior, you are a revolutionary.'

I was surprised to see how readily Mother Jerome embraced the idea of embroidery lessons when I went to talk to her a few days later. 'That,' she said when I went to ask her permission, 'is a far more suitable activity for young women. Father Beaubois has mentioned that a relative of his has left a small bequest, to be used to provide useful occupational skills to women of irregular life and slaves.' In truth, it was hard to see how she could object, since the Jesuits had allowed the Ursulines to establish the Convent in New Orleans on the condition that their school would take in prostitutes and slaves, but I had anticipated some resistance. She added, 'A third of their wares could be destined for use here in the Convent. As regards the rest, we'll have to see.'

This was unexpected good news. If she had said that all the linens had to be handed over to the Convent, the project no longer made sense. I wondered idly if Father Beaubois had brought pressure to bear. But I thought it was best not to get into specifics about what would happen to the remaining two-thirds. 'Thank you for your generosity, Reverend Mother,' I said.

Mother Jerome nodded at me. Her old eyes were shrewd as well as kind. 'You're a good girl, Sidonie,' she said. 'I have seen that you genuinely care for your students. And as Our Lord said, 'As you do it to the least of these, you do it unto Me.' She turned around and opened the large dark armoire in the back of her study. From it, she removed some lengths of cotton fabric. 'The Convent will provide the cloth for the first lessons, so all that has to be bought is embroidery thread. I know that there is a small haberdashery down by the river, where you can buy some, though the quality may not be what one would desire.' She folded the cloth and handed it to me. I was touched by her unexpected generosity. She then handed me some coins. 'These are from the legacy Reverend Father Beaubois mentioned. I shall expect you to keep accurate records of expenditure.'

'But of course, Reverend Mother,' I said. "Perhaps, if we ever earn anything from selling our embroidery, Father Beaubois could use it to help the poor.' I neglected to mention that the poor I had in mind were my students.

That very afternoon I went to talk with Berthe. The kitten Ouragan was curled on a cushion behind the counter and looked plump and contented. Berthe was attending customers, the usual mix of shopkeepers' wives, servants, and the slaves whose mistresses were the wives of rich plantation owners. She looked happy as she bustled about, totting up bills, weighing rice and flour, and gossiping about local events. Finally, though, there was a lull, and the two of us were alone.

'Berthe,' I asked, 'is there ever a demand for fine embroidered linens here in New Orleans?'

Berthe pushed a stray wisp of hair to one side. She was perspiring in the heat. 'Oh yes,' she said. 'The problem is that they have to be imported from France, and of course that takes months. The cost of shipping means that the price I'd have to ask would be too high for all but the wealthiest patrons.' She raised an eyebrow. 'Why do you ask?'

I leaned down to stroke Ouragan, who was winding himself around my legs and purring loudly. 'I think there may be a solution. I am going to teach my students embroidery, and in a month or two we should be able to provide some embroidered linens for sale. Bedsheets, pillowcases, handkerchiefs. Would it be possible to sell them here in your shop?'

Berthe grinned. 'Of course it would,' she said. 'The shop would have to receive part of the profits. Say thirty per cent?'

'It's a deal,' I said, and we shook hands. Thirty per cent was a lot, but there really wasn't any alternative. She was shrewd, was Berthe, but I was learning fast that in business, shrewdness is essential. We would have to work hard, since a third of our profit would go to the Convent and another third to Berthe's shop. Still, a third of the profits was better than nothing.

I left the shop and headed down to the river. The sun was glancing off the buildings, and most of the debris from the hurricane had been cleared. I could hear the buzzing of bees in the garden beyond the wall to my left, and the clucking of chickens. At the haberdasher's, I bought some embroidery thread in soft tones of blue, rose pink, pale yellow, and green. Some brightly coloured thread was on sale for a remarkably low price, bright yellow and red and blue, and I couldn't resist adding them to my basket. The stock in paler colours was limited, but if the idea prospered, and if fine ladies actually bought our linens, we could arrange to have embroidery thread brought over from France on the next ship.

The following day I distributed thread and some cheap remnants of cloth as well as thimbles and embroidery needles among my students. Their faces were a study. 'Ladies,' I said, 'we are going to learn embroidery. And if it all goes well, we will be allowed to keep a third of the profits.'

'That,' said Palmyre, 'I will believe when I see it.' But she smiled, as did Nanette. Little Clotilde hardly ever spoke, but she did now. 'I learn fast,' she said.

Chapter 9

Sister Immaculata

After the hurricane, it took a while for things to get back to normal. I was still determined to build my nest egg, and was concerned that, now that Armand Ardoin and Joelle were in France and were married, one source of income had dried up. I continued to run errands for the nuns and earned money bringing in clandestine sweets, and even once a dog-eared copy of a novel. Novels were strictly forbidden in the Convent, given their worldly and lascivious nature, but one of the Casket Girls, Jeanne, loved them and read them in secret. Where she found money to pay for it, I do not know, but somehow she did. And, of course, when I went to buy food and supplies for the Convent, I sometimes persuaded the shopkeepers to give me a small commission in order to ensure our continued patronage.

My feelings about the Convent and the Ursuline order to which I belonged had become more complicated since I arrived in Louisiana. True, the Order had given me refuge when my parents died. And I was still convinced of my own unworthiness and was all too aware of my propensity to sin. But the warmth of the Louisiana climate seemed to seep into my bones, and the need for self-mortification and atonement seemed less urgent somehow. I had even begun to wash myself regularly, though I was aware of the danger of falling into the sin of vanity. But I was surprised at how good it felt to be clean, and I was determined that the next time I went to buy meat for the Convent, the butcher would not think I stank. In daydreams, I saw myself behind the corner of my own shop. I knew I'd be far more successful than that fat cow Berthe, with her smug moon face and her burly moustachioed husband.

Suddenly the voice of Sister Fidelis broke into my reverie. 'Immaculata, Sister Helene is poorly, and I need for you to fetch some things for me from the herbalist.' Since the hurricane, there had been a spate of illness among the nuns and the Casket Girls. Most of these were treated with herbal medicines: valerian and lavender for sleeplessness, lime-flower tea for female troubles, corn tassels and cherry stems for kidney problems. Sister Helene was one of the oldest nuns, and I'd noticed her increasing tremors and the greyish colour of her skin. I was pretty sure she wouldn't last the summer.

I gathered my basket and walked down the street, turning toward the river. The herbalist, like Sister Helene, was very old, but unlike Sister Helene she was spry and alert, with malevolent black eyes. Her shop was tiny and dark, and was crammed to the ceiling with plants and decoctions of every description. It was whispered that she used some herbal remedies that she'd learned about from the Indians. She was known as 'Tite Jeanne, and I suspected that she'd been a witch back in France. 'Back again, black crow!' she screeched when she saw me. 'What ails the good Sisters now?'

'One of the older nuns can't sleep, and her hands shake,' I replied 'Tite Jeanne reached under the counter, and took out a cloth bag. Into it, she put the leaves of three different plants.

'Give her tea made with these,' she said. 'It won't cure her, but it will make her sleep soundly.' She looked at me. 'So how are the Casket Girls faring?' she asked. I knew she loved gossip. 'Are the suitors queueing up to take them off your hands?'

'Some have married, yes,' I replied. 'I expect you know that Berthe has married a grocer. Another one, Elisabeth, married a trapper who lives down Atachafalaya way. And, of course, Joelle married a planter, Armand Ardoin. They went to France for their honeymoon, but will be back soon.'

'Armand Ardoin, eh?' Tite Jeanne smiled, and there was a malice in her smile I didn't understand. 'And he took his bride to France. Interesting choice.'

'Why?' I asked.

'I wonder if he took her to meet his relatives.'

'He probably did,' I said primly. 'Introducing her to his family would be the most suitable thing to do.'

'Eh *bien*.' 'Tite Jeanne's eyes sparkled. 'Do you know about Armand Ardoin?'

'Just that he's a wealthy slaveowner, with a plantation upriver called Les Chenes,' I said. I wondered what she was getting at.

'Armand Ardoin inherited his land from his father, who received a grant in the time of Governor Iberville. He

139

married and had a son. Later, he took his bride back to France when his second son was born.'

'I see,' I replied. I couldn't understand why this silly old woman found this so interesting. I wished she would get to the point, so I could leave.

'Of course, there might have been speculation what colour the children would have be.'

At this, my ears pricked up. 'Why?' I said. 'What do you mean?'

'Tite Jeanne shrugged. 'Ardoin *père* brought his wife here from St. Domingue. And she was a beauty, all right, with long black hair and dark eyes. Some said she had African antecedents. But, of course, M. Ardoin doesn't like to talk about that.'

My eyes widened. 'I see,' I replied. I took out some coins from my purse and handed them over. 'How did you come to hear about this?'

'I came to New Orleans from St. Domingue.' Suddenly it was as though a shutter had come down to veil her eyes. '*Bonjour*, Sister.'

'Merci, Tite Jeanne,' I said, and went back out into the street. As I walked along the riverfront, my head was buzzing. This could be an exceptional opportunity. If this information was true, and I had no reason to believe it wasn't, M. Ardoin would go to considerable lengths to conceal it. Even if it wasn't true, the rumour that he might have African blood would make him a pariah in New Orleans society.

I smiled to myself. All good things come to those who wait. I began to imagine my *charcuterie*, full of delicacies, with elegant patrons queuing up outside. I had heard that Joelle and Armand Ardoin would be returning in the next month.

Sidonie

I was surprised and delighted to see how quickly my students had taken to embroidery in the fortnight since we had begun. Clotilde showed real talent: her stitches were meticulous and painstakingly even. Nanette's work wasn't quite so perfect, but she was persistent and clearly was trying hard to improve. Palmyre, however, was a revelation. From the beginning, she was reluctant to stick to the dainty floral motifs I gave them, and instead stitched beautiful bright pictures of exotic flowers and birds in vivid colours: scarlet, indigo, bright yellow, emerald green.

'These are beautiful,' I told her. 'But I'm afraid that the kind of client who would pay for our work will be looking for something a little more French and sedate.' She sighed, but then I continued, 'If you can embroider some bed linens that we can sell easily, perhaps we can talk to Berthe about marketing these different designs as decorative tapestries. They really are quite unusual, and the colours are lovely.'

What was most exciting for me, though, was Joelle's impending arrival. She and her husband and Armand Ardoin's brother Jean had sailed from Le Havre three months ago, and would go first to St. Domingue, where the Ardoin family had a sugar plantation, then on to New Orleans. I wondered how she was, and whether she was having an easy pregnancy. An ocean voyage is not easy at the best of times, and for a woman expecting a child, I imagined it would be very difficult indeed. But I remembered that Joelle wanted a baby more than anything else.

As we sewed in the sunlight of the courtyard, I began to hum under my breath. 'You sound happy, Sidonie,' said Nanette. 'Have you got a beau?'

I laughed. 'Not yet,' I said. 'I'm happy because my friend Joelle is coming back to New Orleans. She and her husband are returning from their honeymoon in France, and will go on upriver to New Orleans to their plantation Les Chenes.'

'Is she the pretty blonde one?' asked Nanette. 'I always knew she'd marry well. Men like that kind of rosy pink softness.' She sniffed. 'Not that it will last long in this climate, particularly once she starts popping babies out. Then, of course, he will stray.' She shrugged. 'You, on the other hand, have the kind of looks that will last.'

'Me?' I laughed out loud. I knew I was far too thin, with dark hair and unexceptional grey eyes.

'Yes,' she said. 'You have a face that people remember.'

This, of course, was nonsense. I hoped that Nanette was wrong about Ardoin and the possibility that he might eventually become interested in other women. 'Actually, Joelle's expecting a baby this spring. She's asked me to go stay

142

with her when the little one is born. So we need to have everything in place with our embroidery project before then.'

Palmyre had gone silent. I noticed that her face had gone the colour of putty. 'Is anything wrong, Palmyre?'

She looked at her hands. 'When is the date of their arrival?'

'I don't know,' I replied. 'With transatlantic voyages, it's hard to tell. It'll depend on the winds, and then they're spending some time in St. Domingue. But I would imagine that they'll want to arrive in time to settle in before the baby's born.'

I noticed that Palmyre's hands were trembling. 'Poor girl,' she said. 'She has no idea.'

I wondered if Palmyre was remembering her own lost baby, or perhaps the suffering of childbirth. I was tempted to ask her to tell me what it was like so that I would know what to do to help my friend when the moment came. I had heard vague things about what happened when women gave birth, about screams and blood, and that was when it went well. So often it didn't. But I didn't want to rake up painful memories for Palmyre. I wondered if I would ever have a child of my own.

Father Beaubois poked his head around the kitchen door. 'Bonjour, mademoiselles.' I noticed that his face was brown from all the outdoor work he'd been doing with the butcher, M. Cormier. He smiled. 'You are a hive of domestic industry.'

'We're hoping to have the first sheets and pillowcases ready for sale in a week,' I replied. 'We're very grateful to our anonymous benefactor.'

He approached and glanced at Clotilde's work. 'Beautiful, and very delicate,' he said. 'Not that I am a connoisseur in these matters.' When he saw Palmyre's embroidery, however, his eyes widened. 'This is extraordinary,' he said. 'Are these African birds and plants? The vegetation reminds me of St. Domingue.'

Palmyre rose. 'If you will excuse me, Reverend Father, I am not feeling very well. I am very grateful to you and to M. Cormier for rebuilding my cabin.' She turned away brusquely and left.

'*Pauvre petite*,' said Father Beaubois. His eyes were sad.

'You were in St. Domingue, were you not, Reverend Father?' I asked. 'Did you know Palmyre there?'

Father Beaubois sidestepped the question. 'There are half a million slaves in St. Domingue, Sidonie,' he said. His tone was cold, and I knew not to press him further. 'Now I must go and prepare for evening Mass.' But then he softened. 'It is good to see what enthusiastic entrepreneurs you have become.'

'I only wish that my Natchez student Coahoma was able to take part as well,' I said. I thought of her often, and wondered about her fate after the Natchez uprising. 'Do you have any idea what may have become of her?'

144

'I'm afraid I haven't,' he said. 'Many Indians were killed, of course. And I know that many of the women and children were sold into slavery.'

I shuddered. I remembered Coahoma's bright eyes as she told us the story of the Pleiades. I could not bear thinking of what might be happening to her, if indeed she had survived.

Sister Immaculata

As Sister Fidelis and I peeled potatoes and carrots, I smiled to myself. The news about Armand Ardoin's parentage had cheered me up very considerably, and the dream of my own *charcuterie* no longer seemed so unattainable.

'You're very cheerful today,' said Fidelis. 'It's good to see you smile, Immaculata. God has been good to us, and we should all be happy to have survived the storm.' We'd heard that more than two hundred people had died in the flooding downriver.

'Indeed, Sister,' I replied. 'The Lord be praised.' She looked at me and raised an eyebrow at this unexpected piety. She knew that I was not given to praising God for anything.

'I need for you to fetch me some things from the market,' Fidelis said. 'Joelle and her husband are arriving in three days. She's in the family way and is going to stay with us for a while, while her husband will go upriver to prepare for her arrival. They say he's brought over furniture and crystal chandeliers from France. Young Joelle has done well for herself.'

145

'That's as may be,' I thought. I wondered what colour Joelle's baby would be. A fine comeuppance for her if it was born coal black. Now I understood why Sidonie had been going around with a stupid smile on her face. Not that I had seen much of her lately, now that I thought about it. She was always closeted with those tarts and slaves. I'd heard that she'd been reprimanded about her classes, and had been given a last chance teaching them sewing. I didn't think the nuns would turn her out, but she'd done nothing to find a husband and something would have to be done about her eventually. Probably thought she was too good for the local merchants and laborers, with all her airs and graces.

I picked up a basket and headed for the market. There, I bought some cherries and strawberries. I loved fruit tarts, and now that Joelle was coming, the sentimental old nuns would try to tempt her appetite with pies. If she couldn't eat them, they would not go to waste. Since coming to Louisiana, I'd rounded out a bit, and my body was less bony and angular. I also bought some fish, which was cheaper than meat just now. Prices had risen since the hurricane, since so much livestock had drowned. After this, I went on to the ironmongers to pick up some nails for Father Beaubois and Pierre Cormier and headed back to the convent.

Father Beaubois wasn't around when I returned, but Pierre Cormier was. I hadn't had a chance to speak to him since the hurricane. He was sawing wood in the courtyard of the Convent and had removed his shirt. The muscles in his arms gleamed with perspiration, and I was reminded of the statues of St. Sebastian I'd seen back in France, the beautiful young man martyred with arrows. The arrows Pierre Cormier was struggling with were Louisiana mosquitoes, and he slapped them now and then, cursed, then went on with his work.

'*Bonjour,* Monsieur Cormier,' I said. 'I see you're hard at work, as usual.'

He put down his saw. 'Did your shop make it through the storm?' I asked. I still hadn't had the chance to go have a look, since I'd been rushed off my feet running errands and cooking for Fidelis.

'Part of it was destroyed,' he said. 'Father Beaubois has said that if I help with repairs to the Convent, he'd provide timber to rebuild my shop. He's a good man, even if he is a priest.'

'Why do you say even "even if he is a priest?"' My voice sounded prissy, even to my own ears. 'Of course, priests are good. They are men of God.'

Cormier spat on the ground. 'Most of them are parasites and lechers. Hypocrites one and all, who live off the poor.'

I made the sign of the Cross. This, of course, was blasphemy. But then I told myself to practise some Christian charity. After all, priests and nuns were human too. I knew this all too well as I gazed at the black hair on Pierre Cormier's naked chest.

'When will your shop reopen?' I asked briskly. 'We need to stock fresh provisions, and the Sisters are growing weary of bean stew.'

Cormier laughed. 'I can imagine,' he said. 'I'm sure the winds blowing through the Convent just now make the hurricane pale in comparison.'

I wanted to be offended at the notion of farting nuns, but this made me laugh. I tried to turn my laugh into a coughing fit.

Cormier went on. 'I'm going to do it right this time. In New Orleans, there's work for carpenters and joiners just now repairing storm damage. I'm going to work hard and build up a reserve, and then I'll look for some more land where I can raise pigs and cows and chickens for slaughter and sell eggs as well. And then I'll rebuild my shop. For now, I'm just selling the odd chicken if I can find one.'

'This sounds wonderful,' I said. 'I wish you every success, M. Cormier.'

'And then,' he said, 'I shall bring my fiancée Annette over from France.'

I turned on my heel and headed toward the street. 'Good luck,' I said through gritted teeth. I should have known there would be an Annette. I imagined her as fat, comely, with black hair and rosy cheeks. Like a prime sow. What a fool I had been to dream that Pierre Cormier would ever think of me as a potential wife and business partner. I had stupidly allowed myself to believe that here in Louisiana, I could be a flower rather than an ugly unwanted weed. Pathetic. I would always be Zezette, the dirty little black-haired witch growing up amid manure and paternal beatings.

I looked at the wrought iron railings along the street and saw rainbow arches dancing around them. They could, of course, be tears, but I never cried. But it could mean that I was about to have a spell. Just my luck that I would have one of my funny turns right now. I turned around and headed back to the Convent, eager to get there before my limbs began to thrash and before the dark shadows returned and closed in.

Chapter 10

Sidonie

It was late when Joelle and Armand Ardoin arrived, and the December night was chilly. I heard voices, then the sound of heavy trunks being dragged over the cobblestones. Mother Jerome had ordered that a room be set aside especially for Joelle. The rationale, I suppose, was that Joelle now was a Married Woman and was thus a woman of Experience, which might be unsettling for the rest of us innocent creatures.

This, of course, was nonsense. I threw on a cloak and went out into the corridor to greet my friend. Joelle was standing in the light from the lamps. Her hair was dripping, since it was raining outside. She looked exhausted, and I noticed the soft curve of her belly.

I threw my arms around her. 'You must be so tired, Joelle,' I said. She hugged me back. 'I certainly am. It's a very long trip, Sidonie. But it is so wonderful to see you.'

I took her arm and led her to her room. Mother Jerome was bustling around, but she saw how glad Joelle was to see me, and how exhausted she was. 'Sidonie, you may help Joelle settle in, but be sure that she goes straight to bed. I'll have Sister Fidelis make some tea. Have you had anything to eat, child?"

'No,' Joelle replied. 'But I'm really not hungry. What I want more than anything else just now is to lie down, please.' I saw that she was shivering.

Mother Jerome headed for the kitchen. I helped Joelle take off her dripping cloak, and drew the curtains. 'Is Armand with you?' I asked.

'He and his brother Jean have gone directly upriver,' she said. I noticed that there was a strange tone of relief in her voice. 'He's brought over many things from France for our house and wants to be there to supervise when they're unloaded.'

'That sounds exciting,' I said. 'You're going to have one of the most beautiful houses in Louisiana.'

'I hope so,' she said. She sat on the edge of the bed and took my hand. I was surprised by the strength of her grip. 'Sidonie, you promised that you would be with me when the baby's born. I know that it's a big thing to ask, but it would mean so much to me.'

'Of course I will,' I promised. 'Now, put on your nightgown and get under the blankets.' She did so obediently, like a child. There were dark shadows under her eyes, but I could not be sure if they were really there or were only a trick of the flickering lamplight.

Joelle smiled weakly. 'You will like Armand's brother Jean,' she said. 'He and Armand are very different.'

I tucked her in under the coverlets. I'd made the bed with some of the first sheets my students and I had

151

embroidered. Mother Jerome returned, bearing a steaming pot of tea. Joelle was propped up on pillows, and the colour had begun to return to her face. Mother Jerome shooed me away. 'Off with you, Sidonie,' she said. 'You girls will have time to catch up tomorrow. Joelle needs her rest.'

I leaned over and kissed Joelle's cheek. 'Good night, *Cherie*.' I said. 'Sweet dreams, and *á demain*.'

When I returned to my own shared room, I was not prepared for what awaited me. Sister Immaculata was lying on her bed, with her eyes rolled up into her head, thrashing violently and lashing out at something I couldn't see.

'Mother Jerome!' I shouted. Mother Jerome came running. She called for Sister Fidelis, and the two of them held Immaculata's convulsing limbs. From their demeanor, I had the feeling that this had happened before. She seemed inordinately strong, and in her thrashing, she struck Fidelis below the eye. Finally, the convulsive movements subsided, and Immaculata fell into what looked like a deep sleep.

'Poor lost soul,' said Mother Jerome softly. 'Sidonie, don't discuss this with anyone, please.' Since the other girls were at evening mass and confession, I was the only one who had witnessed Immaculata's fit. She turned to Sister Fidelis. 'I wonder,' she said, 'if it might be best to ask Father Beaubois to perform an exorcism.'

I found this idea terrifying. To me, it seemed that Immaculata was lonely and disturbed, and this was what made her act so unpleasant to everyone around her. I found it hard,

152

though, to believe that there were devils within her. But I knew as well that exorcism was a rite established by Church authorities, and in the Convent I had been brought up to believe that they knew what they were doing. It was all very confusing. But Immaculata was not much older than I was, and I felt sad that she was ill so far from home.

Sister Fidelis rubbed her cheek. 'She certainly seems extraordinarily strong, and that is one of the symptoms of demonic possession.' I knew that Fidelis would have a bruised face the following day. Immaculata had fallen into a restless sleep, and moaned from time to time, though I could not make out what she was saying. I sat and took her hand, and eventually her breathing became more regular.

The following morning dawned bright and sunny. I went out to the garden to pick flowers and brought a bouquet of lilies in to Joelle. She greeted me with a smile. 'Did you sleep well?' I asked.

'I certainly did,' she replied. 'The trip upriver was the most difficult part of all. But now I'm here. It is so good to see you all.' She looked at the new plants which were just breaking through the soil. 'I was so worried about you when I heard of the Indian uprising. Were those Indians you taught involved? I was afraid they'd murdered you in your bed.'

'They were involved, but as victims,' I said. I told her about the massacre of Indians by the French authorities, of the wrong village. 'I've heard that my student may have been sold into slavery, if she survived.'

Joelle shuddered. 'On our return voyage, we stopped briefly in St. Domingue, where Armand has a large sugar plantation. I am still haunted by what I saw there. I'd always thought that slavery was necessary, that Africans were like children who needed to be treated with discipline as well as love. But this was something else again. Still, let's not talk of sad things, or of such horrors. How are our other friends? Is Berthe happy in her marriage?'

'She certainly seems happy enough,' I said. 'She took refuge here during the hurricane, and I gave her a little cat I rescued. She's helping out with a project I've devised to help my students earn some independent income.' I went on to explain our embroidery project.

Joelle smiled, but her eyes were sad. 'What a wonderful idea. And how right you are that economic independence is the root of everything.' She straightened up. 'Still,' she said, 'I remind myself that I am a very lucky woman.'

'Tell me about Paris,' I begged.

'It was wonderful in many ways,' Joelle said. 'Armand insisted that I have many beautiful dresses made, and I went with him to look at furnishings for our house. He wants for Les Chenes to be the most beautiful and opulent plantation in the Mississippi Valley.'

'He must be delighted that you're giving him an heir,' I said. Joelle sighed.

'One would think so,' she said. 'And at times he does seem happy at the prospect of a son. But at other times, he looks so strange...He almost seems fearful.'

'Fearful of what?' I asked.

'If only I knew,' she said. 'Still, I'm sure when the baby comes, it will all be fine.'

'Has it been hard for you?' I asked. I blushed. I had no idea what pregnancy must be like. I knew that expectant mothers were supposed to remain at home in seclusion, covered in flowing garments that concealed their state.

'The first months were,' Joelle replied. 'I couldn't keep food down, and my sense of smell was heightened. I couldn't bear the smell of some of the servants, and sometimes when Armand came home at night, he smelled of a heavy cloying perfume that made me sick. But after three months this passed. And the moment when the little one moved within me...' Her eyes filled. 'There really are no words to describe the joy. It makes it all worthwhile.'

This made me feel wistful. 'I wonder if I will ever have a family.' I said.

'Of course you will,' said Joelle, and she patted my hand. 'When you come to Les Chenes, I will have some dresses made for you. You have lovely eyes, and with the right clothes you will turn heads.'

'The thing is, Joelle,' I said, 'that I don't see many men here whose heads I'd want to turn. They all seem terrified at the idea of a wife who actually has a brain. I know that I can't stay here forever with the Sisters, but the alternatives aren't terribly appealing. I don't see myself as the wife of a fat ironmonger, or of being buried in the country as a farmer's wife.' I blushed, thinking this had been a bit tactless. 'Of course, Les Chenes will be different. I'm sure you'll make a lovely home there, full of people who can carry on an interesting conversation.'

Joelle smiled. 'I would love that,' she said. 'In Paris, the ladies of the aristocracy often host literary salons. Armand used to go to a salon of the Duchesse de Neuilly, but he never took me with him. I suppose he felt that I 'd be unable to say anything meaningful.' She sighed. 'I so wish I'd paid more attention in our literature classes. There are times when I feel like an ignorant, I country girl.' But then she brightened. 'When you come to stay with me, perhaps we could read together, and you could teach me things. I know that Armand's brother Jean is interested in literature, so he could join in. We can have our own salon.'

'That sounds wonderful, *Cherie*,' I said. 'Now I must leave you and go work on some embroidery with my students.'

Sister Immaculata

When I woke up, I saw that my face was cut and bruised. I knew I must've had one of my fits. I wondered what triggered them. Perhaps I really was cursed and inhabited by devils. But I had a strange memory of someone holding my hand. It wasn't the butcher's big rough hand, since the skin

156

was so soft. I recalled in a rush Pierre Cormier's remarks about his fiancée and was surprised by a feeling of grief and loss. Which was stupid of me, since you can't lose what you never had.

I rose, and my limbs ached in every joint. When I went to put on my habit, the cockerel and monkey charm fell from an inside pocket. I thought of the money I'd paid for it. Love. Money. Luck. Stupid of me to believe this superstitious nonsense. I might not have love or luck and probably never would, but what I did have was a little money in my secret cache. I went down to the kitchen. It was nearly time for breakfast, and Fidelis was stirring porridge on the big wood stove. I saw that one of her eyes was purple and swollen shut.

'*Bonjour*, Fidelis,' I said. 'What on earth happened to you?'

'Nothing,' she said. Her eyes were weary but kind. 'You were unwell last night, but Mother Jerome and I put you to bed.'

This filled me with foreboding. I'd had previous episodes, but thought that by going off and hiding nobody would know. I lowered my eyes. 'Thank you,' I said.

Later, as I served breakfast, I noticed that Father Beaubois and Mother Jerome were deep in conversation, but they went silent when I approached. I didn't like this one single bit: clearly something was afoot. After breakfast, they went to Father Beaubois's study. If they were going to discuss me, I knew that the consequences would not be good. In silence, I followed them down the hall.

It wasn't easy to make out what they were saying, but with my ear pressed against the door I could hear their words. 'I have never been comfortable with the rite of exorcism, Reverend Mother,' Father Beaubois said. 'I know that the Church sanctions it, and indeed Sister Immaculata is tormented and in need of help. But I am not sure that this is the best way to go about helping her.'

Mother Jerome said. 'Reverend Father, if indeed Immaculata is possessed by the Devil, we must act quickly. The reputation of our Order is at stake. You know, of course, of the events that took place in an Ursuline convent in Aix-en-Provence around a hundred years ago.'

'Yes, I have heard things,' Father Beaubois said. He sounded weary.

'You know the case of Madeleine de Damandolx, who was an Ursuline nun. She was only nineteen, poor girl, when she began to have violent fits. Once, in a rage, she even destroyed a crucifix!'

Father Beaubois sighed audibly. 'Yes, and she confessed her relationship with Father Louis Gaufridi. Other nuns began to exhibit the same symptoms, and the situation at the convent in Aix was getting out of hand. There was an attempt at an exorcism, but all that produced were accusations that Father Gaufridi was a devil worshipper. They tortured him until he confessed, but then he retracted his confession at his trial. It did him no good: he was dragged through the streets of Aix, strangled, and then his body burnt at the stake.'

I heard Mother Jerome gasp. 'Reverend Father: with the greatest respect, this dreadful tale illustrates why we should deal with this swiftly. If Immaculata is indeed possessed by the Devil, and if these fits are contagious, she could contaminate the whole Convent. Our reputation would be destroyed.'

Father Beaubois's voice was stern. 'Reverend Mother, this is not a course of action to be rushed into lightly. The punishment of Father Gaufridi is hardly an example of Christian love and charity, and confessions obtained by torture are not to be trusted. Immaculata is disturbed, and this must be addressed with compassion, but I shall need to think of how best to proceed.'

'What are the symptoms of demonic possession?' Mother Jerome asked.

'Abnormal strength,' Father Beaubois said. 'Unnatural body movements. Blasphemies. Something called the Devil's Mark.'

I peeked through the keyhole. Mother Jerome was making the sign of the Cross. 'The Devil's Mark,' she gasped. 'Have you noticed that dark mole under Immaculata's nose? And when she had her fit, she was unbelievably strong. She hit Fidelis so hard that her eye is swollen shut.'

I heard the noise of a chair being pushed back and hastened away down the corridor. I knew that I was in great danger. If I was to escape the Convent and buy my own little plot of land far from here, I would have to act swiftly. The Inquisition was not as powerful as it once was, I knew, but its tentacles could reach as far as New Orleans.

I'd heard that Armand Ardoin's overseer would be coming to escort Joelle up to Les Chenes soon. I would have to seek out an opportunity to speak with him in private so that he could transmit my proposal to Ardoin.

It felt as though the Convent was closing in on me. I went to Sister Fidelis, and asked her very meekly if I could run any errands for her.

'Actually, I need some ginger, and some cane syrup,' she said. 'I've just been given a recipe for ginger cakes from a parishioner.' She gave me some coins, and I headed off toward the market down by the river.

I felt a strange attraction to the great river, as it coiled and eddied and flowed down toward the Gulf like a great brown snake. I liked snakes and had never been afraid of them as so many girls are. On the farm back in Brittany there were adders, and I thought the pattern of their scales was beautiful as they lay in the sun. Here in Louisiana the snakes were bigger, like everything else. On the voyage here, I'd seen cottonmouths in the swamp, with their white monster mouths, and diamondback rattlers. I felt a certain kinship to these creatures who seemed to attract nothing but loathing. In the Biblical tale, Eve had seen the charm of the Serpent, and had been seduced by his power. The sunlight glancing off the river was like jewelled snake scales. When I had my own land, I would never kill snakes.

Chapter 11

Sidonie

In the days when Joelle was waiting to proceed upriver, I decided that it would be good for her to join our embroidery group. Back in the Convent in France, she had shown real aptitude for embroidery. Her stitches were precise and perfect, and she loved embroidering fruits and flowers. I thought as well that this would take her mind of the discomfort she would feel travelling upriver, and of the impending birth.

When I suggested this, Joelle reacted with delight. 'I'd love to,' she said. 'I really mustn't complain, since Armand has been so generous, but there are moments when I long to have something useful to do.' She paused. 'But we will have to be discreet. Armand might object to my consorting with *putains* and slaves.'

'If the Ursulines hadn't taken you and me in, Joelle, who knows what might have happened to us,' I said in exasperation. 'We really mustn't cast stones.'

'I know, I know,' she said. Her face was sober. 'You and I have been very lucky, Sidonie, *malgré tout*. There but for the grace of God...'

So Joelle began to take part in our sessions in the small room adjoining the courtyard. I arranged a comfortable chair for her and introduced her to my students. 'Clotilde, Nanette, Palmyre, my friend Joelle, who has just returned from her honeymoon in Paris. She is staying here for the next three days while her husband continues upriver to prepare for her arrival.'

Initially, my students were tongue-tied, but this soon passed. 'Paris is beautiful, is it not?' Nanette said. I could hear the longing in her voice. Joelle told them of the beautiful Parisian boulevards, of the glittering salons. Clotilde was timid, as always, but I could see how she gazed at Joelle's elegant dress and delicate shoes. Palmyre, however, was silent.

'I think I shall embroider a sheet and pillow for my little one's cradle,' Joelle said. 'I am expecting a baby in the spring.'

Palmyre's expression was extraordinary: a mixture of wistfulness, something like anger, and a certain compassion that touched me deeply. 'This is your first child, *n'est-ce pas?*' she asked.

'Yes,' said Joelle with a smile. This morning she looked far more rested and tranquil, and the roses were back in her cheeks. 'I cannot wait to see if it's a boy or a girl.'

'If you are here for only three days,' said Palmyre, 'it will be difficult to finish this in time. I am happy to help you, if you like,'

Joelle's smile was radiant. 'That is ever so kind,' she said. 'Yes please!' They agreed that Palmyre would embroider the sheets and Joelle would work on the pillowcase. Joelle chose a soft blue thread, and the two set to work. It made my heart glad to see that the sophistication of Paris had not taken away Joelle's open, childlike response to things. Nanette and Clotilde stitched away.

'Some good news,' I told them. 'Berthe has told me that she has sold five sets of linens. When I can, I'll go to her shop and will receive the money, and after her portion and the Convent's are deducted, I'll divide it equally between you.'

'It seems hard that two-thirds of the sum will be taken before it comes to us.' Nanette made a sour face. 'Rather like my former trade, when I only got what was left over after the Madam and the pimp had had their cut.'

I blushed and glanced at Joelle. Like me, she had led a protected life, at least until she married Armand Ardoin, and I was concerned that she might be shocked at Nanette's occasional coarseness. But Joelle surprised me. She said, 'Nanette's right. It does seem wrong that others should profit from your embroidery.' Under her softness, Joelle had a steely sense of justice.

'I know it seems unfair, and perhaps it is,' I said. 'But the fact is that this is, for now, the only way we can do business. Remember that here we don't have to rent accommodation or pay for our food and lodging. And it will allow you all to perfect your embroidery skills and will give us useful information about what the ladies of New Orleans are looking for and what will sell.'

'You have become quite an entrepreneur, Sidonie,' Joelle said. 'The role of Madam suits you.' Her gaiety was infectious, and the other girls laughed. Their needles flashed. Sunlight poured through the windows.

'What was that infernal racket last night when we were at evening mass?' asked Nanette. 'I heard thumping and shouting.'

'One of the nuns was taken ill,' I said. The girls looked up from their work.

'What was the matter?" said Clotilde.

I paused. 'It's hard to describe,' I said. 'Her limbs were flailing about, and her eyes were rolled up in her head.'

'Poor thing,' said Joelle. 'I think all the nuns are a bit mad.'

Nanette shrugged. 'I once had a client who had similar fits. He was one of the nicer ones, but sometimes he would have seizures like the one you describe. We had to be careful that he didn't swallow his tongue.'

'I think this person must be ill,' I said. 'What kind of illness it is, I don't know. Mother Jerome and Father Beaubois were talking about a possible exorcism.'

At that, the girls sat up straight. 'An exorcism?'

Clotilde looked confused. 'What is an exorcism, Sidonie?'

It was easy to forget how young Clotilde was. I tried to explain in terms that would not frighten her, but that wasn't easy. 'Exorcism is a ceremony that tries to help people who are suffering and having fits. Priests carry it out to remove their devils.'

Joelle shivered. 'I would like to believe that people are born good, not evil.'

Nanette and Palmyre looked at her pityingly. Nanette was the first to speak. Her voice was drenched in weariness. 'Believe me, Joelle, there are people with devils inside. I've known a few.' Clotilde was mute, huddled in a corner of her chair.

Palmyre was silent for a moment. But then she said gently, 'Joelle, you are lucky to be able to believe in goodness. But you will have to be very strong, because there really are devils in this world. Believe me, I know.' She turned away. The room had fallen into shadow, and I could not see her face.

'Right,' I said briskly. 'This is not the kind of conversation we should be having in front of an expectant mother. We have five more sets of linens to finish for Berthe by the end of the week. Clotilde, how are you doing on the handkerchiefs? Nanette, have you finished the petals on that pillowcase? Joelle and Palmyre, you must hurry up and stop dawdling if you want the baby's sheet and pillow to be finished before it arrives!'

In the distance, I could hear church bells tolling.

Sister Immaculata

The morning arrived when Joelle was due to leave the Convent, in the company of Armand Ardoin's overseer and one of Ardoin's female slaves. I had overheard, in conversations, that the overseer's name was Louis Bertrand. He was due to

166

arrive at the Convent early and would supervise the transportation of Joelle's belongings from the Convent to the boat on which they'd travel upriver. I knew that my best chance to talk with him would be when the boat was being loaded.

I was up before dawn. I crept out of the Convent, without making the slightest noise, and walked down the deserted streets toward the river. I knew that Bertrand would moor his boat there at the pier. It was lucky that I knew my way, because mist was rolling in from the river. The city, shrouded in fog, had an eerie feel, and I shivered.

On approaching the docks, I saw Ardoin's shallop moored there. The boat, like his plantation, was called Les Chenes. There was a hooded figure on the deck. I drew nearer, and called out, 'Monsieur Bertrand?'

He started, turned abruptly, and saw me. 'What on earth do you want, Sister? The docks are not safe in the dark. No place for a nun.' His voice was gruff.

'I want to arrange a meeting with M. Ardoin.' I said. I tried to make my voice sound confident, but to my vexation it trembled slightly.

Bertrand came down to the pier. He smelled of sweat and something rank I couldn't identify that reminded me of sulphur. His left arm hung at a strange angle.
'And what is this meeting about, pray tell?' I didn't like the mockery in his tone.

I drew myself up. 'I can only discuss it with M. Ardoin in person,' I said. The fog billowed around us.

He laughed and spat at the ground. 'Sister, M. Ardoin is a very busy man. If you want to ask for a donation to your Convent, or to some worthy cause, write him a letter. But now I have work to do, so if you'll excuse me—'

I interrupted him. 'It's not about a donation, but about a matter of vital interest, that affects his reputation.' I liked the sound of that phrase.

Bertrand turned on his heel to face me. He looked directly at me, and I noticed that his eyes were grey and strangely lacking in light. They reminded me of the eyes of a dead fish. 'I'm afraid M. Ardoin would require more information before agreeing to meet with anybody,' he said. His voice was silky.

'Perhaps M. Ardoin is not as white as he pretends to be,' I said softly.

'What exactly do you mean, Sister? 'Bertrand asked. He stared at me and stepped forward. 'That is a very dangerous insinuation to make about a man as wealthy and powerful as M. Ardoin,'

'I have information that his mother has African blood,' I replied. 'Of course, I would be willing to negotiate with M. Ardoin. There really is no need for this information to be made public, and of course I would hate to damage the reputation of such an eminent person.' I was rather proud of the way I'd phrased this veiled threat.

For such a big man, he moved remarkably swiftly. He hit me hard, so hard that my head snapped back, and everything went hazy. I felt him pick me up from the ground and carry me aboard his boat. The stench of his body made me retch, and he slapped me hard. Below decks, he tied me to a chair. The rope hurt my wrists, and I cried out. I smelled the pungent reek of a cigar and saw its glowing tip.

'Now, Sister, you are going to confess your sins. Pretend that I'm a priest!' He guffawed. 'You are going to tell me every single detail about the source of this ridiculous accusation.' He went behind me and ground out the cigar in my right palm. I screamed. 'No one can hear you, Sister,' he said gently. 'Sound doesn't travel in the fog.'

I must have fainted, but revived when he burned me again. I could smell my own charred flesh.

'So,' Bertrand continued. 'I'm a good Catholic, and the last thing I want to do is to continue to harm a nun. You really must tell me everything you know. Who told you this pack of lies?'

I was trembling so hard I could hardly speak. I could feel the snot rolling down over my lips and felt vaguely vexed that since my hands were tied, I couldn't wipe it away. 'It w-was 'T-tite Jeanne,' I stammered.

'And who might 'Tite Jeanne be?' He lit another cigar.

'T-the old witch who lives not far from here, by the river. She sells herbs and potions.' For the first time, I thought that I might die. 'M. Bertrand, please let me go!' I begged. 'If you do, I promise to go far from here. I will never breathe a word of this. Please don't hurt me anymore.'

Bertrand laughed. With the tip of his cigar, he made the sign of the Cross on my palms. 'The Stigmata, Sister,' he said. He then did other things I cannot bear to remember. After it was over, he said nothing, but untied my hands, and took me in his arms. It almost felt like what I imagined a lover's embrace would be. For a moment, a wild hope came to me that he would let me go. He strode to the end of the pier.

I felt my body falling through the air. The river coiled around me, hissing, silken, teasing. The water chilled me to the bone. My habit was heavy and billowed around me like the black toadstools that used to grow on graves back home in France. I felt the ripples close over my head, choked, breathed in the darkness. The black water came to claim me, and I sank blissful into its embrace.

Chapter 12

Sidonie

Joelle departed shortly after breakfast. 'Remember your promise, Sidonie!' she cried, as she waved goodbye from the coach. Bertrand, Armand Ardoin's overseer, a rough-looking man with a twisted arm, had come to fetch her after taking her belongings to the boat. He had arrived an hour late, but did not apologise for keeping her waiting. I prayed for my friend and thought of her and the baby and the hard journey upriver.

Breakfast was late, because Immaculata was nowhere to be found. 'Where can that silly girl be,' Sister Fidelis grumbled to Mother Jerome.   'She has grown far too fond of roaming the streets on her own.'

After breakfast, I set to work with my students. We were all rather subdued, particularly Palmyre, who had remained all day in her cabin and only emerged after Joelle's departure. Suddenly, we heard loud knocking at the Convent door. Mother Jerome went to find out what the matter was. Outside stood a horse and cart. On the cart was a body, partly covered in a rough canvas sheet.

The man driving the cart was a local farrier. He removed his hat. 'Reverend Mother, there's been an accident. One of your nuns fell into the river. She's in a bad way.'

Mother Jerome gasped. She stepped forward, and gently pulled the canvas back, revealing Immaculata's face. Her eyes had rolled up in her head, and foam dripped from the side of her mouth.

Mother Jerome's voice trembled. 'Yes, she is one of ours. Where was she found?'

'Down by the docks,' said the farrier. 'Some fishermen found her when the current brought her up against the pier. If it hadn't been for them, she'd have drowned. Reverend Mother. What shall we do with her?'

Mother Jerome drew herself up. 'Bring her in, of course.' She instructed the man to carry Immaculata into the Convent and deposit her in her bed. Taking some coins from her purse, she handed them to the man. Then she turned to us. 'Fidelis, Sidonie, Martine, bring hot water,' she said briskly.' Martine was one of the cloister nuns, whom I'd rarely seen. She was a pale wisp of a girl with a reputation for piety.

Fidelis turned toward the kitchen. 'Sidonie, bring me some scissors,' she said. Her eyes were full of tears, and I wasn't deceived by her brisk tone. I fetched the scissors. Fidelis began to cut away the sodden habits from Immaculata's body. They were soaked and stained with river mud.

Fidelis and I looked down at Immaculata's face. She was unconscious, although she moaned when we touched her. Despite the heat, her skin was cold, and she looked more dead than alive. I looked at her hands, and gasped. My knees buckled, and I had to sit down. There were small round burns on her palms in the shape of a crucifix. My head began to spin.

'Miracle!' Fidelis cried. She made the sign of the Cross and knelt.

Fidelis and I had not noticed Father Beaubois come in. He came up behind us, and Fidelis rose quickly and hastened to cover Immaculata's unclothed body. 'There is nothing miraculous about this, Sister,' he said. His face was grim. 'Sister Immaculata was tortured.'

Both Sister Fidelis and I were at a loss for words. Finally, she regained her voice. 'With the greatest respect, Reverend Father, surely that cannot be true.'

'I'm afraid it can, Sister,' replied Father Beaubois quietly. 'And it doesn't stop there. Another woman was found dead near the river this morning.'

Our mouths opened wide. 'Who was it, Father?' I asked. My voice was shaking.

'An elderly herbalist known as 'Tite Jeanne,' he said. 'Her body washed up downstream, but there were marks around her neck that indicate she had been strangled before she went into the water.' He looked down at Immaculata. 'Poor lost soul,' he said. 'We must keep her safe, because she may be in great danger.'

He left, and we set about washing Immaculata's arms and legs. I was surprised to find tears running down my cheeks. 'I feel guilty that I've never liked Immaculata,' I confessed to Fidelis. 'She's always been unpleasant to me. But I should have

173

remembered that it's easy to be kind to people who are good to us, but it's the difficult ones who show us whether we're really capable of Christian charity.' Fidelis continued with her labours and nodded. Her eyes too were wet. 'She's always been angry, child. And yet she is in such need of tenderness. I think we have all failed her.'

I looked down. Around Immaculata's neck was a chain with a small wooden ornament, made of two intertwined figures. 'What is this necklace?' I asked. Fidelis shrugged. I removed it gently and placed it in the bureau by Immaculata's cot.

A fortnight went by, and then another. Since Immaculata was in no condition to do so, I was expected to do most of the shopping for food, and I was so busy that there didn't seem to be enough minutes in the day. Immaculata had hardly spoken since her return to the Convent, and she lay in bed listlessly, staring at the wall. Her skin was even paler than usual, and there were dark circles under her eyes. Since we shared a room, I heard her turning restlessly in her bed at night and feared she might have another of her fits. Once she woke me when she cried out in her sleep, but I couldn't discern what she was saying. The wounds on her hands had begun to heal, but her spirit seemed mortally wounded, and I longed to be able to help her. Feeling a bit silly, I brought flowers from the courtyard and put them in a vase on the table by her bed. Occasionally, I read to her from one of my books of poetry, though I wasn't sure if she heard me. There were moments when I wondered if she would ever return to us, and others when her gaze disconcerted me with its awareness. One thing I knew: she seemed to be in mortal fear, quivering when she heard noises in the corridor.

Besides all this, I was increasingly nervous about being present at the birth of Joelle's baby. What I wanted more than anything was to be useful to my friend, but I knew absolutely nothing about childbirth and what it involved. One day, as my students and I sat over our embroidery, I asked Nanette if she knew anything about what to do. I knew that Palmyre did, since she'd had a baby of her own, but I couldn't bring myself to broach the subject in front of her, since I knew the pain that it would cause.

'Babies?' asked Nanette. Her mouth twisted. 'The best thing you could do would be to drown it at birth. Particularly if it's a girl.'

I tried to remain patient. 'Nanette, I've promised to help Joelle. She said that her husband was trying to find a midwife for the moment when the baby comes, but if he can't, then I'll need to know what to do.'

Berthe had come in silently and had overheard the last bit of conversation. 'Sidonie, if you come with me, I'll show you how babies are born.'

Berthe had become a good friend. She was shrewd and pragmatic, and of course was a keen tradeswoman and negotiator, but she had a warm heart. Married life suited her. She had gained some weight around the middle, and her complexion was glowing. I liked her earthy humour, and her frankness. The nuns deemed certain topics inappropriate for my virgin ears, but I knew that I could rely on Berthe to explain things without beating around the bush. Also, I could justify visits to her shop by combining them with errands for Fidelis

When we reached the shop, Fidelis beckoned me to a room in back of the counter. 'I'll bet that you had no idea that your kitten Ouragan was a girl.'

I blinked. Ouragan was lying on a blanket in the corner. She looked sleek and well fed, and remarkably plump. Then the penny dropped.

'Oh!' I said. 'She's going to have kittens! I was surprised and a little worried, since the little cat was hardly more than a kitten herself. She looked twitchy and restless, and was licking her abdomen.

'I think it will be today or tomorrow because of how she's behaving,' said Berthe. 'When it begins, I'll run to the Convent to fetch you.' We were only two streets away.

Sure enough, that very afternoon Berthe popped her head around the door. 'Sidonie, it's time! Hurry!' I left a note for Sister Fidelis that I had gone to buy rice. Berthe and I ran back to the grocery.

We arrived just in time. Ouragan was lying on her side. She rose to a half-sitting position and seemed to squat and strain. We saw a little head emerge, then a whole kitten, enveloped in a gelatinous caul. Ouragan began to lick it, and we heard a small shill meow. She gnawed on the umbilical cord, then ate what Berthe told me was the afterbirth. At that point I felt a bit queasy, but told myself not to be ridiculous. Berthe placed the kitten at Ouragan's teats, and it began to nurse. 'This may take a while, Sidonie,' Berthe said. She prepared me a cup of strong tea.

Four more kittens arrived, about ten minutes apart. The last one was small, and Ouragan was tired. Her licking seemed less vigorous, and the sac enveloping the kitten remained unbroken. Berthe acted swiftly, puncturing the sac and rubbing the tiny kitten gently with a towel. 'This is to make him breathe,' she said. She was rewarded with a feeble meow. 'Where did you learn to do this?' I asked in admiration.

'I grew up on a farm,' Berthe laughed. She placed the last kitten by its mother's nipples. 'With people it's not much different. Except that you shouldn't expect Joelle to eat the afterbirth!' That image made me dissolve in laughter, laced with terror. She went on to explain what happened with human birth, what was the same and what was different, and how I should cut the cord.

Blushing violently, I asked how babies were started in the first place. When I was growing up in the Convent and my monthly bleeds began, an elderly nun had provided me with white cloths to place within my knickers, but had failed to explain what was happening. At first, I thought I was bleeding to death. Berthe was wonderfully matter-of-fact about this, and about what humans did to make a baby. My first reaction, when she told me, was to burst out laughing. 'That's ridiculous!' I said. 'Do people have to do that every single time they want a baby?'

Berthe laughed. 'When you love somebody, it's the most wonderful thing there is. And you do it again and again and again, not just to make babies.' I turned even redder. This was hard to imagine, but despite the fact that their marriage had begun as a very pragmatic arrangement, the relationship between Berthe and her plump grocer husband was warm and lusty and very physical.

It was all a bit overwhelming. 'Hopefully, Armand Ardoin will have arranged a midwife!' I exclaimed. But at least I had an inkling of what was in store, and what to do if there wasn't one.

I returned to the Convent, and on entering my room, found Sister Fidelis and Sister Martine at Immaculata's bedside. They were talking as though she wasn't there. Their expressions were intent, and there was something about the scene I didn't like at all. Sister Fidelis looked at the scars on Immaculata's hands and made the sign of the Cross. She turned to Sister Martine. 'I do fear this poor soul is possessed by the Devil' Sister Martine nodded assent, though she was such an insipid girl that she would have agreed with anything. Fidelis continued, 'The rites of exorcism should be performed as soon as possible, though of course it is for Father Beaubois to decide. Demonic possession is not to be trifled with, and it would not do for diabolic spirits to gain a foothold here in the convent.' She sighed. 'Poor tortured creature.'

At that, I could not remain silent. 'Sister Immaculata is ill, not possessed!' I said. 'That kind of talk is very dangerous. She has been badly hurt, but her body is mending. Surely the very least we can do is exercise a little Christian charity.' I was surprised to find that my face was flushed, and my heart was beating hard.

Sister Fidelis was outraged. 'Sidonie, our Faith recognises the existence of the Devil, and exorcism is a rite sanctioned by the Church to cast devils out. We are concerned for Immaculata's immortal soul. These things are for others older and wiser to you to decide.'

I looked down at the floor. I was simmering in fury. Immaculata could be difficult, as I well knew, but she was in great danger, and not just from the person who had attacked and tortured her. I knew that Fidelis was a kind person at heart, but she was frightened, and I was coming to learn that fear can make kind people do very cruel things.

Chapter 13

Sister Immaculata

They think I can hear nothing. Fools. I can, but I am hiding behind my eyes. They have no idea of the darkness and danger that exist out there in the world.

I can't remember much of what happened down by the river, nor do I want to. I recall the smell of my own burning flesh, and of a cigar, and of choking on dirty river water. In the Convent, I remember somebody washing me, and flinch because I hate the idea of being naked. For a long time, I drifted in and out. The first thing I saw when my eyes were able to focus were some flowers on the table by my bed. I don't know who bothered to leave them there. Still, their scent helped take away the stench of terror that lingered in my nostrils.

I remember as well, a voice reading poems. Through slitted lids, I glimpsed Sidonie. Why she did this, I do not know: she's never liked me, and I never liked her. I always thought she was a jumped-up pretentious little schoolmarm with ideas above her station. I've never had time for poetry and that sort of nonsense, but I have to confess that I found the rhythm of the words and the rise and fall of her voice soothing.

But then I overheard something. Fat old Fidelis and that ridiculous prim Martine were asking whether I had devils within me. I know, of course, that I have, and that what happened was divine punishment for my evil nature. So no argument about that. But I didn't like the way the conversation was heading. What took me by surprise was that Sidonie waded in and took up cudgels on my behalf. She has a temper, that one. Still, this was the first time in my life that anyone has ever stood up for me. Even though she's wrong, and even though I do believe in devils, more now than ever before, I have to confess that I felt something that was alarmingly like gratitude. This is a sign of weakness, and I cannot afford to be weak and let my barriers down.

After this, I decided it was time to get better. If Louis Bertrand ever comes back for me, or if the nuns decide to hand me over to exorcists, I want to have my wits about me. So, I began to sit up, then take a few steps, then short walks down the corridors. The other nuns gave me a wide berth. This suited me well. Clucking, patronising old hens. I hate them all.

Sidonie

I should have known that my comments about exorcism would provoke a reaction. The following day, I saw Sister Fidelis deep in conversation with Mother Jerome. Mother Jerome then went to Father Beaubois's study, and the two were closeted there for nearly an hour. I heard raised voices and wondered what they were saying. That afternoon, I saw Father Beaubois deep in conversation with Pierre Cormier, the butcher, in the courtyard. The two men had become friends when they were working together to rebuild the Convent. I know it isn't nice to eavesdrop, but I couldn't resist. They were talking about what to do about Immaculata.

Father Beaubois said in a low voice, 'I have a favour to ask, my friend.' Cormier raised an eyebrow, then nodded. 'One of our nuns is ill. You may have heard of a woman being killed down by the river. I think the same person attacked Sister Immaculata. There are other problems as well, and I think she may be in danger. For all these reasons, I would like to send her away from New Orleans for a while.'

'I'm sorry to hear that,' said Pierre Cormier. 'I like Immaculata. She drives a hard bargain. But yes, I had heard news of this. People talk in the shop.'

Father Beaubois went on. 'You have a bit of land on the edge of town, *n'est-ce pas*, with a small house?'

'Yes,' Cormier responded. His expression was wary.

'Would it be possible to send Immaculata there for a while? She could go with Palmyre, one of our slaves, who could take care of her while she recovers. She is very vulnerable here in New Orleans.'

Cormier thought for a moment. 'The cabin there is very small and is not very fancy. This might be possible for a brief time. My fiancée is due to arrive from France in a month, and then I shall need the house. Annette would not like to find another woman installed there, even if she is a nun.' He smiled.

'That would be very helpful,' Father Beaubois said. 'By the time your fiancée arrives, Immaculata will almost definitely be able to return to the Convent. I hope that by then the danger

182

will have passed. There are things that I suspect, but cannot prove. Perhaps by then I shall have some clarification.' He rose. 'Thank you, my friend.' I drew back from the door and returned silently to my room.

Sister Immaculata

On a sunny morning Father Beaubois summoned me to his study. 'Immaculata, I have arranged for you to be sent to convalesce at a place in the country.'

This struck terror into my heart, since I thought he meant the insane asylum. But he went on, 'I believe you know the local butcher, who is a friend of mine.'

I blushed to the roots of my hair and nodded.

'He has kindly agreed to allow you and the slave Palmyre to go to the little house on his farm in the country.'

'Surely it isn't necessary to send Palmyre!' I exclaimed. 'I am much better, Reverend Father. I can care for myself.'

'You will do as you are told, Sister,' he said sternly. 'Remember your vows of obedience. And remember the proprieties. It would cause comment if you were to go to M. Cormier's house unaccompanied.' He looked at the scars on the palms of my hands. 'It may not be safe for you to remain here. And you may not be the only one in danger.'

This did make me think. I'd noticed how Palmyre always went to ground and stayed in her cabin when Armand Ardoin and his overseer were around. 'Yes, Reverend Father,' I said, without much good grace. I didn't like the idea of living, even for a brief spell, in the love nest that Cormier was preparing for his fat stupid Annette. I'd never seen her, but I knew she would be fat and stupid. Men like women like that, a good armful of flesh. But I had nowhere else to go.

'You will only be staying there briefly,' Father Beaubois said. 'M. Cormier's future wife will be arriving from France soon, and then we'll think about bringing you back to the Convent. I will arrange for you to be taken there day after tomorrow.'

I left Father Beaubois and returned to my room. There, I looked at the amulet hanging above my bed, and my mouth twisted. 'Luck, love, money.' Ha! But at least I do have a little money. One day I will have my own shop and will leave all this. For good.

The night before Palmyre and I were due to leave, acting on an impulse I could not account for, I took the amulet and put it on Sidonie's pillow. On a piece of paper, I scrawled, 'Thank you.' I still find her annoying, but she took up for me. I may not be lucky, and I'll never find love, so I thought I might as well pass it on.

Chapter 14

Sidonie

The day came when I was due to depart for Les Chenes to be with Joelle. I was surprised by how reluctant I felt to be leaving the Convent. I was often impatient with the nuns, it's true, but the Convent was really the only family I'd ever known. Although most of the nuns were fond of me, I knew that Mother Jerome would be relieved at my departure, since I and my heretical opinions would now be somebody else's problem.

My students were downcast at my departure, but I was convinced that the embroidery project would continue to give them focus as well as a small independent income. We'd agreed that Nanette would deliver the finished linens to Berthe, and that Berthe would see that the appropriate share of the profits reached the Convent. I knew that I would miss my students, who had become good friends.

Palmyre was uncharacteristically subdued. She beckoned and called me aside.

'Sidonie, you and Joelle are in great danger at Les Chenes.'

I hardly knew what to say. I knew that Ardoin was difficult, and I knew that Joelle's marriage had had its ups and downs. But the word 'danger' seemed a bit melodramatic. 'What on earth do you mean, Palmyre?' I asked.

'There are things it would be dangerous for me to say,' she replied. She lowered her eyes. 'I knew Ardoin and his overseer in S. Domingue.'

'Really?' I exclaimed. 'Tell me more.' I had always had the feeling that the key to some of Ardoin's behaviour could be found in his past in the West Indies.

'That is all I can say for now,' answered Palmyre. She glanced at the amulet hanging from my neck, and her eyes widened. 'Where did you get this?'

'It belonged to Immaculata,' I said. 'It came as a bit of a surprise, but she gave it to me and left it on my pillow. I've heard that she's leaving for the country later today to recover from her illness.'

'In my country, it is supposed to bring us love, luck and wealth,' Palmyre said.

'Well it didn't for Immaculata, except perhaps for wealth,' I replied. I knew that she had managed to make quite a bit of money running errands for the sisters, and kept it in a sock under her mattress. 'I wear it to remind myself to be kinder. I never liked Immaculata, but I've discovered that she isn't so hard and cold as she might seem. Besides, you never know.' I smiled.

'Father Beaubois has arranged for me to go with her,' said Palmyre. 'He thinks we both may be in danger.' She sighed. 'You've been a friend to me, Sidonie,' she said. 'There has not been much friendship in my life.' She grasped both my hands

186

and looked into my eyes. 'Promise me that you will never mention my name to Ardoin or to Louis Bertrand.'

'I promise,' I said. 'But why all the secrecy?'

She looked into the distance, and then took a deep breath. 'When I arrived in S. Domingue, I was bought by Ardoin. His overseer took me to his plantation, and up to his bedroom. There, he raped me. Ardoin looked on. He seemed to enjoy watching.' She was trembling.

I recoiled in horror. 'My friend, I have no words. I don't know what to say.'

'My baby died on the boat from Africa,' she continued in flat tones. 'My husband was sold to a different plantation when we reached St. Domingue, but I heard that he escaped. I never saw him again. For a long time, I was in a daze, and Bertrand kept me as his concubine. He is a vile man who delights in cruelty. But I was determined to escape and one night I did. I managed to stow away on a boat heading to New Orleans, posing as the servant of a priest. Father Beaubois is a very good man, and he helped me at huge risk to himself. But now you will understand that Armand Ardoin or Louis Bertrand must never find me. I vowed that one day I would take revenge for the death of my child, and for what happened to me and others, when I was strong enough. If they do find me, and if they try to recapture me, I will kill myself. But I shall kill them first.' Her eyes flashed. I had no doubt that she would do as she said.

I reached out and and hugged her. Initially, Palmyre stiffened, but then relaxed into my embrace and hugged me back.

The next morning, I waited in the door of the Convent. The January dawn was cold. My few possessions fit into a small portmanteau, and I left the small trunk or *cassette* with my trousseau at the Convent, since it didn't make much sense to bring it upriver. I'd been told that one of Armand Ardoin's female slaves would serve as chaperone on the journey. After what Palmyre had told me, I was very glad of this. I was terrified at the idea of being alone with Bertrand, but was determined to keep my promise to Joelle. Father Beaubois, Mother Jerome and Sister Fidelis had come to see me off.

'Godspeed, Sidonie,' said Father Beaubois. 'Do give my regards to Joelle and to her husband. I know your presence will mean much to her. You will be in our thoughts and prayers. You are a brave young woman, and a loyal friend.' He went on, 'I am glad that there will be another woman to accompany you on the journey. However, I have spoken to Armand Ardoin, and he has given me assurances that you will be well treated at Les Chenes and will be respected by his overseer M. Bertrand and delivered safely.'

Mother Jerome, to my surprise, embraced me. There were tears in her eyes. 'Take care of yourself, little one. I shall be praying for you. And very best of luck to Joelle when her time comes.' She dotted her eyes with a lace handkerchief. 'Do send us a letter to let us know how things are, and when to expect your return.' Fidelis said nothing, but her eyes were wet.

We heard horses' hooves. It was Louis Bertrand. The carriage drew up, and my small trunk was loaded onto the back. Bertrand said nothing, but made a brusque gesture indicating that I should climb in. He was short, with a barrel chest and bandy legs, and one twisted arm hung down by his side. After hearing Palmyre's story, it was hard not to show my revulsion when I looked at him. Within the carriage was a female slave, huddled in the corner. She said nothing, but gave me a tenuous smile. I waved farewell to Father Beaubois and the nuns, and we set off to the port.

There, my portmanteau was loaded onto Ardoin's boat. 'It will take us two days to reach Les Chenes,' Bertrand said. 'Your cabin is below. I would advise you to remain there. The slave Clemence will sleep on the floor outside your door. You will find bread, cheese and water.' He smelled of tobacco and of something else I couldn't identify, and my skin crawled. I went below, and fingered Immaculata's amulet. I was suddenly aware of how very alone and vulnerable I was.

During the voyage upriver, I heeded Bertrand's advice and stayed below decks most of the time, emerging from time to time for a breath of air and a glimpse of my surroundings. The river was like a living thing, brown with undulating diamond ripple scales. On the banks, Spanish moss dripped from the trees. It felt like a haunted place, with unseen eyes watching us. I could hear the calls of strange birds. Once, near the bank, I saw a long brown form splash into the river and shivered. I tried repeatedly to engage the slave Clemence in conversation, with no success. She was small in stature, with expressive eyes and an air of kindness, and I was perplexed by her silence. But most of the time I remained in my cabin, passing the time by knitting a blanket for Joelle's baby.

Late in the afternoon on the second day, I felt the boat bump against something, and went up to deck. Bertrand was throwing a rope around a post on a wooden pier. Waiting by the pier was an open cart, with a slave holding the horses' reins.

My portmanteau was loaded onto the cart. Louis Bertrand sat behind the driver, and I sat with Clemence in the back of the cart. Joelle had told me that the house was set back from the river on a peninsula. The road was a dirt track. Flanked on either side by live oaks. The effect, in the gathering dusk, was sinister.

Suddenly in the distance I saw clouds of birds, clustering around something in the trees. At first, I couldn't discern what it was, but as we drew closer I saw to my horror a box-like thing made of timber, resembling a cage, hanging from one of the trees. In it was a black man. The birds had managed to penetrate within the slats of the cage and had pecked out his eyes. His cheekbones were visible, and his body was covered with lacerations. He was still alive. His flesh in some places hung in tatters. Underneath the cage was a pool of blood. I could hear his moans, and heard the word, 'Water.'

I felt as though I was about to faint. But then I tugged hard at Louis Bertrand's sleeve. 'For the love of God, M. Bertrand, we must cut this poor man down at once and take him to a doctor,' I cried. At my side, I felt Clemence shudder.

Bertrand brushed me off as though I were a fly. 'Drive on,' he told the coachman.

'Have you no pity, monsieur!' I shrieked. At this, Bertrand turned around and looked me in the eye.

'You know nothing, little girl. This slave raised his hand against me three days ago. To do so is punishable by death. We have to set an example, to keep the other slaves in line.' He paused. 'You will say nothing to your friend, in her delicate condition.' I could hear the threat in his voice and recoiled. The menace radiating from him was palpable.

I pulled my cloak around me and closed my eyes in horror. I could not close my ears to the groans of the dying slave, though, and they haunted me even after they became inaudible as we lurched down the track to the house. I was trembling and in a state of shock as we approached, but realised that I would need to keep my wits about me in order to protect Joelle and her baby. I tried to be attentive to my surroundings.

Les Chenes was an imposing house by any standard. It was set at the end of a horseshoe-shaped drive, and was two stories high, clad in timber painted white. There were verandas on all four sides of the house, with Corinthian columns the height of two floors. It was rapidly growing dark, and above our heads the moon was hidden behind scudding clouds.

When we stopped in front of the house, a tall African woman emerged. She wore a yellow *tignon* around her head. Her eyes were deep-set, and her cheekbones were prominent. I descended and turned to say farewell to Clemence. She opened her mouth to try to answer, and I saw that the reason for her silence was that she had no tongue. It had been cut out.

The tall woman led me to what would be my room. It was beautiful, with high ceilings, white walls, and large windows. I discerned Joelle's taste at work here, in the soft blue and white tones of the curtains and the canopy of the four-poster bed. There was a bureau on which a tray with refreshments had been laid out. I turned toward the woman with a question in my eyes.

'Madame has been unwell, and is resting,' she said. 'She will see you at breakfast tomorrow morning.' She turned and left.

After what I'd witnessed, I could not bring myself to eat. I wondered how much Joelle knew about horrors like those I had just seen, and whether Armand Ardoin had sheltered her from them. I hoped, for her sake and for the baby's sake, that he had.

That night I tossed and turned, but finally fell into a fitful sleep. The following morning dawned bright and sunny. I could not escape images of the dying African, which kept running through my mind. I washed my face and hands in the basin and made my way downstairs.

The entrance hall was imposing, with a stairway at the end leading to the upper floors. The balustrade was in elaborately carved mahogany, and in the stairwell was a crystal chandelier. I noticed that the windows were all made of glass, unlike ours covered with thin muslin in New Orleans. There was a portrait of a man with dark hair and eyes, and a pointed beard, with a strong resemblance to Ardoin; I deduced that it must be his father. I heard voices in an adjoining room and tapped timidly at the door.

'*Entrez*,' I heard. It was Joelle's voice. She sounded tired.

I opened the door and burst into the room. 'Here at last, my friend,' I cried, and embraced her.

There were dark circles under Joelle's eyes, but her smile was radiant. 'Darling Sidonie,' she said. 'You cannot imagine how delighted I am to see you. Have you had breakfast? Was the journey awful?'

I didn't want to tell her just how awful. 'It was long and tiresome, but I'm here now,' I said. 'How have you been?' I looked at her belly. She was carrying the child low. Berthe had told me back in New Orleans that this was a sign that things were about to start happening. I sat down at the table and helped myself to a flaky croissant.

Joelle sighed. 'Being so very pregnant is not pleasant,' she replied. 'I look like a beached whale.' Her blonde ringlets

193

were lank and her eyes were tired. Given her volume, I wondered for the first time if there was more than one baby.

'Are there any twins in your family? Or in Armand's? I asked.

'Not in mine, certainly!' she exclaimed. 'Armand doesn't talk much about his parents or grandparents. His brother Jean is arriving next week.' She winked at me.

That wink persuaded me that she knew nothing of the dying slave. Joelle was light-hearted and carefree by nature, but she had a compassionate heart and a sense of justice. I knew that she would be horrified at what I had seen. 'The woman who showed me to my room last night said you'd been unwell,' I said.

Joelle shrugged. 'Just tired of being pregnant,' she said. 'That was Octavia, our housekeeper. She and Armand coddle me far too much.' She rose. 'Let me show you the rest of the house.'

I heard a noise on the veranda. Armand Ardoin entered, and handed his riding crop to a house slave. He saw me and inclined his head. 'Welcome to Les Chenes, Sidonie.'

'Thank you,' I said. 'It is very impressive.' This seemed to please him. I continued, 'Joelle is going to show me around.'

'I'm afraid that won't be possible just now,' Armand said. 'We must ensure that she rests.' He nodded, and the housekeeper emerged. 'Madame is going to lie down for the rest of the morning,' he said. His tone implied that he would not countenance any disagreement. Joelle flushed, and her lower lip jutted out in a pout, but she did not challenge him, and the housekeeper Octavia accompanied her back to her room. I was disappointed for my friend, whose need of fresh air and exercise seemed obvious to me. But on the other hand, it suited me just then to be left to my own devices.

Armand continued, 'I have matters to attend to for most of the morning, but in the afternoon I will show you the house. I'm afraid that you will have to entertain yourself in the meantime.'

'But of course,' I said demurely. 'I shall sit outside and finish the little blanket I'm making for the baby.' He turned to leave and went out through the front door. Some minutes later, I heard the noise of horses' hooves vanishing in the distance.

Carrying my knitting with me, I went outside. Taking advantage of the fact that Octavia was occupied with Joelle, I slipped away and headed down the drive toward the dirt track we had come in on the night before. I tried to be unobtrusive as I walked among the trees bordering the drive. There were so many questions in my mind: what on earth had the slave done to suffer such a ghastly punishment? Was Armand Ardoin aware of what his overseer had done?

I walked on and, turning the corner, arrived at the place where I'd seen the cage hanging from the branches. I had scissors in my reticule and had formed vague plans to cut the man down and try to give him succor in some way, perhaps help him escape. But there was nothing there: the cage, and the man, had vanished. I blinked and asked myself if I had imagined it all. But then I saw the stains of dried blood on the ground and knew that what I'd seen was real.

I turned and headed back to the house. On reaching the veranda, I saw that Octavia had emerged from Joelle's room. I approached her and asked, 'Is Madame indisposed?'

'Yes,' she replied. Octavia's voice was soft and melodious, in accentless French. There was something austere about her demeanour. I estimated her age as around thirty. Clearly, she was not given to light-hearted conversation. But I persevered.

'I would imagine that being pregnant cannot be easy,' I said. 'Do you know if M. Ardoin has arranged for a midwife to be present at the birth?'

Her face went still, and I thought that, somehow, I had offended her. 'M. Ardoin will discuss this with you, if he wishes to do so.'

She turned suddenly as she heard a child's voice. Approaching the veranda was a girl of about twelve. '*Maman,*' she asked, 'should I help with the washing later?'

Her face was the face of Armand Ardoin, though her skin was the colour of honey. I managed not to betray my shock. After all, I thought, the child could have been fathered by Armand's father, or by his brother. Whatever the case, I found it horrifying that the men of the family would take advantage of slave women.

I knew I was unsophisticated and naïve about these matters, but not so naïve that I couldn't distinguish right from wrong, and this was wrong in every way. I found it hard to look at Armand without remembering Palmyre's horrifying story of what had happened to her.

Octavia answered her in an African language I didn't understand, and the child turned and left at once. In the distance I saw the overseer and shuddered. Octavia noticed my revulsion. Armand Ardoin was riding at his side.

'M. Bertrand and the Master go over accounts every morning,' she said.

'Octavia, I am going to rest for a bit,' I said. 'M. Ardoin is going to show me the house and grounds after lunch.'

'I'll have lunch brought to your room,' she replied tonelessly.

This state of affairs really was not satisfactory at all. If I'd come to help Joelle and keep her company, it didn't make sense to prevent me from seeing her. I resolved to bring this up with Armand later.

After a light lunch in my room, I went down to the entrance hall. Armand was in his study. I peeked in and tapped lightly at the door. It was a pleasant room, lined with books. I knew that in order to help Joelle, I would have to try to be pleasant to him. '*Bonjour*,' I said.

'Bonjour, Sidonie,' he replied. He sounded weary.

'May I look at your library?' I asked.

He raised an eyebrow. 'But of course,' he said. 'Although I think most of them will be a bit deep for a young woman like you.'

I smiled and walked over to the bookshelf. If Armand Ardoin thought he could intimidate me, he could think again. Many of the tomes were unappealing treatises about agriculture and animal husbandry, but I was delighted to spot some old friends, and my eyes lit up. 'Moliere's *School for Wives*,' I exclaimed in delight. 'And Racine's *Andromaque*!'

'You know these books?' Armand replied incredulously.

'Yes,' I said. 'These editions are beautiful.' I touched the leather binding with reverence.

'Never did I expect to find a *Femme Savant*e or a *Precieuse* under my own roof,' said Armand drily. It was my turn to be surprised by his apparent knowledge of Molière's plays *The Learned Ladies* or *The Affected Young Ladies*. He added, 'Not that I have seen either play. I don't think much of women with intellectual pretensions. But my brother Jean is a bit of an intellectual and a pedant.'

'He sounds charming,' I said. 'I would have imagined that you and Joelle attended many glittering salons in Paris where these things were discussed.'

'But of course,' he said airily. 'Not that Joelle understood anything.'

I didn't like this at all, but decided to opt for flattery and guile. 'I would think that, as mistress of a house as beautiful as Les Chenes, your wife would be expected to have her own literary salon.'

Armand laughed. 'Yes, here among the squirrels and raccoons and alligators.' But then he turned pensive. 'You may be right, though, that it is time for Joelle to improve herself and acquire a veneer of intellectual sophistication, as befits the mistress of Les Chenes. As long as she remembers her place as a woman.'

'And what might that be, Armand?' I said, my face the picture of innocence.

'As wife and mother, of course,' he said. 'Perhaps the two of you could discuss a few appropriate books from time to time, without taxing yourselves too much.'

'If you wish it,' I said. I thought that this way I would at least have an excuse to see Joelle and talk to her. 'Armand, I have a question for you. Has a midwife been arranged for Joelle?'

'We live in the middle of the wilderness, Sidonie,' he replied. His expression was stern. 'As you will understand, there are no doctors in the area. My housekeeper Octavia, however, does have some experience as a midwife.'

I tried hard to conceal my reaction to this. After seeing Octavia's child, and noting her resemblance to the Ardoins, I felt that for her to preside at Joelle's confinement was inappropriate to say the very least. Then I remembered what had happened to Palmyre and told myself that something similar might have happened to Octavia. 'Actually, I have a little experience in these matters myself,' I lied.

'Excellent. Then you will be able to help Octavia,' he replied. 'Now, let me show you a bit of the house and grounds. I don't have much time to spare, so it will have to be quick.'

We emerged into the entrance hall, which ran from the front to the rear of the house on both floors. The morning sunlight caught the crystal chandelier and created hundreds of dancing rainbows. 'Oh, how lovely!' I exclaimed. Armand smiled. 'It's French crystal. Only the finest for Les Chenes,' he said. 'The stained-glass panel in the front door was also brought from France.' I noticed the unusual pattern, and commented on it. 'Isn't that the form of a Celtic cross?' I asked.

'Yes,' Armand replied. 'They say it's to ward off evil. My brother insisted that we choose this pattern. Superstitious nonsense, in my view.' From the entrance hall doors led to a gaming room, a large formal parlour, a dining room with a long mahogany table, Armand's study, and even a ballroom. I could see that Armand took pride in his mansion. 'How long has it taken you to build the house?' I asked.

'Four years,' he said proudly. 'I began work immediately after my father died four years ago. Before then, there was a small house made of wood. A cabin, really. Our other plantation in St. Domingue has a much larger house.'

We went out the back door, and he gestured toward a long low building adjoining the house, which contained the kitchens. In the distance were the slave cabins. Even further was a lane which Armand told me led to the overseer's cottage, down by the river. 'How many slaves work here, Armand?' I asked.

He shrugged. 'Around a thousand,' he said. 'Of course, my overseer deals with all of that.' He pointed to the adjoining fields. 'We're now beginning to plant sugar instead of indigo. A far more lucrative crop.' We turned back toward the house. Behind I could see that a formal garden had been laid out, with a fountain in the middle and concentric paths fanning out. Back home in France, it would have taken many years to establish a proper garden, but here in the Louisiana climate plants seemed to grow and bloom overnight. The contrast between the strict formal patterns and the exuberance of the vegetation created a strange effect. I recognised camellias, lilies, azaleas, and several magnolia trees.

'It's very beautiful,' I said truthfully. I wondered if Armand was insensible to the fact that so much of this beauty was the product of so much human suffering.

That evening I chatted with Joelle after dinner. She seemed more animated than the day before. I soon discovered that this was because of the imminent arrival of her brother-in-law, Jean. 'You'll like him, Sidonie,' she said. 'The two of you can talk of books and that sort of thing. Tomorrow evening we will all dine together.' I could see that the prospect cheered her up considerably. She twirled a curl around her index figure. 'Of course,' she went on, 'I shall look like an elephant in this state. But there's no reason for you not to look pretty.' She began to pull dresses out of her wardrobe. 'Perhaps the grey silk? No-that would make you look washed out. And the red wouldn't suit your colouring.' She paused. 'But this blue-green satin...'

Joelle lay a dress out on the bed. The colour reminded me of sea foam. The bodice was narrow, low-cut, edged with white silk. 'Isn't it a little décolleté? I protested.

'Nonsense,' Joelle said gaily. 'You must try it on now to see if it fits. If it doesn't, Clemence is also a seamstress and she can do alterations. But tomorrow evening we shall dine in style.' She reminded me of a child with a new doll, though the vision of myself as dress-up doll seemed remarkably silly. But I decided to humour her and slipped the dress over my head.

I could hardly believe what I saw in the mirror. For the first time in my life, I thought that I might actually be able to look pretty. Joelle's smile was radiant. 'I told you so, Sidonie!' she said. 'The colour matches your eyes. And the white trim brightens up your skin. The low-cut neckline makes you look quite voluptuous.'

I laughed out loud. Voluptuous I knew I was not. Indeed, I am quite flat-chested. But the cut of the dress pushed up my breasts and made me look as though I actually possessed a décolletage. 'If you say so, Chère.'

'You're thinner than I used to be before I became a whale,' Joelle said with a sigh. 'So, I shall ask Clemence to take this in around the waist so that you can wear it tomorrow night.'

'But that might ruin it!' I exclaimed. 'You mustn't spoil such a beautiful dress. After the baby is born, you can wear it again.'

Joelle shrugged. 'Armand will buy me others,' she said. She yawned. 'But now I must go to bed and get some rest if I am going to be in good form for tomorrow's dinner. Jean will arrive early tomorrow afternoon.'

We embraced, and I went to my room. It was hard to sleep. I could not forget the dying slave, or Clemence's tongueless mouth. I wondered if Joelle knew the reason for her maid's silence. At the same time, I had to confess that I was excited about meeting Ardoin's brother, Jean, the following evening, and delighted that I'd be wearing a becoming dress when I did. This made me feel horribly guilty. How could I be so superficial and vain when I was surrounded by all these hidden horrors?

Chapter 15

Sidonie

The following day dawned sunny and bright. I spent most of the morning in my room reading. To have the run of Armand's library was luxury indeed. Around noon, I heard a clattering of horses' hooves, and voices as baggage was unloaded.

Later, I went to Joelle's room to dress for dinner. Clemence had taken in the beautiful blue dress at the waist, and it fit as though it had been made for me. Joelle clapped her hands. 'Exquisite!' she said. 'Now, you must let Clemence put your hair up.'

I wasn't at all used to being waited on, and this felt strange. I'd washed my hair the night before and had screwed it in a knot. But resisting Joelle was like standing in the way of an avalanche, and I let myself be carried. She called for Clemence.

'*Bonjour*, Clemence,' I said. 'Thank you for doing my hair.' She smiled timidly and nodded. Her eyes were large and amazingly eloquent, and I reasoned that they would be, since she used them to communicate. She brushed my hair gently with Joelle's silver-backed hairbrush, and then drew it back from my face and with deft flicks of her comb, shaped it into a chignon at the base of my neck. When that was done, she held up a mirror and gestured to me, indicating that I should look.

I did not recognise myself. 'My goodness me!' I exclaimed. In the mirror I saw, not a gaunt and gawky bookworm, but an unfamiliar being who actually resembled a sophisticated Parisienne. This, for me, was a miracle on the magnitude of the loaves and the fishes. Joelle laughed out loud in delight. 'How elegant you look, darling Sidonie!' she cried.

Joelle looked lovely herself. Clemence had tied pink ribbons into her golden curls, and she was wearing a flowing silk overdress in tones of pink, white and green. Her skin was glowing, and the listlessness I'd noted when I arrived had disappeared at the prospect of an elegant dinner in distinguished company. I smiled at her. 'What would the nuns back in the Convent say if they saw us now?' I asked.

'Mother Jerome would probably faint dead away in shock at the sight of our plunging necklines!' Joelle giggled. Pregnancy had filled her out and had made her breasts firmer and rounder. 'Here's a fan.' She handed me a fan made of carved sandalwood.' We are going to dine in the gaming room, because the table in the dining room is far too large for only four of us.' She took my arm, and we descended the stairs.

Waiting in the entrance hall were Armand and his brother Jean. Armand looked very distinguished, in a blue satin dinner jacket trimmed in gold brocade. My eyes went to his brother.

'Jean, may I introduce Sidonie, a friend of Joelle's who is visiting us,' Armand said. Jean bowed. He was taller than his brother, with unruly black hair and dark eyes and a neatly trimmed beard which gave him a rather saturnine air. He dismissed me with a glance and embraced Joelle. 'You look radiant, if I may say so, dear sister.' I decided that I heartily disliked him.

We moved into the gaming room, where a small table had been set in a corner. The silver cutlery glinted in the candlelight. Joelle was in her element. She nodded to a slave who was standing in the corner, and he brought porcelain dishes with clear consommé.

'It is good to see that Joelle has the company of a friend,' Jean said. 'I understand that both of you were *filles á la cassette,* and came to New Orleans on the same ship?' I thought I detected a disparaging undertone.

'Indeed we were, monsieur,' I replied, head held high. 'Joelle and I were already friends back at the convent in Rouen.'

Despite his supercilious air, Jean seemed to be aware that it was incumbent on him to make polite conversation. 'Do you miss France?' he asked, suppressing a yawn.

I thought for a minute. 'Yes, some things,' I replied. 'I miss the cool breeze from the sea. And I miss the flowers. But Louisiana is home now.' I was surprised to hear myself say this, but it was true. I turned Jean's question back on him: 'And do *you* miss France, monsieur? What led you to come back to Louisiana?'

He shrugged. 'I felt that it was only right to come help my brother. Running two large plantations, here and in St. Domingue, is no easy task.' A shadow crossed his face. Armand saw it, and intervened. 'In the company of two beautiful ladies, there are far more interesting things to discuss than farming.' He went on, 'Our little Sidonie has intellectual pretensions.'

I reddened. I did not like being called 'little Sidonie' one single bit. For the first time, I saw a spark of interest in Jean's eyes. He turned to me. 'Do you enjoy reading, mademoiselle?'

'I love reading,' I said. 'I would never call myself an intellectual. I only wish that I could. Joelle and I were educated in a convent, and our access to books was limited. I have only read what few plays were in Mother Superior's library, and a few smuggled novels. But I enjoyed studying classics and history.'

Armand rolled his eyes. 'You must learn, my dear, that even if you do read these things, you should keep quiet about them if you want to find a husband. Men, generally speaking, do not find women with strong opinions attractive.'

Jean spoke out. 'There are many men, it's true, who don't like a challenge, and who look for pretty, shallow girls. But an intelligent woman who is beautiful and who also has a mind of her own is a wonderful thing.' I went beet-red. I knew that he could not possibly be talking about me.

We began on the second course, pheasant in a sherry sauce. The manservant had been topping up our glasses with wine, and I knew my cheeks were flushed.

Joelle too was feeling the effects of the wine. She said, 'Perhaps not all women are looking for a husband. Marriage is not every woman's goal, you know.'

A silence fell. Armand's face was dark. 'Most women are sensible enough to know that marriage offers them protection and economic well-being, though not all women are grateful for these things.'

I wanted to come to Joelle's rescue, without making Armand even angrier. 'Obviously, I cannot form a reasoned opinion about the virtues of marriage, since I have never been married myself. But from my limited reading, it seems to me that the best marriages are marriages between equals.'

'What can you possibly mean?' he asked. His voice was silky.

I thought for a moment. 'I mean between people with common interests, with a similar degree of intelligence, and ideally who are both economically independent.'

Armand laughed out loud. 'I have never heard such nonsense.' His expression was ugly. 'If that were so, my own marriage does not make sense. If what you say is true, I should have looked for a rich heiress rather than an impoverished Casket Girl.' Joelle went white. 'But, of course, Joelle and I are blissfully happy because she does not share these absurd ideas, and she knows that she depends on me for everything. As for you, Sidonie, I can only ascribe them to your youth and naivete. Once you have learned the ways of the world, you will realise the idiocy of your views.'

Jean moved to defuse the tension of the moment. 'Armand, I believe that the moment has come for us to have cigars and port. Perhaps the ladies are ready to take their leave.' I seized the opportunity. 'Yes, it's late, and Joelle must not get overtired. Good evening, messieurs.' I gently led my friend to the door, and we went up the stairs to her room.

When we closed the door, Joelle turned to me. She was shaking in fury. 'Yes, I *do* share your 'absurd' ideas, Sidonie,' she said. 'How *dare* Armand throw my origins in my face! Yes, you and I are Casket Girls, but he knew what he was getting when he married me. Sometimes I wonder if that's the reason he married me. Since I have no money of my own, I have to put up with anything he dishes out. The other women, the insults, the rest.' Her shoulders slumped, and she began to cry.

I put my arms around her. 'It'll be all right, Joelle,' I said, in the tones one would use to comfort a child. I was not convinced, however that it really would be all right. Joelle was proud and spirited, and I had seen how much it wounded her to be treated with open contempt in front of guests. But Armand's comments had made me wonder as well. If indeed he was so wealthy, why had he chosen an impecunious girl rather than holding out for a more affluent wife? It was all very strange. 'None of this is good for the baby,' I told Joelle firmly. 'So, it's off to bed with you. Tomorrow morning I'll come by to see how you are. And since Armand has said we can discuss books, I'll bring a few, though we don't necessarily have to stick to bookish matters.'

The following morning, Octavia came to tell me that we would all be breakfasting together. I found this surprising and wondered whether it was yet another attempt to control Joelle and supervise her conversations, or whether Armand had seen that human contact was beneficial to her. I had feared after the previous evening's scene it would be awkward, but it seemed that there was a tacit understanding that we would not refer to this.

It was a beautiful sunny morning, of the sort that make one glad to be alive.

Joelle, however, looked as though she hadn't slept well, and her eyes were ringed with dark shadows. I too hadn't slept well, because my thoughts kept returning to the image of the slave in the cage, and to the horror that ran beneath all of the obscene luxury of my surroundings. Armand and Jean spent most of the meal discussing the plantation and their activities for the day, but then Jean turned to me. 'Do you ride, Sidonie?'

'Not really,' I confessed. 'But I have always wanted to learn.'

'Then I shall teach you,' he said. He looked at his brother. 'I shall take Sidonie out this afternoon on the old brown mare. She's gentle and very safe for an inexperienced rider.'

Armand nodded absently. My impression was that he preferred the idea of my riding (and possibly breaking my neck), rather than staying at home and inculcating revolutionary ideas to his allegedly submissive wife. It would not have surprised me to discover that he'd asked his brother to do him this favour. I smiled at Joelle, and we chatted about friends back in the Convent while Armand and Jean discussed the price of indigo. I was glad to see that her appetite had returned. Attalie, the cook, had made beignets, and the taste of these warm pastries dusted in sugar reminded us both of New Orleans.

After breakfast, Joelle and I went upstairs, and spent the morning reading. I'd found a volume of poems by the poet Pierre de Ronsard. Joelle sat in the window seat, and the sunlight fell on her golden curls as she read in a soft clear voice about Ronsard's crimson rose:

> Alas! See how in such short time
> her beauties have been lost.
> Nature, evil stepmother, lets her last
> only from dawn till dusk.

She sighed. 'You know, Sidonie, it's true. Youth, beauty, love, are all such transient things.'

'They are,' I admitted. 'But I love the last verse.' I read back to Joelle:

> If you believe me, love,
> While time still flowers for you
> in freshest newness
> take full advantage of your youthful bloom:

For as with this flower, old age's doom
Will blight your beauty.

'This poem's so dark, Sidonie,' Joelle said. 'I hate to think of getting old and ugly.' She shivered.

'So do we all,' I acknowledged. 'And yet the truth of the matter is that, if we're lucky, we grow old. And then we die. What I like is the last bit, about living to full advantage while we are young. Both of us have lost family to epidemics, and nobody knows how long we are going to live, but what matters is living for the day and making the most of it.'

Joelle smiled tremulously at me. 'How right you are that we should live for the day. In the end, what really lasts are family and true friendship.'

'Enough philosophizing,' I said briskly. 'Let's continue with our knitting for the baby.' Our needles flashed as we sat in the sunlight.

Sister Immaculata

The slave Palmyre and I were taken to Pierre Cormier's cabin in the country the night before Louis Bertrand came to fetch Sidonie. Mother Jerome clearly did not approve of this arrangement and looked on with tight lips as we departed. It was a dark night, and the woods were full of strange sounds.

When we arrived, Pierre Cormier was waiting for us. He had prepared a room for us to share. The cabin, as Father Beaubois had said, was small and lacking in comforts. I imagined, with a tinge of grim satisfaction, Fat Annette's reaction when Cormier brought her to this shack on the edge of town. Still, it was a refuge, for now at least. And it was good to be away from the convent and the furtive glances of people who thought I was the Devil. That night I slept more soundly than I had in months.

Palmyre was, as usual, quiet. She seemed to share my relief at being away from New Orleans. That first morning, Cormier had gone in to New Orleans and left us to our own devices. We looked around and were not impressed by what we saw. Palmyre shrugged. 'Sister,' she said, 'shall we attempt to improve this place a bit?'

I nodded. There was hardly enough space to swing a cat. There were three small rooms, cubicles really: two with low cots and a narrow room with a pot-bellied stove in the corner where Cormier must do his cooking. There was also a porch. He had left some bread and cheese for us. He'd told us that he would spend most of the week in town tending his shop and would come out from time to time to bring us food and check on us. He left a rifle propped up behind the door.

Palmyre drew some water from the well, and we set about sweeping, dusting, and mopping floors. After that, we ventured outside. There was a vegetable patch, overgrown with weeds. 'Men!' I said. 'Absolutely useless.' Palmyre glanced at me, and I thought I detected the hint of a smile. This seemed impertinent to me, and I didn't smile back. Though I have to say, she worked as hard as I did, and that's a lot. We weeded energetically for the next few hours. The heat was intense, and soon we were both dripping with sweat. But I felt a certain strange contentment in the repetitive movement of weeding. Underneath the vegetation, there were rows of potatoes, tomatoes, and squash. Some were stunted because the weeds had smothered them and shut out the light, but I knew that now they would flourish.

Out back, we discovered three pigs in a makeshift sty. They were rough-bristled grey creatures, with small glinting eyes. I wondered if they were boars that Cormier had captured and penned. But they seemed plump and well cared for. If there's one thing I know about, it's pigs. One day I shall have pigs of my own.

Pierre Cormier may have his Annette, I thought, but I don't need anyone as long as I've got myself.

Sidonie

After lunch, I went downstairs to meet Jean. I'd abandoned any pretensions to glamour, and was back in my everyday clothes, with my hair skewered back into a knot. Jean greeted me with a sardonic smile. 'So, Sidonie,' he said. 'Are you ready for a bit of equine adventure?'

I smiled. 'Yes, as long as the adventures aren't too adventurous!' If truth be told, I was looking forward mightily to escaping from the heavy atmosphere in the house, but I wasn't too sure about riding. We went out to the stables, where a groom was holding two horses. One was a spirited grey gelding. The other was a fat placid mare. Jean pointed toward her.

'This is Belle, the horse you'll be riding today,' he said. 'She's a good old girl and is very gentle.' She whickered softly, and Jean gave her a lump of sugar. 'I see that you are old friends,' I said.

He laughed. 'Indeed, we are,' he said. 'Armand and I learned to ride on her.'

Jean helped me mount, and then leapt up to the saddle of the grey. We set out down the path, at a sedate pace. I was grateful that he did not attempt to trot or gallop. Belle's steady walk was like a rocking chair, and I began to relax.

'How old were you when you went back to France?' I asked. 'It must've been hard to leave Belle behind.' The mare twitched her ears at the sound of her name.

'We were three and five years old,' Jean replied. 'Our father did not want for us to grow up in New Orleans.' I could see by his expression that the memories were not pleasant ones.

'That must have been hard,' I said. 'To leave home so young. But at least you had your mother and father, and each other.' I thought of the cholera epidemic and the early deaths of my own parents.

'Actually, we didn't have both of our parents,' he said. 'My father remained here to run the plantation as well as our property in St. Domingue, which is my mother's home. My mother did go with Armand and me. We were educated privately at home by a Jesuit tutor.'

'That explains your interest in reading,' I said. 'The Jesuits, like the Ursulines in the Convent where I grew up, are said to be excellent teachers.'

'Father André taught us well, but he was a strict disciplinarian,' Jean replied ruefully. 'When we got Latin declinations wrong, he would pull our ears and slap our faces. I have hated Latin ever since.'

'What subjects did you enjoy most?' I asked. I'd disliked Jean on sight, but it felt oddly pleasant to talk as we rode along.

'Literature and history,' he said without hesitation. 'But I also enjoyed fencing and archery.'

'I wish girls had been allowed to do fencing,' I sighed. 'Which writers did you like best?'

'Without a doubt, Molière,' Jean replied.

At that, we were off. We spent most of the ride in a spirited discussion of Molière and his plays. Finally, Jean asked me, 'Would you like to try a trot?'

'Why not?' I replied, casting caution to the winds. Jean touched Belle's flank gently with his crop, and she went into a bone-jolting trot. He tried to show me how to post, to stand in the stirrups and sit. This, riding side-saddle, was not easy, and I held on for dear life. The old mare must have been feeling her oats, because she then broke into a gallop. That, strangely, was easier. The rolling gait of the horse reminded me of the rocking movement of the waves when I came to Louisiana on the *Gironde.*

'Well done, Sidonie,' Jean laughed. 'I'll say this for you: you're game, at least.' I knew that the following day I'd be stiff and aching and would discover muscles I never thought I had. When we got back to the house, I was weary but content. And I was determined to show Jean a thing or two and become a good rider.

Chapter 16

Sister Immaculata

Over the following weeks, Palmyre and I settled into a pattern. We would work in the garden in the morning, before it became too hot, and after lunch would clean the house. At first, I didn't feel very strong, but the activity did me good, and I did what I could. In the afternoons, we would sit on the porch in the shade. Palmyre had brought along some embroidery thread in strange bright colours. She would work on her embroidery, and I would simply rock back and forth dozing. I tried to read books of devotionals, but came to the conclusion that they were boring. When we arrived, Palmyre was thin, with a haunted air, but here she began to fill out. She was all right, for a slave; she didn't talk much, and that suited me. I too gained weight, thanks to good country air. There were no mirrors, so I couldn't see how I looked, but told myself that vanity was a sin. Sin was not something I needed to worry about in this godforsaken place, I thought.

Little did I know. Late one afternoon, Pierre Cormier arrived. He was weaving on his feet and reeked of liquor. 'So, Sister,' he snarled, 'how is the rural idyll suiting you?'

'Quite well, thank you,' I snapped. 'Palmyre and I have tidied up this pigsty of a cabin of yours and tended the real pigsty outdoors. We've also managed to salvage that jungle you call a garden. When your bride *Annette* (I said the name in mocking falsetto tones) arrives she will be grateful to us.' Palmyre had gone fishing down by the river, and was nowhere in sight.

Pierre Cormier sat down heavily at the table in the makeshift kitchen. He glared at me. 'Annette won't be coming.'

'Oh really?' I said tartly. 'Did the prospect of married life in Louisiana with you not appeal to her?'

To my horror, tears began to slide down his face. Sometimes liquor takes men like that, makes them maudlin. 'She's run off with someone else. My cousin.' He lowered his face into his hands and wept, then began to retch up all the filthy liquor he had consumed.

I wet a cloth in the bucket by the stove and went over to him. I held his head against my chest as though he was a small child and began to dry his tears and clean the vomit from his face and neck. The weeping stopped. Then it all changed. He turned toward me and pulled me down to him. He kissed me hard, and I kissed him back, harder. He touched my breasts, then lifted me up to the table in a swift movement and pulled my habit up around my waist. We coupled there on the table, and there was nothing gentle about it. On the farm, I once saw foxes mating, and this was similar: feral, snarling, full of anger and something else I couldn't identify. I knew that my lips would be swollen and bruised from his kisses, and knew that my fingernails had left claw marks down his back.

When it was over, he pulled away, adjusted himself, and went out to the porch. I splashed cold water on my face,

219

and felt a smile rising to the surface. I did not feel one ounce of repentance and lifted my face to the sun.

Sidonie

At Les Chenes, the days settled into a routine. The baby was due in March, so
Joelle was unable to do very much. Every morning, I would go up to her room, and we would chat about poetry, or Joelle's plans for the baby, or about the New Orleans. I thought that Joelle sounded homesick for the Convent. I wondered what would happen when I returned to New Orleans, and feared she would be lonely, but reassured myself that she would have the baby to occupy her time and energy.

One morning a letter arrived from Mother Jerome.

My dear Sidonie,

I trust that you have arrived safely at Les Chenes. And that all is well with you and with Joelle. Is she keeping well? I hope so, and hope that the two of you are remembering your daily devotions. A child is God's greatest gift to us, and I am sure that dear Joelle will inculcate Christian principles in her little one.

Here, all is much the same. Your students seem to be doing quite well with their embroidery project, though they keep themselves to themselves. Their linens are selling quite well, and Nanette has passed on to the Convent the amount we agreed.

Sister Immaculata has been unwell and has gone to convalesce in the country with the slave Palmyre as companion. Please keep them in your prayers.

One sad bit of news is that Josiane, one of the Casket Girls, has passed away. I know she was your friend. We had hoped that the warm climate and country air would be beneficial for her and heal her consumption, but it was not meant to be. May she rest in peace. A mass was said for her soul this morning.

Please write to let us know how you are.

Yours in Christ,
Mother Jerome

Poor Josiane, I thought. I had never really known her well, but I'd liked her; she was a gentle soul, and the news of her death came as a shock. I remembered the ridiculous rumours that had circulated about her when she'd coughed up blood, and the accusations that she and all the Casket Girls were vampires. People can be so cruel.

Les Chenes

Dear Mother Jerome,

Thank you for your letter. It was lovely to hear from you, and to have news of the Convent. I think of you all so often. I was very sorry to hear of Josiane's death, and hope that Sister Immaculata is not consumptive as well. If you see

221

her, please tell her that I shall be praying for her recovery. If she would like to write to me, please tell her that I would like that very much.

Joelle's baby will be born soon. She is doing reasonably well, though my impression is that she will be relieved when the child is finally here. We spend the mornings knitting clothes for the little one and reading poetry. One bit of news is that Joelle's brother-in-law Jean Ardoin arrived recently. He seemed at first a little distant and arrogant, but he is teaching me to ride. I am determined to become as good a rider as he is.

Please give my best to all the Sisters and to Father Beaubois, and to Berthe if you see her. And please pray for Joelle, that when her hour comes it won't be too difficult. I am a little apprehensive about the impending birth, and hope I will know what to do.

Yours,
Sidonie

Sister Immaculata

After my strange encounter with Pierre Cormier, everything changed. Instead of waiting until the end of the week, he began coming to the cabin nearly every day about noon. I wondered who would be minding the butcher's shop, but didn't much care. Palmyre was discreet, I'll give her that. When she heard the noise of horse's hooves, she knew to make herself invisible. I had cast my habit aside, because of the heat, and spent most of the time in the long cotton petticoat I wore underneath. Pierre would come in and grab me by the hand, and out to the woods we would go. There we made love in every possible way: standing up against the trees, with the pine bark biting into my back; lying on the ground; on all fours like dogs. Once we even swam in the river naked and then made love on the bank, 'though I was afraid of alligators. We didn't talk much, and at the end of the day we would return, spent and mud-stained, to the cabin, and Pierre would take his leave. Occasionally a shadow would flit over his face, and I wondered whether he was feeling guilty. If he was, the guilt wasn't enough to make him stop. Once he shook his head. 'This is like a fever.'

One day he looked around the cabin when he arrived, and blinked. 'You and Palmyre have made this quite pleasant,' he said. I smiled.

. 'Have you thought about getting more pigs?' I asked.

'I haven't had time to think about it,' he said. 'But yes, I probably should.'

'If you do, I could tend them for you,' I said.

From time to time I wondered what was happening upriver. Sidonie was far too outspoken for her own good, and I'd seen what happened when people like Bertrand and Ardoin were challenged. I hoped that she would keep her mouth firmly shut. She's a bookish little madam, but she was kind to me, and I feel that I'm dangerously on the brink of liking her.

Sidonie

In the following weeks I would go riding in the afternoon with Jean, while Armand was closeted with the overseer. My impression was that both of us were glad of an excuse to escape from the Big House, and little by little something like a friendship began to emerge, though I often found Jean maddening. One afternoon, as we approached the river, I gathered up my courage.

'Jean, may I ask you something?'

'But of course,' he replied. We pulled our horses to a stop, dismounted, and sat on a bank overlooking the river. Jean raised a quizzical eyebrow.

I took a deep breath. 'How much does Armand trust Louis Bertrand?'

He looked directly into my eyes. 'Why do you ask?'

I plunged in. 'When I came here from New Orleans, as Bertrand brought me on a cart up to the big house, I saw something horrific. I still have nightmares about it.' I described the dying man in the cage and finding the bloodstains on the ground, though the cage had vanished.

Jean looked into the distance. He hesitated, then began to speak. 'Bertrand is more than capable of a horror like what you describe. I've just come here from our plantation in St. Domingue, and heard similar stories there. At first, I dismissed them as fabrications of the slaves, things they'd made up about a stern taskmaster. When I mentioned them to

Bertrand, he laughed, and said he was following the dictates of the Code Noir.'

'What on earth is the Code Noir?' I asked.

Jean sighed. 'You really don't want to know, Sidonie.'

'Yes I *do* want to know,' I said angrily. 'I think the problem is that too many of us just don't want to know.'

'Very well, then,' he said. 'Since you ask. The Code Noir was promulgated by King Louis XIV in 1685. It provides a legal framework concerning relations between slaves and their owners. For example, it is legally permissible for masters to chain and beat slaves, but not to torture or mutilate them'

'But why?' I said weakly.

'Because they're property,' Jean said. His tone was one of cold fury. 'One can't be allowed to damage one's property. And there's more.'

I felt cold inside, and raised my eyebrows.

He went on. 'If a slave runs away and is recaptured after more than a month, the punishment by law is to cut his ears off. If it happens again, his hamstrings are cut, and he's branded. And if it happens a third time, he can be killed.'

Jean saw that tears were streaming down my face. He took my hand. 'My dear Sidonie, forgive me. I am so sorry, but you did ask.' He produced a large linen handkerchief.

When I'd wiped away tears and was able to speak, I asked, 'How much does Armand know about Bertrand's punishments?'

'That's what I've been trying to find out,' Jean said. 'My brother is a good man at heart.' On that I had reason to disagree after hearing Palmyre's story, but held my tongue. 'But he tends to avoid confrontation. And, of course, he knows that our family's economic welfare is dependent on running the plantations well, and making a profit. So he tends to look the other way. But if he does know, I must convince him that this has got to stop.'

'I know that I am currently enjoying Armand's hospitality, and that I should not criticise my host,' I confessed. 'But after what I've seen, I've come to think that slavery is abhorrent. And I don't think it will continue indefinitely.' I went on, 'Two of my students in New Orleans are slaves, and they've become my friends. What do you think yourself, Jean, about the system?' I asked. 'Are you happy to live knowing that your lifestyle is based on the suffering of others?' I realised how self-righteous I sounded, and flushed.

'As for whether the institution of slavery will continue, who is to know,' Jean said. 'I agree with you that it is loathsome. I have many reasons for this opinion, some of which you don't know about. I do want to help my brother and be loyal to my family, but it's becoming clear to me that I am going to have to make some difficult choices soon. There are some new ideas in France, and it's not impossible that I might return there one day to practice as a lawyer, and get involved and try to change things. '

I looked out at the river. 'How involved have you been with the running of the plantations?' I asked.

'Very little,' he admitted. 'I was at the Sorbonne until relatively recently, and don't have much of an idea of what's going on, though I do find the institution of slavery abhorrent. When I was in Paris, I was exposed to some new ideas. Of course Armand dismisses these as intellectual fripperies, and he attacks me for enjoying the fruits of slave labour and living in grand style in Paris while criticising the institution.' His mouth twisted. 'With some justification, I must confess.' Jean rose, and reached out a hand to help me back to my feet. 'We must head for home before it gets dark.'

In the following days, meals were not pleasant occasions. Armand was surly, and I was convinced on several occasions that before coming to the table he had been drinking. Jean tended to remain silent, as did Joelle. My mornings with Joelle were tranquil, although she spoke with a febrile gaiety of the balls that would take place at Les Chenes, of the dresses she would wear, of her ambitions for her child. Her boudoir was a pleasant place, with soft blue and white curtains in *toile de jouy*, and it was good to sit there with my friend as the sunlight poured through the windows.

One day I was surprised to receive a letter from Immaculata.

Dear Sidonie,

I heard from Mother Jerome that you seemed lonely and would like to hear from friends in the Convent. I'm not exactly a friend, I know. I always thought you were a bit above yourself...you always only seemed happy if you felt you were superior to the rest of us. I know I'm not as educated as you are, but I used to think that with your book learning you looked down on me. But I remember when I was ill that you stuck up for me, and that's something I'll never forget. I'm now staying at the butcher's house, along with Palmyre the slave. For a slave, she's all right. She certainly isn't afraid of hard work. I am feeling much better, and like taking care of the pigs. Write to me if you have time.

Immaculata

I was touched that Immaculata had written to me. But her observation that I only felt happy if I could look down on people hit a nerve. Perhaps I really had let my sudden elevation to the status of teacher go to my head, I thought ruefully. I love helping people, but there's a pride linked to that, particularly since I do *not* like asking others for help. Immaculata was difficult and thorny, but her powers of observation were uncomfortably sharp. I wrote back that same afternoon:

Dear Immaculata,

It was really good to hear from you. Joelle and I miss the Convent, although her house is beautiful. The baby will be born soon! I hope I will know what to do. I'm glad to hear that you're on the mend. Palmyre's a good person, and she hasn't had an easy life, but then who has. Please keep Joelle and the baby in your prayers.

Sidonie

What I most looked forward to at Les Chenes, though, were my afternoon rides with Jean. In February and early March, the azaleas were in bloom, and the paths we rode on were edged with clouds of pink and fuchsia and purple flowers. As we rose, we spoke of everything and nothing: our respective childhoods, books we'd read, music that we loved. I discovered that Jean was passionate about philosophy. We talked endlessly about human nature, about whether people were innately good, or whether we were all born, as the Church would have it, in a state of Original Sin. Jean believed passionately that people were good at heart, and that it was the world that corrupted their goodness. I, on the other hand, was a bit more sceptical; I had, after all, been brought up in a Convent, where an awareness of Evil and the doctrine of Original Sin were drummed into us from an early age. But I believed that we had to face and acknowledge our own darkness if we were ever to move beyond it and gain redemption for ourselves.

Our conversations, however, were not always intellectual. Jean loved to tease me about being so serious and bookish. I retaliated by laughing at his idealism. We spent most of our time laughing, and the banter did my soul good. I began to notice other things: the way his hair curled at the back of his neck; a tendency for his brows to draw together in the heat of a discussion; the occasional melancholy I saw in his eyes; and his stubborn pride.

Chapter 17

Sidonie

Late one March morning, I saw Joelle grimace. 'What's wrong?' I asked.

'Nothing,' Joelle said matter-of-factly. 'Just a touch of indigestion.'

That afternoon, as Jean and I were riding in the forest, a rabbit darted out, and Belle bolted. I was thrown over her head and landed with a thump in a pile of leaves. Jean leapt from his horse and ran over to me. 'Are you hurt, Sidonie?' he asked.

I raised myself up on one elbow and tried to dust myself off. 'The only thing wounded is my dignity,' I said. I felt like such a fool. Jean began, with the utmost gentleness, to pick twigs out of my hair. His expression was unreadable.

'You looked lovely at dinner the night after I arrived, Sidonie,' he said. 'But I like you even better like this.' He rose, and held out his hand to help me up.

His words had left me speechless. But for a very attractive and intelligent man to say that he liked me just as I am was a bewitching thing indeed.

We remounted. In the distance I saw a horseman approaching at breakneck speed. It was Armand. On his face was a look of terror.

'It's Joelle!' he shouted. 'The baby's coming!'

When we reached the house, I raced up the stairs to Joelle's room. My friend's face was ashen. Octavia stood by her side. She had tied a length of sheets to the bedposts, for Joelle to hold on to when she had to push. 'When did this start, Octavia?' I asked.

'Not long after lunch,' she replied. I berated myself for having gone riding. I should have realised that Joelle's 'indigestion' was the onset of labour pains. I said so to Octavia. She smiled at me gently. 'Mlle. Sidonie, it's a first baby, and these things take a while. But it's good that you are here, because your presence will reassure your friend. She's a brave woman. Most would be screaming their lungs out by now.'

At that moment Joelle let out a low groan. I reached out for her hand, and she gripped it so hard that it hurt. I could see large drops of sweat on her forehead. But I knew my friend well, and knew that her pride meant that she would only let out a cry if she was being tortured beyond endurance. 'How often are the pains coming?' I asked Octavia.

'Not as often as they should be,' she replied. 'The baby probably won't be born until late tonight, or even early tomorrow morning.'

I shuddered. But then I decided it was time to do something practical. 'What may I do to help?' I asked. I'd had my reservations about Octavia, but was reassured by the kindness I saw in her eyes, and by her calm unflappability.

'For now, just stay at her side. And you could fan her,' Octavia replied.

'That would be so lovely,' whispered Joelle. The pain had subsided, for now at least. It was an unseasonably warm day, and her blonde curls were matted. Her face had a transparent look that filled me with fear.

Sister Immaculata

One morning when I got up to prepare breakfast, the room began to spin. I thought at first that one of my funny turns was coming on, but this was different. My sense of smell was much more intense than usual, and I felt nauseated. I managed to make it to the porch before I vomited.

Palmyre looked up from the table. I was surprised at the expression in her eyes. It looked very much like pity. Why a mere slave would pity me, I had no idea, but I did not like it at all, and I drew myself up. 'Stop dawdling, Palmyre, and help me draw water from the well!' I barked.

But then something occurred to me. My courses had not come for the last two months. I'd always been irregular, so attached no importance to this. I remembered my nausea in the mornings, my exaggerated sensitivity to smell. My belly had developed a gentle bulge, but I attributed this to the large amounts of food I was eating. The realisation that I was pregnant hit me between the eyes like a bullet.

My hands began to tremble. If I was expecting a baby, I would have to leave the Convent. The nuns would not brook the slightest whiff of scandal, so they would try to hush it up. I had no visible means of support. But then a strange feeling of

233

calm began to steal over me, coupled with the absolute conviction that I wanted to have this baby, whatever it took. What Jacques Cormier would think of this, and what he would or wouldn't do, I had no idea. But I knew I'd manage on my own if I had to.

Sidonie

The shadows lengthened. I tried to keep Joelle distracted between bouts of pain by talking about Rouen, and about New Orleans and the Convent, and about Berthe and my students. I wondered what Palmyre and Nanette and Clotilde were doing, and whether Immaculata was really on the mend. It was strange that she hadn't said much about the butcher whose house she was living in, but I imagined that she would be busy with other things: Immaculata never was one to sit still. And I thought of Coahoma, and prayed that she hadn't been sold into slavery. I remembered those we lost, those who'd died in the epidemic, but tried hard not to think of death. The prospect of summoning death into the room by merely thinking of it was utterly terrifying. There was a rank smell of sweat and the rusty smell of blood, and I could hear the buzzing of a fly.

Between pains, Joelle looked up at me. 'Sidonie,' she whispered, 'if anything happens to me, promise me that you will take care of my baby and keep her safe.'

'Nothing's going to happen to you, darling.' I held tight to her hand. 'But 'her'? Do you think it's going to be a girl?'

'I know she is,' she said. The sweetness of her smile made my heart clench. 'I want her name to be Marie.' Her eyelids closed.

Octavia indicated with a movement of her head that she wanted a word with me. We stepped out into the hall. 'I don't like this at all,' she said in a low voice. 'It looks as though the baby is coming feet first.'

I whitened. 'What can we do?' I asked.

'There isn't much we can do,' she said. 'If this goes on much longer, mother and baby will die. The only possibility would be to cut Joelle so that I could try to turn the baby. Could you please go tell M. Ardoin? I'd need his permission.'

I raced down the stairs and knocked at the door of the study. Jean came to the door in a cloud of cigar smoke. Behind him, in a chair, sprawled Armand. There was an overwhelming smell of brandy.

'I must speak at once with Armand,' I said.

'I'm afraid that won't be possible,' Jean replied. He too smelled of brandy, but was enunciating his words clearly. 'My brother is asleep.'

'Well wake him up!' I cried in fury.

'Sidonie, Armand is unconscious,' Jean said. 'He has had too much to drink, and I apologise on his behalf. What's happening with Joelle?'

I explained as quickly as I could. Jean paled. But then he straightened up. 'I'll take responsibility,' he said. 'We must do everything in our power to save Joelle and the little one.

Octavia knows what she's doing, and she has delivered many babies here on the plantation.'

I raced back upstairs. 'Octavia, M. Ardoin is unable to give permission, but his brother Jean has,' I said. 'And I agree with them. What do you need?'

Octavia looked exhausted. Beyond her, I could hear Joelle's moans. I could tell that she was steadily growing weaker. 'Boiling water. A pair of scissors, a needle, and some thread.' I ran down to the kitchen and fetched the items.

'Sing to me, Sidonie,' Joelle asked in a thready voice. I thought of her singing during the epidemic, and was overcome with emotion. But nonetheless, with tears rolling down my face, I sang her song:

Orleans, Beaugency
Notre Dame de Paris
Vendome, Vendome.

I cannot remember much of what happened next. I can recall smells: the coppery smell of blood, the cloying scent of lilies in the corridor. And sounds: Joelle's groans, and one ear-splitting scream, followed by silence. I remember the swift skill of Octavia's movements, a baby's thin reedy cry. I vaguely remember holding the little one in my arms as Octavia tended to Joelle and disposed of the afterbirth. What I cannot forget was the transparency of Joelle's face against the pillow and the look of wonder in her eyes as she saw the darkness close in.

When it was over, I went downstairs. I did not bother to change my dress, which was covered with bloodstains, as were my hands and arms. Armand and Jean were in the study.

I entered. Armand sprang to his feet. I could smell the liquor on his breath. 'Has the baby arrived?' His words were slurred.

'Yes,' I said.

'Is he...dark?'

'It's a beautiful little girl,' I said. 'Congratulations.'

'A girl,' he said. His mouth twisted.

'And Joelle?' asked Jean.

I looked Armand in the eye. 'Your wife is dead,' I said.

Chapter 18

Sidonie

The following days passed in a haze. Octavia and I washed Joelle and prepared her body for burial. She had died without the last rites, and this troubled me, but I believed with all my heart that anyone as kind and generous as my friend would go straight to Heaven, with or without the aid of priests. She was interred in the small plantation cemetery, beside the grave of Armand and Jean's father.

Joelle's pine coffin seemed absurdly small. The graves were above ground, like most in Louisiana, because of the proximity of the river. I was in a daze and could not shed a tear. My heart ached at the idea of leaving my friend in this eerie place, amid ghostly trees with trailing tendrils of Spanish moss. I prayed that she might rest in peace there, and vowed to keep my promise to her to keep her baby safe. Octavia had given me a white flower from the garden, and I left it on the grave.

Armand had been drinking, but he held himself erect. Jean held his brother's arm, and I could see sorrow etched on his face. After the coffin was placed within the raised mausoleum, we returned to the house.

I felt dazed with grief, but knew there were matters we'd have to address. 'Armand,' I said, 'there are some urgent matters to be dealt with. We must arrange a wet nurse for the baby.' Armand still had not seen his child.

Armand shrugged. 'Sidonie's right,' said Jean. 'Perhaps Octavia would know of someone?'

'I'll ask her,' I said. I tried to make my voice gentle. 'Armand, would you not like to see the baby? She is such a sweet little thing.' That, at least, was true. Since Joelle's death, Octavia and I had taken care of Marie. Despite the tragic circumstances of her arrival into this world, she was a tranquil little soul. I had no previous experience of babies, but it is fair to say that when she looked up at me, I fell in love. I was bewitched by her delicate vulnerability, and by the fact that she was all I had left of my closest friend.

'Very well,' Armand said tonelessly. 'I suppose I must.' I went upstairs and brought the baby down in my arms. She was dressed in one of the chemises Joelle had embroidered for her. Armand squared his shoulders, breathed deep. He stood up and came over to me, and peered into her face.

The baby looked up. Her eyes were dark and fringed by long black lashes. Her hair was jet black and curly, and her skin olive. Despite her colouring, there was something of Joelle about her. I thought she was utterly beautiful. My heart ached at the idea of this little one growing up without a mother, and I thought of what a wonderful mother Joelle would have been, and of what she told me when we were arriving on the ship to New Orleans, of her ambition in life to have a family of her own, with babies she could love and protect. I remembered the Ronsard poem we'd read together, and reflected that Joelle

239

would never grow old and lose her beauty. This thought did not bring much consolation.

There was no light in Armand's eyes as he looked at his child. He heaved what sounded to me strangely like a sigh of relief. 'Speak to Octavia. She'll arrange something.' I saw that Louis Bertrand, the overseer had entered noiselessly. He stared at the baby, and I instinctively moved to block Marie from his view. Even before I had seen the man in the cage, I'd found Bertrand repellent; something about the man made the hair on the back of my neck stand on end. Armand turned on his heel and the two men headed toward the study.

I went out to the veranda and saw Jean. The two of us went to the garden, and sat on a bench in the shade. The scent of the flowers was intoxicating, and there were butterflies in colours I'd never seen before. It was hard to think, in such idyllic surroundings, that a tragedy such as the one we'd just lived through was possible. This, I thought, is Louisiana, all this beauty with all the horror bubbling underneath.

Jean smiled gently at me and took my hand. 'I know today has been terrible for you, Sidonie,' he said. 'You and Joelle were such close friends. More like sisters, really. I wish there had been time for me to know her better.' He sighed. 'Her death is such a waste.'

'Yes,' I said. 'But she's left a beautiful little daughter.' There were tears in my eyes, but I blinked them back. 'But Jean, Armand's reaction to the news of her death was bizarre, and it made me angry. He did not even ask how Joelle was. And I thought it was very odd that his first question was whether the child was dark.'

Jean sighed. 'People react to bereavement in different ways, Sidonie,' he said.

I liked the fact that Jean was loyal to his brother, and my hand felt warm in his. But I pressed on. 'Indeed they do. Still, I found his reactions strange.'

Jean looked at me intently. He seemed to be wrestling with himself. Finally, he said, 'Sidonie, there are things you don't know about. Things related to my family. If you knew them, you might not want to hold my hand.'

'What on earth can you mean?" I asked. 'Of course I'd want to hold your hand.' I blushed violently and berated myself. Men, I'd heard, did not like girls who were forward.

Jean paused, and drew breath. He said, 'My mother has African blood.' He continued, looking into the distance, 'My father met her in S. Domingue, She was very beautiful, and they fell in love. But it was not possible for them to live as man and wife in St. Domingue or in New Orleans, so they went to get married in France. The danger of discovery wasn't so great there. Armand and I were educated in France, and our mother remained with us. My father had to be in Louisiana and in St. Domingue to run our family's plantations, but he came to see us from time to time.'

Jean's tone had been detached and unemotional, but I could imagine the two lonely little boys in France, wondering why their father came so seldom to see them. And later, the two young men in New Orleans, knowing that the discovery of their secret would mean that they would be outcasts, and that New Orleans society would be closed to them. My heart went out to him. I took his hand and chafed it between my own hands, as if he were a child who needed to be kept warm.

'To those who love you, these things don't matter,' I said.

He looked slant at me. 'And do you love me, Sidonie?' he asked.

I took a very deep breath. 'Yes,' I said.

Jean gathered me into his arms and kissed me hard. I could feel how fast his heart was beating. He looked into my eyes. 'I have loved you from the moment that I met you, and then when you learned to ride despite being terrified at first. I love your courage, and your loyalty.'

I smiled. 'That means we owe a lot to Belle, then. I shall bring her carrots from the kitchen every day.' And then I felt a touch of sadness. 'We also owe so much to dear Joelle. I wonder what will become of little Marie.'

'Armand is in no fit state to reach decisions just now,' Jean said. 'You and I will have to take steps to ensure that Marie is taken care of. I know that Armand is preoccupied with matters related to the plantation, and to discontent among the slaves.'

I leaned my head on his shoulder and looked up at him, "My friend Palmyre, a slave who was one of my students in the Convent, told me about something horrible related to your overseer. She told me that he raped her, and that she fled from S. Domingue to New Orleans.' I didn't mention what Palmyre had said about Armand's looking on, because I knew that Jean would be torn between loyalty and revulsion.

Jean shuddered. 'I have never liked the man,' he said. 'I hate the way he deals with the slaves. And I hate his influence on my brother. Something will have to be done.' He looked at me, and I was stunned and delighted at the tenderness in his eyes. He folded me into his arms and kissed me again.

Sometime later, we walked back toward the house. When we reached the veranda, we heard shouts. They were coming from Armand's study. Jean banged hard on the door, then opened it and went in. I went upstairs and found Octavia.

'Octavia, we'll need to find a wet nurse for the little one.' Marie was crying loudly, a thin high wail, and I thought she must be very hungry. 'Do you know of anyone who could do this?'

'I do,' she said. 'I'd already thought of this. There's Claudette. She had a baby a fortnight ago, but the little one died.' She took Marie into her arms and rocked her, trying to soothe her. 'She was my daughter's wet nurse. I didn't have much milk.'

'Your daughter is a beautiful little girl,' I said. Octavia looked hard at me to discern whether I was being sarcastic, and when she read in my face that I was sincere, she smiled. 'Yes, she is. And clever, too. I know that you are a teacher. I have

243

been trying to teach her to read and write, though because of my responsibilities I don't have much free time.'

'What a wonderful thing for you to do,' I said. Octavia could hear the admiration in my voice. 'How did you learn to read and write yourself?'

'From a woman who was M. Ardoin's mother's lady's maid in St. Domingue. We had to have our lessons at night,' she said.

'Why was that?' I asked.

Octavia looked at me pityingly. 'No master wants his slaves to be able to read and write,' she said. A shutter seemed to come down over her face.

'What happened to your teacher?' I asked.

'They found out about our lessons,' said Octavia. 'She was sold. I never knew what happened to her. And I was told never to read again, never to teach anyone else, because it would give us ideas above our station.' Her eyes were alive with anger. 'I was brought to Les Chenes not long thereafter.'

I was horrified by this. 'What is your daughter's name?'

Octavia seemed startled by my question, and hesitated. But then she answered, 'Marthe.'

'Would you like for me to help with Marthe's reading lessons?' I asked. I was outraged that a child should be deprived the chance to learn.

'That would be dangerous for you,' she replied.

'Oh I don't think so,' I said airily. I tried to be diplomatic. 'M. Ardoin seems to be sunk in grief and won't notice a thing. We could tell him that you and I are caring for the baby, which of course we will be. But that won't take all our time.' I knew that given the amount Armand Ardoin was drinking, he would be unlikely to notice anything at all. At least, that is what I was relying on, because I'd come to Les Chenes as a friend and companion to Joelle. Now, with her death, there was no real reason for him to allow me to stay on.

Octavia thought for a minute. Then she said, 'That would be wonderful. But we must be very, very careful. You aren't the only one who would be in danger. If M. Ardoin or Louis Bertrand get wind of this, Marthe and I would both be sold.' She was attacked by a fit of coughing, but straightened her shoulders and left.

Chapter 19

Sidonie

The following morning, a letter arrived for me, from Berthe:

Dear Sidonie,

I hope that all is well with you. Joelle's baby must be due any day now! I hope that our midwifery sessions with Houragan will stand you in good stead.

Speaking of babies, I have some news that you will not believe. Sister Immaculata has left the Convent, and has married the butcher Pierre Cormier! Rumour has it that she is in the family way. The wedding itself was all a very hush-hush affair. Father Beaubois married them, and Mother Jerome is going around with a face like thunder. I saw Pierre Cormier the other day, and he looks like a bullock going to the abattoir: completely stunned, but not unhappy. Immaculata, on the other hand, is very full of herself, and seems to have taken charge of the butcher shop. I saw her the other day behind the counter. She was humming, and looked positively smug! Whoever would've thought it.

Nanette and your students are still producing fine linens, and they're selling well. And my own business is going well too. But we miss you. When are you coming back to New Orleans?

Love, Berthe

Clearly the sad news about Joelle had not reached New Orleans yet. Mail delivery on the river was erratic, I knew. I wondered if Immaculata had received my letter. But my jaw dropped when I read the news about her. After the initial shock, though, I felt a certain admiration for her gumption, and for the courage with which she had pursued her dreams.

Over the following weeks, Octavia and I spent the mornings looking after little Marie. Claudette, the wet nurse who suckled her, was a tall rangy woman whose eyes were pools of sorrow. She worked in the big house as a laundress, and Octavia's daughter Marthe was learning to iron under her supervision. This made it easy for both of them to come to us. Initially, Claudette was taken aback when I spoke to her, since wet nurses were usual regarded as part of the furniture, but soon she and Octavia and I began to get to know each other.

'How long have you been at Les Chenes, Claudette?' I asked one morning. She adjusted her blouse to allow Marie to nurse. 'Five years,' she replied.

'And where did you come from? I hope you don't mind my asking.'

'From Senegal.' A tear began to trickle down her face. 'I came over on a boat from Africa to New Orleans, and was brought to Les Chenes.'

'One of my students in New Orleans went through something similar,' I said. 'They began as my students, but became my friends.' I went on to describe Palmyre and the others, and told her of Palmyre's dreadful journey.

Octavia had gone very still. 'Palmyre, did you say?'

I raised my eyebrows quizzically. 'Yes.'

A strange smile spread across Octavia's face. 'I once knew a Palmyre, in St. Domingue. She was a conjure woman.'

'My friend Palmyre was in St. Domingue,' I said. 'Perhaps she's the same person. My friend was Yoruba. What's a conjure woman?'

Octavia looked at me in amazement. 'You are a very unusual young woman, Mademoiselle Sidonie,' she said. 'Few white people would have a clue about what 'Yoruba' is. They say we Africans all look alike.'

'Not really,' I said. 'I know that I am young and naïve and relatively uneducated, but I don't think I'm particularly unusual. I'm just fascinated by people, that's all, but I have so much still to learn. But you haven't answered my question. What's a conjure woman?'

Octavia hesitated. 'A conjure woman is a woman who knows a great deal about plants,' she said. I remembered Palmyre back in the Convent, and the care with which she tended the garden. Octavia continued, 'Conjure women also have powers that others don't.' She turned away. 'I must go check supplies in the kitchens.'

After this, Octavia and Claudette were both more open with me. Over the coming days, I came to look forward to my sessions with little Marthe. She was a bright child, and eager to

248

learn while the baby slept in her cradle or was suckled by Claudette. In the mornings, as sunlight cast patterns across the carpet of Joelle's room, we would sit together and I would read to her, with my finger underlining the words. In Armand's library, I'd found a book of fairy tales, which Marthe loved. We made it into a game, and I told her that it was important to keep our game a secret. She was thin, with big dark eyes, and it was good to feel her lean close to me while we read.

One morning Octavia and Claudette spoke of the discontent among the slaves at Les Chenes, and of the unspeakable actions of Louis Bertrand, the overseer.

'He likes young women, and takes them to his cabin,' Claudette said. 'By young women, he means children. If they come back, they are broken. Often, they do not return.'

Octavia looked at her daughter, and I saw the fire in her eyes. I knew that she would go to any lengths to protect Marthe and Marie, just as I would. She was wracked by another fit of coughing, and I realised that she really was not at all well.

Claudette went on. 'Sometimes he takes older girls, and tells them he's using them as 'breeders''

I was horrified. 'Surely this cannot mean what I think it does?'

Octavia looked at me pityingly. 'Mademoiselle Sidonie, it is so blindingly obvious. Louis Bertrand wants to have his own land and slaves one day. He is trying to build up his 'stock'.'

I recoiled. It was becoming clearer and clearer to me that Joelle would never have wanted her daughter to grow up surrounded by this horror. Something had to be done. But I was only a friend of Marie's dead mother, and had no legal authority over her. I was at a loss about the right course of action.

Octavia's eyes flashed. 'This will not go on forever. There are *quilombos* in the swamps, and they are growing.'

'What are *quilombos*?' I asked.

'I will tell you only because I trust you,' she said. 'They are communities of slaves who have escaped. One day they will rise up against their owners.' She saw my eyes widen. 'But we will remember those who were good to us,' she said.

Despite the circumstances of her birth, Marie was a remarkably placid baby, and seemed to thrive. My moments with Jean, amid caring for Marie and teaching Marthe, were precious indeed. It was not easy for us to find opportunities to be alone. There was little time now for leisurely country rides, but we met on occasion in the garden. He spent much of his time with Armand, and at times I could hear raised voices coming from Armand's study. Armand continued drinking heavily, and on some days he did not leave his room. It was as though his child did not exist.

Jean, however, would pop into to the nursery when he could. I reflected that most men of his background would find an interest in babies unmanly. Jean, was, of course, initially terrified of holding a baby, but soon learned how to hold his little niece, and was as besotted with her as I was. It was good to see him lean back and smile as Marie nestled in his arms.

One day, as we walked around the garden, I gathered up my courage. 'Jean, there's something I must ask you.'

'But of course, Sidonie,' Jean said. I thought he looked very tired.

There was no easy way to say it. 'I've noticed that Marthe, Octavia's little girl, has a remarkable resemblance to the Ardoins. I haven't dared mention this to Octavia.'

Jean sighed. 'My father was a bit of a womaniser,' he said. 'He spent long periods of time alone, because my mother was in France with Armand and me. Marthe is his child. She is my half-sister.'

I was appalled by this. 'Did your father force himself upon Octavia?'

Jean drew back. His voice was cold. 'I am not privy to my father's private thoughts or actions.' I knew that I'd gone too far and had offended him. Jean was a proud man, and family loyalty ran deep.

'Forgive me,' I said, reaching for his hand. 'It is all such a tangled web. And I know that the Bible says judge not, lest ye be judged. But my heart aches for Marthe and children like her, who don't seem to belong anywhere and who under the law are their father's property. I've grown fond of Octavia. She's a devoted mother to Marthe, and she tried her hardest to save

Joelle, despite everything.' My voice broke as I spoke the last words.

Jean took me into his arms. 'I am finding it hard if not impossible to defend my family's actions, my love, and it is tearing me apart.'

I leaned into his chest. 'Is your brother managing to cope with the loss of Joelle?'

Jean's voice was hard. 'Not really. I've had some difficult conversations with him. I've mentioned the man in the cage, and other things that have come to my attention. Bertrand seems to be out of control, and I know he meets up with a local farmer who is equally cruel, and, I think, dangerous. I've suggested to Armand that we emancipate the slaves, sell the house and the land, and return to France. '

My heart sank within me at the idea of Jean's returning to France. I wondered where I fit in that particular equation, if fit I did. But I had to acknowledge that this would be the ethical course of action. 'What did he say?'

'It was hard to get much sense out of him,' Jean replied. 'He began to shout at me, to say that this would impoverish the family, that to do so would amount to a repudiation of our father. Ever since we were children, Armand would always shout when he knew he was wrong. But whatever the consequences, this is the only moral choice. And with the sale of the land, the family would not be left destitute. But as the eldest, the deeds are in Armand's name, and nothing can be done without his consent.'

'What a tangle,' I said. 'I know that I am being selfish, but the idea of your returning to France would break my heart.'

Jean smiled down at me. There were tears in his eyes, and the tenderness in his voice took my breath away. 'I would never leave you, Sidonie,' he said. 'It would do me the very greatest honour if you would consent to be my wife. Though at the moment I have nothing to offer you.' I kissed him hard.

We headed back to the house. 'There's just one more thing,' Jean said.

'And what is that?' I asked.

'Be very careful with Louis Bertrand,' he replied. 'The man is not only sinister, but unhinged.'

'How do you mean?' I asked.

Jean thought for a minute. 'He has always been malevolent, but sane. He was aware of the possible consequences of his action, and that seemed to rein him in at least a little. Now I think he may be losing his reason.'

'What leads you to think so?'

'He's drinking even more than usual, and talks to himself. What's eerie is that he seems to be hearing voices...we can't hear them, but he acts as though there really is someone there, and as though he hears a response to his ravings. At times he seems to think that he is being persecuted by unknown enemies.'

This was chilling, but I was determined to know the worst. 'Is there anything else I need to know?'

Jean looked grim. 'I don't know what was said, but I have the impression that he's been threatening Armand. With what, I do not know. It could be that he knows about our mother's origin, or he could be blackmailing him about something that happened in St. Domingue.'

My first thought was to protect those I loved. 'Jean,' I said, 'I think that we must begin to devise ways to escape from Les Chenes should that become necessary.'

Jean held me close. 'I cannot desert my brother, Sidonie,' he said. I could hear the desolation in his voice. 'But if anything happens, promise me that you will take yourself and the girls to a place of safety.'

The following morning I was playing with Marie. There was something so soft and delectable about baby skin. I leaned over and nibbled on her toes as I was changing her, and Immaculata's amulet of the monkey and the cockerel fell out of my collar.

Octavia paled. 'Where did you find that, Sidonie?' she asked. She had stopped calling me Mademoiselle Sidonie long ago.

I slipped the necklace over my head and handed it to her. 'It belonged to one of the nuns in the Convent. She was called Sister Immaculata. It was given to me, and my friend Palmyre told me that if ever I needed her help, I was to send her this amulet.'

'This amulet is supposed to bring its wearer love, luck and money,' Octavia said. 'It is a Yoruba symbol. Where did Sister Immaculata get it, and what happened to her?'

'She left the order and married a butcher,' I said. 'So perhaps the amulet did work its magic. I have no idea where she got it.'

'I'd hold this close if I were you, Sidonie, and use it if you need to,' she said. There are some strange things going on here on the plantation.' A shadow crossed her face.

'What kind of things?' I asked.

'Three men were taken to the overseer's cabin last night,' Octavia said. 'They have not returned. People are angry.'

I shivered. 'I worry about Marie and Marthe,' I said.

'So do I,' said Octavia. 'But we will keep them safe from danger.' Her expression of calm ferocity left me in no doubt that she would do whatever it took to achieve this. 'I think that your friend Palmyre is the woman I once knew.'

Chapter 20

Sidonie

After Joelle's death, I stopped dining with Armand and Jean, and gave the excuse that I was needed in the nursery. This was a sacrifice, because I loved every minute of Jean's company, but Armand was often incoherent and sometimes I sensed a current of hostility beneath a thin layer of civility. That night I found it hard to sleep. There was a full moon, and I could hear a crow cawing in the distance. From my window, I could see the oaks in the drive, and the wisps of Spanish moss floating in the breeze. In the moonlight, it created a ghostly effect.

Suddenly, from the direction of the study, I heard raised voices. A shot rang out. My thoughts flashed to Jean's words about Louis Bertrand. Throwing on a cloak, I crept down the stairs and out the door to the garden. Hiding in the shrubbery, I peeked through the French windows that opened from the study to the veranda.

What I saw filled me with horror. Armand's body lay on the floor. Blood and fragments of bone were spattered against the wall. Bertrand was holding a flintlock rifle. He was weaving on his feet, and pointing the gun at Jean. I could see spittle dribbling from a corner of his mouth. But then he made a brusque movement, indicating that Jean should sit, and began to tie him to the chair. I could not hear Bertrand's words.

So far as I could see, Jean had not been injured, but I was terrified that he might come to harm.

I remembered my promise to Jean that I would take the girls to a place of safety. Clutching my cloak around me, I ran as fast as I could to Octavia's room, which was attached to the kitchens, and banged on the door.

Octavia opened it, blinking. 'What on earth is wrong, Sidonie?'

I was shaking so hard I could hardly speak. 'Bertrand has killed Armand,' I gasped. 'He is holding Jean prisoner in the study.'

Octavia paused. Then she began to give orders. Even in my state of shock, I was impressed by her air of cold command. 'Take Marie, Marthe and Claudette to the coach house' she said. 'Bertrand will never go there, because he thinks it is haunted.' I nodded. She went on, 'Then, return to the house, and wait in the garden outside the study.'

I did as she said and raced back to the nursery, glancing into the study window as I did so. Bertrand seemed to be ranting and shaking a fist at Jean, who was tied to the chair. He had, thank God, laid the gun on the table. I woke Claudette, and between the two of us we crept down the back stairs, Claudette holding Marie in her arms, me guiding Marthe. Marthe was sleepy and bewildered, but I told her in a fierce whisper to keep silent. We made our way to the coach house, which was at some distance from the main house. In the back, over the carriages, there was a small room for the coachman, and I left Claudette there with the two girls, and made my way back to the house. There, I stationed myself outside the study, as Octavia had indicated.

Suddenly, I smelled smoke, and heard Octavia's voice. She was banging at the study door, and was shouting. 'M. Bertrand! Fire! The house is on fire!'

Bertrand, with an oath, opened the door and left the study. The French windows had been left unlocked. I ran up and opened them. Jean had been bound and gagged, and there was a bloodstain on his left sleeve. Taking a letter opener from Armand's desk, I stepped over his dead body and went to cut Jean's ropes and untie his gag. I could smell smoke in the distance. Taking Jean by the hand, I led him out through the French windows.

I could tell that Jean had lost a lot of blood. But I urged him on, taking him by his good arm, through the trees in the moonlight. Smoke was billowing from the house, and I could see the flickering of flames. Finally we reached the carriage house. Jean was so weak that he could not climb the stairs, and I had to call for Claudette to help carry him to the upper room.

There, I removed his shirt. There was a flesh wound on his upper left arm, but fortunately the bullet had only grazed him. I rummaged in the drawers of a crude wooden bureau next to the bed, and to my delight came across a bottle of brandy, which I surmised had probably been pilfered from the main house. I poured two fingers of brandy, and gave it to Jean to drink, then poured more brandy over the wound. A muscle in Jean's cheek twitched, and I could tell how much it was hurting, but he didn't utter a sound. I then improvised a bandage. Jean was clearly in shock, and I saw his hands shaking. I led him to the coachman's cot, and covered him with blankets. 'My darling, you must try to rest now' I told him. 'Octavia knows we are here, and she will take us to a place of refuge.' Jean drank deep, and settled down under the covers, turning his face to the wall. My heart went out to him when I thought of the grief he must be feeling for his dead brother.

I went over to Claudette. She was nursing Marie, and I was relieved to see that amid all the horror the little one's healthy appetite continued unabated. Marthe was sleeping in the crook of Claudette's arm. I spoke in a whisper. 'Why does Louis Bertrand think that this place is haunted?'

Claudette looked out into the shadows. 'The coachman tried to escape,' she said tonelessly. 'They cut off his ears. Then he escaped again. They couldn't find him, but one night he returned. He had lost a leg, no one knows how. He hid in the shadows, and fired a shot at Bertrand. He was captured and killed. They put him in a cage.' I realised in horror that this was the man I'd seen en route to Les Chenes.' Claudette continued, 'But they say his ghost haunts this place still. Bertrand never comes here.' She looked disdainful. 'He pretends that he is a strong man, but secretly he is terrified.'

I shuddered. 'What a dreadful story,' I said. I returned to Jean, who was still shivering. Gently, I lifted the blankets and lay down by his side, holding him close, trying to warm him with my own body heat. At last the shivering began to subside, and he fell into a fitful sleep.

When the grey light of dawn began to creep through the windows, I heard a light tap at the door. It was Octavia. Beneath her cloak was a basket of food she'd brought from the big house. We spoke in whispers in order not to wake Jean, Claudette and the girls.

'You are not safe here, Sidonie,' she said. 'After the house burst into flames, Bertrand tried to rally the slaves to put out the fire but many of them escaped in the confusion. The fire destroyed some parts of the house, including the study where the master's body was lying, but the ballroom and entrance hall are still intact, and the kitchens weren't affected because they are separate from the house.' She paused, and looked me in the eye. 'Bertrand is raving mad, and says that he is surrounded by devils and monsters. He has vowed vengeance against the Ardoins and those they love. He is now barricaded in the ballroom'

I shivered. 'Where can we take refuge, Octavia?' I asked.

She thought for a minute. 'In the swamp,' she said. 'Bertrand is terrified of the swamp. There is an island there where you and Jean and the girls can hide until we devise a way for you to escape.'

In all honesty, I found the swamp terrifying myself. But if it was the only way to save Jean and the girls, I would not hesitate, and the swamp it would be. 'How will we be able to find food?' I asked.

Octavia smiled. Her smiled was chilling. 'Remember what I told you about *quilombos*. There's a long tradition of Africans taking refuge in the swamps, and sometimes whole communities of escaped slaves live there. On this island, there's a cabin where a friend of mine lives. Here are fishing poles, so you can catch some fish when you have to. I'll try to bring you food when I can.'

'What about you, Octavia?' I asked. 'You really are in mortal danger yourself.'

She laughed, and her eyes flashed. 'Bertrand is a superstitious man. He is scared of me.'

I raised my eyebrows. 'Why is that?'

Octavia looked longingly at Marthe. 'Have you never wondered, Sidonie, why I do not embrace my daughter, who is what love most in this world?'

Indeed I had found this strange. 'Actually, yes I have.'

Octavia straightened her shoulders. 'As you'll have seen, I have these fits of coughing. Sometimes I cough up blood.'

'Oh, my friend,' I exclaimed, and moved to embrace her. Octavia drew back.

'It's consumption,' she said in matter-of-fact tones. 'But that fool Bertrand thought I was a vampire when he saw the blood on my handkerchief one day. He flees from me when he sees me, and he's convinced that I cannot be killed.'

I didn't know what to say. Octavia's heroism had left me mute, and this dreadful news had saddened me more than words can say. I remembered the gossip about my friend Josiane, who had died of consumption, and the rumours that the Casket Girls were vampires. I recovered my voice. 'I promise you that if anything happens to you, Jean and I will protect Marthe and Marie.'

'I will come tomorrow with a boat,' she said.

Jean had slept fitfully, but I thought he looked better when he woke up. He blinked and looked around in the flickering candlelight. The walls of the cabinet were rough-hewn and soft grey in colour, and the only furniture was the cabinet in the corner and the cot on which he lay. Claudette, Marthe, Marie and I had slept in rag pallets on the floor. He turned to me. 'Sidonie, where are we?'

'We came here last night, my darling,' I reassured him. 'Octavia has brought us here, but she's going to take us to a place of safety until we can summon help.'

Jean shook his head. I could tell that his arm was hurting badly. 'For a moment I thought it was all a nightmare,' he said. 'It all seems so unreal.'

'Can you bear to tell me what happened?' I asked.

Jean shook his head and collected his thoughts. 'Louis Bertrand demanded to meet with Armand. Armand had asked me to go with him, since Bertrand was acting so strangely. He was convinced that Bertrand might be plotting something, and that we might be in danger.'

I shuddered.

Jean continued, 'Bertrand began cursing and shouting. He threatened us with exposure, told us that he would reveal to all of New Orleans that our mother had African blood.' He paused. 'He said if we did not sign documents transferring ownership of Les Chenes into his name, he would cut not only our throats but those of every other white person in the house. He demanded a considerable sum of money. Armand lost his temper, and after a heated exchange slapped Bertrand in the face. At that point, Bertrand reached for his gun and fired.' Tears were streaming down Jean's face. 'My brother was not perfect,' he said, 'but he died bravely.'

I told him about the burning of the house. 'Do you think Octavia started the fire?' Jean asked.

'I think she probably did,' I said. 'It was remarkably resourceful of her. If Bertrand hadn't been distracted and lured out of the study by the fire, he probably would have killed you as well. '

'That house is cursed,' said Jean. 'Good riddance. I wish the whole thing had burned to the ground. Now what we must do is to figure out a way to escape this horror, and give Armand's remains a Christian burial. Marie is Armand's only heir, but she is a minor. As her guardian, I can sell the land and put the money in trust for her. He leaned against the wall, and from his pallor I could tell that he was exhausted.

'And I'll give all the slaves their freedom. None of us needs this poisoned legacy.'

That night we slept fitfully. I thought of Armand's body among the ashes, and of all of the beautiful books which had been destroyed. Shortly after midnight, I heard a soft tap at the door. It was Octavia. She beckoned for us to follow her. Jean and I went down the back stairs of the carriage house, with Claudette carrying Marie and with Marthe walking hand in hand with me. Luckily there was a full moon, and visibility was good. We walked in silence amid the trees, past the slave cabins. To the south of Les Chenes, we came upon the edge of the swamp. It was eerie in the moonlight, and I could hear the hooting of an owl. I trembled, but reminded myself that I had to be strong.

The ground under our feet was soft and moist, and Spanish moss hung from the cypress trees. Octavia pointed the way to the edge of the water. There, concealed under layers of moss, was a rowboat. She indicated that we should get in.

I could tell that Jean was in pain, but he lifted Marthe into the boat, then gave his hand to help Claudette and the baby. I waded to the side and clambered in, trying not to think about the monsters that could be lurking under the dark surface of the water. Octavia was the last to come aboard. In the bottom of the boat, there were oars. She gave one to me, and the two of us began to row.

Off we glided into a haunted landscape. I could hear the calling of strange birds, the occasional cry of a fox, splashes in the distance of large dark things. Suddenly Claudette cried out, '*Feux follets!*' She was trembling so hard that I thought she might drop the baby.

Octavia looked at her sternly. '*Tais-toi*, Claudette! Be silent.' Her authority was such that Claudette pressed her lips together and subsided. I tried to see what she was looking at, and saw dancing lights in the distance. They created a strange effect, flickering among the shadows of the cypress trees. 'What on earth are those, Octavia?' I asked, trying not to let my voice tremble.

'They're called *feux follets*, as Claudette has said,' Octavia replied. 'Some say they are the lost souls of Africans who died here, or during the Middle Passage. Others say they appear when something is rotten. But they can't harm us.' I admired her fearlessness and her cool assurance, and wished I were more like her.

Octavia and I continued rowing. Jean's eyes were closed, and I prayed that he was asleep and not feeling pain. I'd sensed that he was frustrated at not being able to row because of his injury. I'd never rowed before, and could feel blisters beginning to form upon my hands, but kept on as though our lives depended on it. Which indeed might be the case.

Just when I thought I could row no more, we came upon a bit of land rising out of the swamp. In the mist, I could discern a cabin made of cypress boards. There was a light in the window. Octavia descended from the boat, and went up to the cabin. I heard low voices.

Octavia returned. A tall man was with her. Even from a distance, I sensed the dignity of his bearing. His skin was very dark, and his features were strong and beautiful. He was leaning on a stick as he walked, and I saw that one leg was withered. His forearms, though, rippled with muscle. Marthe smiled when she saw him.

'Sidonie,' said Octavia, 'This is Imbangala. He escaped from Les Chenes. He is no friend of the Ardoins, but I have known him since St. Domingue, and he has given me his word that he will help you and keep you from harm. Marthe knows him, since we have taken supplies to him on the island.' She handed him a basket, which I could see was heavily loaded with food. I nodded to the man, and reached for the basket, but he immediately took it from my hands and headed up the path. He motioned for Jean to follow him.

'Imbangala will now help me row back, and will return later with the boat.' Octavia said. I could see that she was exhausted. My eyes filled with tears.

'My dear friend,' I said, 'I will never forget your kindness.' I reached for Immaculata's amulet. 'Is it possible for you to send this to my friend Palmyre, at the Convent in New Orleans?'

Octavia smiled. Her smile was chilling. 'I'll take great pleasure in making sure that it reaches her,' she said. Imbangala returned, and the two of them went down to the boat. They disappeared into the mist.

Carrying the baby, I led Claudette and Marthe up to the cabin. Jean was sitting on a chair, and there was a fire in the chimney I was worried at his pallor and general air of lethargy, though he was trying to put a brave face on things. I settled Claudette and Marthe into their small room on the back of the house, and settled down by Jean. 'You must try to sleep, darling, and to rest and recover,' I said gently.

'You're right, Sidonie,' he replied. His eyes were glazed with fatigue. 'In this state I'm no good to anybody. I'll need to get my strength back, and then we can deal with Bertrand.' He lay down in a low cot in the living room. I covered him with blankets and brought him some of the food Octavia had provided, but he had no appetite. His eyelids lowered, and soon he was fast asleep. When I saw how vulnerable he was, a sudden wave of tenderness grabbed me by the throat.

Chapter 21

Sidonie

The tall African returned around noon. He too seemed tired. He and Octavia had spoken in an African language, so I was surprised and impressed when he spoke to me in perfect fluent French. 'We must change the dressing on M. Ardoin's wound,' he said. 'In the swamp, there is a greater risk of infection.'

Jean looked at him and nodded. 'Thank you,' he said. 'I want to my arm to heal so that I can help. Did Octavia get back to Les Chenes safely?'

'Yes,' he said. His expression darkened. 'I fear for her safety, though. Bertrand has always been cruel, but now he is completely insane.'

'Is he still barricaded in the ruins of the ballroom?' I asked.

'No,' Imbangala replied. 'He's gone back to his cabin. Someone at Les Chenes told me about the fate of the men who disappeared last week. They are now hanging from trees on the path leading up to the cabin. Bertrand has several guns.'

Jean recoiled. 'I give you my word,' he said, 'that I will put an end to this horror.'

'For you to do that,' Imbangala said,' we must keep you alive.' He began to wash Jean's wound with a clean cloth, and then packed it with herbs. 'What are those?' I asked.

'They're swamp plants that can be used to heal,' he replied. 'We used them at home in Africa.'

'Are you from the same country as Octavia?' I asked.

'No,' Imbangala replied. 'I am from Angola. My father was the leader of our people, and my wife was Yoruba. My father arranged the marriage as a strategic alliance between our kingdoms. We were captured by Portuguese slavers, then taken across the sea to St. Domingue and sold to different owners. I escaped from St. Domingue, then was recaptured and sold on the block in New Orleans, then brought to Les Chenes.'

'Were you ill-treated here?' Jean asked.

Imbangala looked at Jean coldly. 'Your brother's overseer had a reputation as a slave-breaker. And I had a reputation for escaping every chance I got. Bertrand knew I was a troublemaker, and that I would not hesitate to incite other slaves to revolt.'

'What happened?' I asked. I was afraid of what the response would be.

'Bertrand decided to cut my hamstrings, so that I could not escape again,' he said in a flat tone. 'He slashed the tendons in the back of my right knee with a knife. I knocked him down and managed to flee, with the help of two other slaves. They brought me to this island. Others have used it before.'

I shuddered. 'What a horrific story,' I said. Imbangala finished dressing Jean's wound and rose

I thought it was best to be direct. 'Imbangala,' I said, 'why are you helping us, and why do you trust us?' I knew that striking an overseer was a death sentence, and though I was horrified and indignant after hearing his story, I was astonished that he had confessed to us what he had done.

He smiled, but there was no warmth in his smile and his eyes were cold. 'You might better ask why you should trust me.' It was true: here we were in the middle of a swamp, two women, a child, a baby, and a man with a wounded right arm. Power was on his side, not ours. But then he went on, 'Octavia is my friend. I've promised her that I will help you, and I never go back on my word.' He added, 'I trust you because Octavia has told me you know a woman called Palmyre, and are her friend. I want to find her.'

My face lit up. 'Do you know Palmyre?' I asked in delight. I explained that she had been my student in New Orleans, and that she and I had become friends.

Jean had remained silent throughout. But now he stood, and looked Imbangala in the eye. 'If we're talking about trust, I know that you may not feel that you have any reason to trust me or even to respect me and my family, after the wrong that has been done to you and others. I cannot undo the evil that already has been done to you by someone acting on my family's behalf, but I solemnly swear that I shall not only emancipate every single slave on Les Chenes, but also commit myself for the rest of my life to the cause of abolition.' I knew that he meant every single word he said.

As he walked out the door with his fishing pole, Imbangala turned to me. 'Octavia asked me to tell you that she's arranged for your message to reach your friend Palmyre. If this is the same woman, yes, I knew her, years ago.'

This cheered me up tremendously. How Palmyre would be able to help me, I had no idea, but I knew that my friend would not let me down. Remembering her terror when Armand and Bertrand were in New Orleans, I felt guilty about asking her for aid.

Over the following days, we settled into a routine. There was a small garden in back of the cabin, and Claudette and I worked there together in the morning, and talked as we did so. After the first day, Imbangala and Jean would go fishing. I could see that the two men, after their initial mutual wariness, were increasingly at ease in each other's company. In retrospect, I don't know why I found this surprising: both were used to being obeyed, and both had an air of command. I didn't think that they would ever be best friends, but I sensed the growth of mutual respect.

Claudette and I took turns caring for Marie, and Claudette suckled her. I was relieved to see that our limited diet of fish and greens and potatoes didn't seem to affect her supply of milk. Marie was such a contented baby, and her laughter was bewitching. Marthe was a very self-contained little girl, but I could tell she was missing her mother. Remembering my promise to Octavia, I continued with our reading lessons. Marthe's quick mind was a delight, and I spent hours telling stories, which served to distract her from the dangers around us.

What was more difficult was that, in such close quarters, Jean and I rarely had a moment to be alone. I was aware every minute of his presence, of the scent of his skin and the tone of his voice, and I could sense that he was equally aware of me. Despite the desperate circumstances in which we found ourselves, there was something magical about sharing this strange, self-contained world with him. I prayed every night that we would be able to leave and to marry, and to make a home of our own, either in Louisiana or in France as he had suggested. Lying with him to keep him warm brought us both moments of piercing sweetness, and at the same time, intense frustration, since with people all around there were boundaries we couldn't cross. When he touched my skin under the covers, I felt alive to my fingertips. I thought of the Convent and of the nuns and their strictures about the Sins of the Flesh. If this was sinning, I reflected, I would happily embrace perdition for eternity.

Increasingly, in these days on the island in the swamp, I found myself thinking about the Church and what I'd been taught to believe. There was so much I loved about it: its concern for the poor, the Biblical exhortations to stand up for the weak and the persecuted. But at the same time, I remembered that the Ursulines had not found it problematic to own slaves. I had learned from my students in New Orleans, and from Octavia and Claudette, that there were so many different and fascinating ways of looking at the world. It was all very confusing. At times, when I looked out on the water of the swamp, the distorted images I saw there reminded me of how all the certainties I'd been taught in the Convent back in France seemed to waver and flicker and throw back different refractions of light and shadow here.

Given the dangers that surrounded us, we knew that we had to be watchful, and we listened for any strange sound that might mean Bertrand might be coming after us. One evening, as we sat around the fire, I turned to Jean and Imbangala. 'Do either of you know where Louis Bertrand comes from, and what has made him what he is?'

Jean spoke first. 'I know very little about him. My father hired him when Armand and I were studying in France.'

Imbangala looked into the fire. 'I have heard from other Africans that he came from a poor background. In St. Domingue, they said he was the Devil.' He stared into the flames. 'Apparently he traded in slaves, and wanted to amass a fortune in order to have a plantation of his own.'

'Ah,' said Jean. 'So, if Marie and I, as the last of the Ardoins, were to disappear, and taxes were not paid on the land, he might think that he could buy Les Chenes cheap.'

'It is hard to know what goes on in his mind,' said Imbangala. 'But you are in great danger, it's true.'

'He will not harm you while there is breath in my body,' I said fiercely, taking Jean's hand. Suddenly there was an unearthly howling in the distance. We all started. Imbangala reached for his gun.

'The *loup-garou*!' Claudette cried. Her teeth were chattering in terror.

'It's not the *loup-garou*,' Imbangala said impatiently. 'It's just a fox, or perhaps a lone wolf.'

'What is the *loup-garou*?' I asked.

'Some people believe that people can take on the form of wolves, but keep their human intelligence, which makes them even more dangerous,' Imbangala replied. 'I can see why some think that the overseer is a l*oup-garou*, since he really is a beast in human form. But if he comes, we'll be ready to receive him.' He walked noiselessly out to the porch and remained there on guard, looking out into the dark.

That night, as we lay in the dark, Jean and I talked softly about the future. 'If we manage to escape from here, where shall we go, my love?' I asked him.

'I wish I knew,' said Jean. 'One possibility would be for us to make our way to France. I could earn a living there as a lawyer, and you as a teacher. In France there is not so much concern for people's background.' I knew that he was referring to his African blood.

'That's true enough,' I said. 'You and the girls could easily pass for white.
But at the same time, that would mean that we would be condemned to a lifetime of deceit. Have you ever thought of settling somewhere else, somewhere remote, here in Louisiana?' Despite everything, I had come to love Louisiana, its luxuriant nature and its easy warmth.

'The need to deceive, to pass, will be the case wherever we decide to live,' Jean said. 'People with African blood cannot exercise certain professions, or vote, or hold civic office, or attend certain schools.' His face was sad. 'I often think that I do not have the right to ask you to join your life to mine, my love. I do not want to condemn you to a life lived in the shadows, always on the verge of discovery and ruin.'

I embraced him tightly and looked into his eyes. 'I'm not afraid.'

Jean looked deep into my eyes. 'Your strength, and your fearlessness, are the greatest gifts I have ever been given,' he said.' He thought for a moment. 'There is a town up the Red River called Natchitoches,' he said. 'Perhaps they need a lawyer.' He looked out into the dark. 'But first of all we have to leave this place, and rid ourselves of this nightmare. Then we can talk about all these things.'

The following morning I was sitting on the porch with Marie in my arms. I had the eerie feeling that we were being watched, but dismissed this and chided myself for being fanciful. Jean and Imbangala finished their breakfast and went outside. I could tell that they were talking about weighty matters, given the air of seriousness on both their faces. I knew that food was running low.

The men returned. Imbangala said to me, 'We are concerned about Octavia. She'd promised to come with food two days ago. We have decided that I am going to go back to

Les Chenes. Jean will stay here to guard you and Claudette and the girls.'

'Please God may nothing have happened to Octavia,' I said. My imagination, always over-active, had been running riot: with visions of Octavia's illness advancing, or of Bertrand overcoming his terror of her in order to do her harm. 'Imbangala, do take care.'

'I am not frightened of Louis Bertrand,' Imbangala said. His smile was like the flash of a razor. He disappeared into the mist, and we were left there looking at the wake of his boat.

'What an extraordinary man,' Jean said. 'He is, you know, a prince in his own country.'

I smiled. 'The reason the two of you get on so well is that you are both used to telling others what to do.'

Jean spent the night on the porch, with the gun on his lap. I stayed inside with Claudette and the girls, and went out from time to time to check on Jean and bring him food or a warm drink. Marie was fretful, and woke from time to time. Again, I had the sensation that we were being watched. It made the skin crawl on the back of my neck.

At sunset the following day, we heard the sound of oars in the distance. Jean tensed and propped the gun against the railing. But it was Imbangala. When he came into sight, I saw the expression on his face and knew that the news would not be good. He moored the boat, and walked up the incline to the cabin.

'What news?' Jean asked.

Imbangala put down his gun. 'Much has happened,' he said.

'Tell us!' I said. 'Is Octavia all right? And what has Bertrand been doing?'

Imbangala leaned against the porch. 'Octavia is dead.'

My knees buckled, and I had to sit down. 'What happened?' I whispered.

'Her illness took a turn for the worse. When she returned to Les Chenes, she took great delight in tormenting Louis Bertrand by appearing at the window. He would make the sign of the Cross, scream 'Vampire!', try to flee. One evening, she was seized by a fit of coughing. Her lungs were haemorrhaging, and blood was pouring from her mouth. She died, and he did nothing to help her.'

'The bravest of the brave,' said Jean. He inclined his head. 'An admirable woman, your cousin. I am sorry for your loss, my friend.' I was crying so hard I could not speak.

'Thank you,' Imbangala said. He went on. 'That piece of vermin believed that she was a vampire. He did not even bother to bury her, but dumped her corpse in a corner of the ballroom.'

I put my hands over my ears.

Jean looked out over the dark waters of the swamp. 'Where is Bertrand now? He must be brought to justice.'

Imbangala let out a harsh laugh. 'Justice? All of his actions are sanctioned by law.'

'As you probably know, I am a lawyer,' Jean said. 'I believe in the rule of law with all my heart. But when there are unjust laws, it is our duty to resist them and try to change them one day. Bertrand must be punished for what he has done to my brother and to your cousin, and to all the others.'

Imbangala swayed on his feet. 'Is there any food left?' he asked. 'I have not eaten for three days.' I could tell that he was exhausted as well as famished, and berated myself. 'There is,' I answered. I went inside and brought back some stale bread, which was all that was left in our depleted stores. Once he had eaten a few bites, he went on with his account.

'I wanted to confront Bertrand,' Imbangala said. 'But I took the precaution of talking to the remaining slaves before doing so, and I am glad I did. Bertrand is not alone.'

'How do you mean?' Jean asked.

'There is a sharecropper who lives upriver,' Imbangala said. 'A poor white man called Jacques Boudreaux.'

'I know who you mean,' Jean said. 'I met him briefly, and was not impressed. I found him servile and treacherous, as well as filthy and unkempt.'

'He is all of those things and more,' Imbangala replied. 'He and Bertrand are both notorious for abusing children. Very young children. According to the other slaves, Bertrand has convinced Boudreaux that we are trying to foment a slave revolt. Though not many of the slaves are left, since most escaped after the fire.'

My mouth fell open. I realised that we really were in mortal danger. If Bertrand and Boudreaux made this accusation to the colonial authorities in New Orleans, Jean was in grave peril if his part-African ancestry was revealed. Imbangala would be executed; Jean would be as well. I was not overly concerned for myself, since the authorities would find it hard to believe that a mere seventeen-year-old girl could be intelligent enough to be an agent of subversion. Still, I didn't want to put this to the test. A slave revolt was every slaveowner's greatest fear, and any hint of one would be suppressed without mercy.

'It gets worse,' Imbangala said. 'The cook overheard Bertrand and Boudreaux talking. They have been spying on us, and are planning to come here in the night to take us by surprise.'

'We'll take the fight to them, rather than waiting here like trapped animals,' Jean said. 'We will trap the *loup-garou* in his den.' Imbangala nodded his assent.

I knew that the news of Octavia's death would hit Marthe hard. My heart sank, but I knew that she would have to be told. She had been playing with some stones in back of the house I went out to her and sat beside her on the ground.

'Marthe, you are going to have to be a very brave girl,' I said. She looked up at me, and I could see in her eyes that she knew what was coming.

'Your mother has passed away,' I told her. 'She was a very good woman, and I know she will be in Heaven with God and his angels.'

The little girl looked to the ground, and tears began to fall down her cheeks. 'I don't want her to be in Heaven. I want her here with me.' She began to sob. 'I hate God and his angels.'

I held her close. 'Your mother was a hero,' I said. 'She loved you more than anything in the world.'

'W-what's a hero?' Marthe asked. 'Is it like an angel?'

'Sometimes, but sometimes not,' I answered. 'A hero is someone who, even though she may be afraid, is willing to stand up for people and ideas she loves and believes in.'

That, for some reason, seemed to comfort the child more than the idea of her mother in heaven, flanked by angels. 'I want to be a hero too,' she said softly.

Chapter 22

Sidonie

The sun was setting, and the tops of the cypress trees were suffused in a strange red light. Suddenly we heard the splash of oars in the distance. 'Go inside, Sidonie, and take cover with Claudette and the girls,' Imbangala said. Jean nodded. They both cocked their guns and took aim. I moved to go inside, but then on tiptoe doubled back and crouched on the porch.

A boat came into sight. In it were, not Bertrand and Boudreaux, but two figures wrapped in black cloaks. When they emerged from the mist, it created an unearthly effect. 'Who goes there?' Jean called out. His voice was not altogether steady.

A female voice responded. 'Sidonie?'

It was Palmyre! I burst past the two men and ran down to the water's edge. 'I knew that you would come, my friend!' I cried, with tears streaming down my face. Clemence was sitting in the boat behind her. I led the two women up to the cabin. Imbangala looked as though he had seen a ghost.

'Palmyre?' he said. 'I thought you were dead.' I was astonished to see his eyes fill with tears. He held out his arms, and Palmyre ran into them.

Later, the story emerged as we all sat around the table. Much of this I already knew. Palmyre had been Imbangala's consort in Africa, and he was the father of her lost baby. Both had been kidnapped and transported to St. Domingue by slavers. There, as we knew, Palmyre had been bought by Armand Ardoin and passed on to Louis Bertrand.

When Imbangala heard this, his eyes flashed. 'I will kill this snake,' he said in calm tones. But Palmyre intervened. 'No,' she said. 'That is a pleasure I shall reserve to myself. It is something I have been waiting for a long time, but I wanted to be sure I was strong enough. Until now, I have been tormenting him from a distance.' She withdrew something from a pocket. It was a small doll, with an uncanny resemblance to Louis Bertrand, withered arm and all. There were pins sticking out from his head.

I shivered, and asked myself if the hallucinations Bertrand had been having were linked with this strange doll. Palmyre saw my glance. 'Don't be afraid, Sidonie. I would never harm you.' She smiled. 'It was hard for Clemence to tell me what had happened, since she has no tongue. But when I saw the *gris-gris* of the monkey and the cockerel, I knew you were in danger. And I remembered how we made drawings for you back in the Convent, so I asked her to draw what was going on.' She handed me a crumpled paper. On it, Clemence had sketched a man with a twisted arm, a knife and rows of oak trees, flanked by a white man, a tall black man, a white woman and two black women, and two children. 'I had heard that Imbangala had been sold to Armand Ardoin, taken somewhere upriver, and killed by his overseer when he tried to escape. But when I saw the tall black man, I wondered and let myself hope that he was still alive.'

Palmyre had asked other slaves if they knew of a plantation whose name contained the word 'oaks', owned or managed by a man with a withered arm. This had led her straight to Les Chenes. She and Clemence had made their way upriver and had been aided on the way by an informal network of slaves and sympathisers. They had encountered en route one of the slaves who had fled from Les Chenes on the night of the fire, and had learned of the deaths of Joelle and Armand Ardoin.

I remembered, in the Convent, how Palmyre had always avoided being seen by Armand when he came courting Joelle, and how she had stayed hidden when Louis Bertrand came to take me to Les Chenes. "You're a very brave woman, Palmyre,' I said to her. 'To come upriver, not knowing what you might find.'

'You would do the same for me,' she said. 'And I knew that the moment had come to act.' She looked at Marie, fast asleep in Claudette's arms. 'Is this Joelle's little one?'

'Yes,' I said. 'She is such a good little girl.' I called Marthe, who was standing tongue-tied in the shadow. 'And this is Marthe, Octavia's daughter.'

'Come here, child,' Palmyre said. Marthe stepped forward, long-legged and tentative like a fawn. She had inherited Octavia's dignity and grace, and would be a beautiful woman one day, with large dark eyes and skin the colour of the finest pale sherry. Palmyre's eyes shone with unshed tears. 'You are beautiful and strong like Octavia. What will become of these girls?'

'Jean and I will keep them and take care of them,' I said. 'If, of course, we manage to get away from here alive.'

'Well we must make sure that you do,' Palmyre said. I could tell that after her long journey, she was exhausted. Claudette and I made up a pallet beside Imbangala's and left the two of them alone.

The next morning dawned overcast, with a low wind stirring the tops of the trees. Jean and Imbangala rose early, and I could hear the murmur of their voices from the porch. When the rest of us awoke, we joined them. They, together with Palmyre, had reached a decision.

'Gather your things,' said Imbangala. 'We are going back to Les Chenes. Sidonie, Claudette and the girls will remain in the coach house, while Jean and I will accompany Palmyre to the big house.'

I was not at all convinced by this. 'Palmyre, you have shown that you are my friend by coming to our rescue. But now please continue to be my friend by understanding that I cannot let the three of you go into danger without me.'

Palmyre frowned. But then she looked at me and said, 'I know how it is to feel powerless, and I would not wish that for you. So yes, you may come. But you must do as I say.'

'What are you planning to do?' I asked.

'The less you know, the better,' Palmyre said gently to me. 'If things do not go as planned, and you are questioned, it is better that you do not know what we were planning to do.' She smiled. 'I don't know if you remember my flower patch back at the Convent. Sometimes flowers have their uses. I am bringing flowers to the loup-garou.' I began to wonder if Palmyre had taken leave of her senses.

We quickly packed up the few items of clothing we had, and had a frugal breakfast. Then we headed down to the shore, and got into two boats, with Palmyre, Claudette, the girls and me in the rowboat, Jean and Imbangala and Clemence in the canoe Palmyre and Clemence had arrived in. Mist rose from the surface of the water, and the swamp seemed dark and menacing in the half-light.

We tied up about half a mile below Les Chenes, and made our way in silence through the woods to the coachman's house. When we reached it, we put the girls to bed. Palmyre remained outside on guard.

Jean was not happy about Palmyre's decision to allow me to take part in the expedition to the Big House. 'You have seen so much horror, my love,' he said. 'I hate the idea that you will be exposed to danger. Besides, we shall need to move quickly and in silence.'

I found this exasperating. 'Jean, waiting back at the coachman's house would be infinitely more terrifying for me. As you've seen, I can move quickly and silently when I have to.

If I hadn't done so when Bertrand tied you up in the study, who knows what might have happened.'

Jean sighed. 'That is of course true,' he said. I could tell that it was not easy for him to admit this. At times he was exasperating, this proud wilful man of mine.

The four of us went silently toward the big house. It was ghostly in the moonlight, with the burnt-out beams of the study silhouetted against the sky. We crouched behind the garden wall. I could detect a faint smell of rotting flesh and tried hard not to retch.

From our hiding place, we could see what remained of the ballroom. It was lined with mirrors, and I remembered Joelle saying in some embarrassment that Armand had wanted his own little Versailles. In the mirrors, in the flickering candlelight, we could see Louis Bertrand sitting with another man at a low table. I had not encountered Jacques Boudreaux before. His face was half-concealed by long, dirty hair. I could see that he had a scar on his upper lip, which exposed his broken front teeth, brown tobacco-stained stubs. His expression was one of singular malevolence. As we watched, he spewed out a stream of tobacco into a spittoon. On the table in front of them was a decanter of brandy. The two men had clearly been drinking for some time.

Palmyre nodded to Imbangala. Silently, he disappeared around the corner of the house. Suddenly, we heard the howl of an animal close at hand. It sounded like a panther, or a big cat of some kind. My hair stood on end.

In the ballroom, both men sprang to their feet. 'What in hell was that?' Bertrand exclaimed. He picked up his shotgun, and the two men went toward the entrance hall. I could hear them firing shots into the night.

Palmyre sprang into action. She raced toward the empty ballroom and opened the French doors. There, she emptied the contents of a cloth bag into the decanter of wine, then returned to our side and remained totally still.

Imbangala emerged through the trees and came back silently to our hiding place. I felt Palmyre slump in relief. His laughter was white in the moonlight. 'I was in no danger,' he whispered. 'They were so drunk that not in a thousand years would they have been able to hit anything.'

From our vantage point, we could see Bertrand and Boudreaux lurch back into the ballroom and slump into their chairs. 'Must've been a wildcat,' Bertrand said. He poured glasses of brandy for himself and for Boudreaux. The two men raised their glasses and drank deep.

For a moment, nothing happened. Then Bertrand began to clutch at his throat. Boudreaux fell off his chair and writhed on the floor. Palmyre crossed the garden, opened the doors, and stepped into the ballroom. We followed close behind. There was an overwhelming stench emanating from the corner.

So, gentlemen,' Palmyre said in silky tones. Her voice, when she pronounced the word 'gentlemen', was laced with irony. 'We meet again.' Her facial expression, in the candlelight, was that of an avenging goddess, and she had never been more magnificent. She looked down at Bertrand and Boudreaux, and spat in Boudreaux's face. 'This is for my child. And for my friend.' She nodded toward the corner, and I saw in horror the outlines of Octavia's decaying body. 'And for me and all the men and women you have abused. I hope that you enjoyed your brandy. It is a very fine vintage, laced with wolfsbane, brought from my garden in the convent in New Orleans.' Her smile was radiant. 'An appropriate poison for a *loup-garou*. Though I think that word is offensive to wolves, who are noble creatures.' Boudreaux twitched, shuddered, and lay still.

Bertrand had fallen to the floor. He stared at Palmyre and blinked. Suddenly I saw him remember, realise who she was, and his eyes filled with dread and fury. Foam issued from the corner of his mouth when he tried to swear at her. 'Not easy to find oneself voiceless, *n'est-ce pas*?' Palmyre said. 'Count yourself lucky. Wolfsbane, in smaller doses, could have taken days rather than hours to kill you. But I have decided to show mercy. Still, you will not die immediately, and your death will be slow and very painful as the cold creeps up your limbs.' She turned on her heel. I could see that she was trembling, but utterly resolute.

Imbangala embraced her. Jean and I were transfixed in a mixture of horror and absolute admiration. Palmyre looked at Octavia's body.

'The very first thing we must do is bury her,' she said. Imbangala and Jean nodded. They pulled down one of the velvet curtains and gently wrapped Octavia's body in it. Jean said, 'My brother must receive a decent burial as well. We will bury them in the Ardoin plot.' This seemed appropriate, since Octavia was the mother of his half-sister. They went to recover what was left of Armand's body from the burnt-out shell of the study.

My voice was shaking. 'What now, Palmyre?' I asked.

She jerked her head in the direction of the dead and dying men. 'Jean and Imbangala can take them to the swamp. I am told the alligators are hungry at this time of year.'

Palmyre remained standing guard over Bertrand and Boudreaux, and I headed back to the coachman's house. It is hard to describe how I was feeling: it was as though I had witnessed these events from a vantage point outside my body. I felt an overwhelming need to speak to Jean about it all. We had just witnessed two murders. And it could be said that we had aided and abetted Palmyre and Imbangala. Killing another human being went against every single thing I had learned from the nuns, and I knew that I should feel guilty. And yet what I was experiencing was a sense of relief, giddy nausea, and a strange exhilaration.

Back in the coachman's house, Claudette was waiting. The two girls, thankfully, were sound asleep. She raised her eyebrows in enquiry, and I nodded. 'The danger to the girls, and to us all, is gone,' I said. She asked no questions. I wrapped myself in an old woollen cloak and sat down in a dilapidated chair. I found that I was trembling hard, and could not get warm. In the distance, I smelled smoke.

About six hours later, as the sun was rising, I heard footsteps. Jean, Imbangala and Palmyre came into view. They came up the steps and Palmyre sank into a chair. Imbangala and Jean remained standing, but I could see that they were exhausted.

'We will rest for a while, but then we must leave,' Jean said. 'Octavia now rests alongside Armand and Joelle.'

'And the others?' I asked. I could not bring myself to mention their names.

Palmyre smiled. 'Do you remember those beautiful purple flowers in my flower patch in the Convent, Sidonie? It was monkshood, which is also called wolfsbane. It is one of the most deadly poisons there is. Imbangala and Jean took the bodies to the depths of the swamp and heaved them into the water. Soon there will be nothing left of them.'

On the horizon, I could see a strange orange light and raised my eyebrows. Jean saw my question, and answered. 'What remained of the house is burning. By the end of the day, it will have burned to the ground.'

I did not ask who was responsible. 'Good,' I said. 'What should we do now? We should leave this place as quickly as we can.'

Jean thought for a moment. 'I will sign a paper emancipating Imbangala and Palmyre.'

Imbangala looked into his eyes. 'For this, we are grateful. But Palmyre and I were born free, and do not need a white man's signature to set us free.'

Jean nodded. 'That is true. But in Louisiana, in the eyes of the law, that is not so. It is important that you keep this document with you, because it will confirm your status as free people of colour.' He looked at Imbangala and Palmyre. 'Where will you go now?'

Palmyre smiled. 'The Louisiana territory is a big place,' she said. 'There are many places far from New Orleans where we could live. Perhaps the Atchafalaya swamps, or the lands to the west near the Sabine River. Or even in the mountains of St. Domingue, where I have heard there are communities of maroons. Some people do manage to escape from slavery.'

This, to me, made good sense. I turned to Jean. 'Where shall we go?" I asked.

Jean took my hand. 'We'll make our way to New Orleans. There, we can get married.'

My face lit up. 'Perhaps Father Beaubois, in the Convent, could perform the ceremony.'

Palmyre nodded. 'Father Beaubois is a good man, and a brave one. When I escaped from St. Domingue, he gave me refuge at the Convent. He has helped other slaves as well.'

Jean continued. 'In New Orleans, I shall take legal measures to emancipate the remaining slaves at Les Chenes, and seek to sell the land on Marie's behalf as her guardian. After that we can go to France, and take steps to adopt Marie

291

and Marthe. I want for you to meet my mother, and for her to meet her grandchildren. There are also some business matters I must attend to. In France, you and I can decide where we want to spend the rest of our lives.'

'Yes,' I said. 'And Claudette can come with us, if she wishes, as nurse to Marie. Clemence will have her freedom, but we could take her as well. Or I could speak to Berthe in New Orleans about employing her.'

Chapter 23

Sidonie

We set out the following day for New Orleans in the same boat that had brought me to Les Chenes. When we were about five miles upriver from New Orleans, we moored briefly and said our farewells to Palmyre and Imbangala.

I embraced her.

'I shall never forget you, my dear friend,' I told Palmyre. 'You have taught me so much about what real heroism is.'

Palmyre reached into her cloak and took out Immaculata's amulet. 'This has already brought you love. May it continue to do so, and bring you luck and riches as well.' She smiled. 'You're a courageous woman yourself, Sidonie. I know our paths, or the paths of our descendants, will cross again one day.'

'That would be a wonderful thing,' I said.

I could tell that Jean and Imbangala were similarly moved. They said their farewells with a gruff masculine embrace, and we cast off once more. I stayed on deck waving until Palmyre and Imbangala were lost from view.

The nuns were not expecting us. Mother Jerome's mouth dropped open when she saw me, and she held her arms open wide. She remembered Jean from Joelle and Armand's wedding, and wept when we told her of their untimely deaths. She and Fidelis both cooed over Marie, and smiled at Marthe, whom we introduced as Jean's half-sister without going into details about her parentage. We told no lies, but I had learned that it is not always necessary to tell the entire truth.

After the initial excitement, Mother Jerome turned to me. 'Sidonie, I am aware that the circumstances were unusual, but it is inappropriate that you have travelled unchaperoned from Les Chenes, with only two children and two slaves for company.' She tutted. 'What might people think!"

Jean spoke up. 'Sidonie has done me the very great honour of agreeing to become my wife.'

That provoked an explosion of delight. The nuns, clucking and fluttering like a flock of happy hens, brought in our few belongings. They agreed to house us until the wedding. Needless to say, I would be lodged at one end of the house, and Jean at another, near Father Beaubois's quarters.

I turned to Mother Jerome. 'Do you think Father Beaubois would marry us?'

'Why don't you ask him yourself?' she replied, as Father Beaubois walked through the door. His jaw dropped when he saw me. His face broke into a smile.

'I'm back, Father,' I said. It was good to see him. 'You have already met Jean Ardoin, my fiancé.' The two men did that male thing of sizing each other up from head to toe. 'Would you be willing to marry us?'

Father Beaubois nodded, and smiled at Jean. 'Of course, Sidonie,' he said. He seemed genuinely happy for us. 'Of course, we shall have to publish the banns in advance.'

Jean said, 'Reverend Father, we would like very much to be on the next boat to Le Havre, which is leaving in four days. Might it be possible to waive the banns? If it is not, we could be married in France.'

I admired Jean's dexterity. He knew full well that Father Beaubois and Mother Jerome would take a very dim view of my travelling across the Atlantic with Jean as an unmarried woman, even though I was his fiancée. Father Beaubois was aware of exactly what was going on, and smiled ruefully. 'Perhaps we can waive the banns, in the circumstances. I could perform the ceremony the day after tomorrow. You will both need to come to confession.'

'If that is the case, there is no time to be lost!' exclaimed Mother Jerome. She beckoned to me, and led me into her quarters. There, she reached into a chest of drawers and took out a length of white silk. 'For your wedding dress.'

I was overcome. I had not dreamed that it would be possible to have a real wedding dress. Mother Jerome smiled. 'Those students of yours have done extremely well with the embroidery project. Perhaps they could make your dress.'

Nanette and Clotilde were hard at work in their improvised atelier, the former storeroom. When I entered with the white silk in my arms, they all rushed up to embrace me.

'We thought you were dead,' Clotilde said. 'And Joelle and the baby?'

I told them of Joelle and Armand's deaths. I felt that the less they knew of the circumstances, the better, and told them the house had burned to the ground and that the causes were unknown. They wept at the news of Joelle, but were delighted that I was going to be caring for her little one, and for Jean's half-sister. I did not mention that Marthe's mother had been a slave.

When I told them of my engagement to Jean, there were shrieks of delight. 'Aren't you a dark horse, Sidonie! Little Miss Bookworm has landed herself a planter,' Nanette exclaimed, half in congratulations, half in naked envy. But when she saw the silk, her eyes lit up. 'Of course you will need a wedding dress.'

'It would be wonderful if the three of you could make it!' I said. Berthe burst through the door. 'Sidonie!' she cried, and enfolded me in a hug. It was wonderful to see her. I had missed Berthe's earthiness and her matter-of-fact way of looking at the world.

'So how is the embroidery business going?' I asked.

Berthe laughed. 'These girls are dynamos. We have been selling many, many embroidered linen sheets and handkerchiefs to the finest ladies of New Orleans.'

Nanette grinned. 'Indeed we have.' I noticed a new pride in the way she held herself. She added, 'If business continues to develop as well as it has, Clotilde and I have saved nearly enough to buy a small house near the docks. You were right, Sidonie, that economic independence is the basis of everything.'

'Is there any news of Coahoma?'

Berthe sighed. 'I went with my husband to deliver some supplies to a plantation downriver, and saw a girl who looked a lot like her in the slave quarters.'

Having seen at close hand what slavery was like, I shuddered. 'I hate to think of what she must be going through. I hope and pray that they will be free one day.' My heart ached for my friends.

'You haven't asked about Palmyre!' Nanette exclaimed.

'No, I haven't,' I said. I hoped that I didn't look too evasive. 'Where is she?'

'We don't know,' Nanette replied. 'One night she disappeared mysteriously, and hasn't been heard of since. We thought she might have jumped into the river and drowned herself.'

'She would never do that,' I said. 'Palmyre is one of the strongest people I know.'

Berthe interrupted. 'Girls, if the wedding is day after tomorrow, there's no time to waste!' She turned to me and shooed me out. 'Sidonie, you must leave now. The dress is going to be a surprise.'

I went in search of Father Beaubois, and found him in his study. I thought he had aged since I saw him last, and his hair was visibly greyer. 'Reverend Father,' I asked him, 'would it be possible for you to hear my confession at some point today?'

'Of course, Sidonie, he replied. 'I shall have to prepare a sermon later, so perhaps I could hear your confession now.'

We went into the Chapel, and I knelt before the confessional and made the sign of the Cross. 'Forgive me, Father, for I have sinned. It has been five months since my last confession.'

I could hear the rustling of Father Beaubois's robes as he took his seat on the bench. 'What has brought you to make confession?'

'I hardly know where to start,' I said. 'Many would say I was the accomplice to a double murder. But I cannot in honesty say that I am sorry.'

I heard a sigh from the other side of the screen. 'Why don't you tell me exactly what happened?'

I drew a deep breath. 'I'm afraid there's a lot to tell,' I said. I told him about the man in the cage, and the bodies of slaves hanging from trees on the path leading up to Louis Bertrand's cabin. I described Octavia's courage, and the fact that she had had a child by Armand, Ardoin's father. I confessed my grief at Joelle's death, and my rage that her life had been cut short. I told him about witnessing Armand's murder. I told him about what had passed between Jean and me. I went on to describe Palmyre's arrival, and our trip from the island in the swamp to Les Chenes to poison Louis Bertrand and Jacques Boudreaux. I paused to draw breath, and continued, 'What I feel most guilty about is that I do not feel any regret at the deaths of Bertrand and Boudreaux. On the contrary, it seems to me that justice was done.'

'Ah, justice.' I heard Father Beaubois sigh. 'That is the difficult thing. Why do you think Bertrand and Boudreaux behaved as they did?'

I was quiet for a long time. Then I continued, 'Perhaps Bertrand suffered as a child, and was prepared to do anything to amass money and make himself invulnerable. And then of course he went crazy. As for Boudreaux, I have no idea. Maybe because he was poor, and afraid of Africans.'

'You're right,' Father Beaubois said, 'that fear is the most dangerous emotion of all, and it makes people do dreadful things. We must try to feel compassion, and try to walk in their shoes in order to understand why they behave the way they do. And then to forgive, if we can.'

'But Father,' I burst out, 'Palmyre lost her baby. She was repeatedly raped by Bertrand. Her husband was hamstrung by him. Surely there comes a point at which there are limits to forgiveness! Because if we forgive, what we're doing is perpetuating a system under which these horrors can occur.' My heart was beating hard.

'I would like to believe that there are no limits to forgiveness,' said Father Beaubois, and there was a quiet dignity in his words. 'Remember the words of Our Lord on the Cross, "Father, forgive them for they know not what they do." The dilemma of the thinking person is to know when it is

299

justifiable to rise up against injustice. There also we have the example of Our Lord, when he expelled the moneylenders from the Temple.'

'For me, it's hard to balance these two things,' I said. 'What I find most difficult is that so many laws—the Code Noir, for example—are unjust.'

'In my view, laws are made by human beings, and human beings are fallible,' Father Beaubois replied. 'If we feel strongly about certain laws and their consequences, it is our responsibility to do all we can to see that they are overturned. But at the same time, we should never forget the humanity of oppressors. So yes, it is difficult to know what the ethical solution is.' I could hear him stirring. 'Can you say in all honesty that you are sorry that you helped bring about Bertrand and Boudreaux's deaths?'

I thought for a moment. I knew that if I were unable to make a valid confession, Father Beaubois might not be able to marry me to Jean. But I drew a deep breath. 'No. They will not be able to harm anyone else. But I am sorry that I lost sight of their humanity, and I'm sorry that I can't do more to end the system that created them.'

Father Beaubois sighed. 'That will have to do for now. You must perform an Act of Contrition, and pray a rosary for their souls. I know that at times the difference between good and evil is hard to discern. What we must strive for is purity of heart.'

The following day I rose early and went for a walk by the river. I thought of Immaculata, whose amulet I wore around my neck. I thought of the ship that brought us here, and of Joelle laughing by my side at the railing. I thought of Coahoma, and prayed hard that she was safe wherever she was. I thought of Octavia, and of Armand, who would never see their daughters grow up to be fine women. I thought of Palmyre and Imbangala, and prayed for their safety and happiness. And then I thought of Jean, and it felt as though the sun had come out inside me.

I walked up the street to the butcher shop. The shop had been painted recently, and the counter had been moved to a corner, in order to accommodate more customers. Above the counter hung chickens and cuts of beef, along with ropes of garlic and stems with bay leaves. Behind the counter was Immaculata, serving a tall woman with pale brown skin, who looked to me like the housekeeper of some affluent family.

I would hardly have recognised her without her nun's habit. Immaculata looked plump, almost sleek, and her belly was rounded. Her hair was tied back neatly in a knot at the base of her neck. She wrapped up a slab of meat in paper and tied it with string, then turned to me. Her eyes widened.

'*Bonjour*, Immaculata,' I said. 'Your shop looks beautiful. It clearly needed a woman's touch.'

'You're right about that, Sidonie,' she replied. 'My husband's a good man, but men have no idea about how to

301

appeal to customers.' Her voice swelled with when she said the words 'My husband.' She continued, 'I'm sure you've heard all my latest news. New Orleans is a village. And I was sorry to hear of Joelle's death.'

'Congratulations, and thank you,' I said. 'I think of her every day.' I went on, 'I've come to invite you and your husband to my own wedding.' I knew that the nuns would find their presence problematic, but quite frankly I didn't care.

She nodded. I knew not to expect effusions from Immaculata. She turned back to her till, then stopped and looked back at me. 'And by the way,' she added, 'I now go by the name Zezette.'

I hastened back to the Convent. At the door, I ran into Berthe. '*Bonjour*, Sidonie,' she said with a grin. 'We have a lovely surprise for you.'

I'd wondered what my wedding dress would be like. I've never been overly concerned about clothes, but I did want to look pretty. I knew it would be white, but that's all I knew. Berthe took my hand and led me in to the atelier, where Nanette, Clotilde and Ottilie were waiting for me.

Spread out on the couch was the most beautiful dress I had ever seen. Berthe looked at me anxiously. 'Yesterday, we were talking about Palmyre and her embroidery. We still had the panels she embroidered, so we made them part of the skirt. I do hope that you like it!'

The dress was made of shimmering white silk. The bodice was simple, with long sleeves and a narrow waist. But the skirt billowed out, and it was covered with colourful embroidered images. One panel was made of Palmyre's image of the Convent, and of the river, of books, and of two smiling figures representing Jean and me under a bright yellow sun. The girls had also embroidered images of a baby and a little girl, of a woman with blonde ringlets, and of a bold dark-skinned woman with light radiating from her head. My eyes glistened.

'It is the most beautiful dress in the world,' I said. 'Thank you, my dear friends.' I embraced each of them in turn.

Our wedding day dawned bright and cool. My friends helped me get dressed, and Nanette did my hair, sweeping it up in a knot and letting some strands trail over my shoulders. When Mother Jerome saw the brightly coloured figures on the skirt, she raised an eyebrow. 'White is the colour of purity,' she said, and frowned. I blushed violently. But then she smiled. 'You look lovely, Sidonie,' she said. 'I will be praying that you and Jean have many happy years together.'

The evening sun was streaming through the windows when I walked into the Chapel holding a bouquet of gardenias from the courtyard. Jean was standing at the altar. When he saw me, his face lit up.

I took my place at his side. Father Beaubois began with the beautiful words of the Mass. We knelt at the altar rail. The words *Kyrie Eleison/Christe Eleison* were full of meaning for me: Lord Have Mercy/Christ Have Mercy/Lord Have Mercy. I prayed for mercy and goodness for us all.

When the Mass ended, we were surrounded by well-wishers. Mother Jerome had arranged for a small reception, with cakes and wine. Zezette and her husband were among the throng, and he raised a glass to toast our happiness. But soon Jean looked at me, and I at him, and we knew that it was time for us to be alone.

Berthe laughed. 'There were some plans for a *charivari,* but I've managed to persuade my husband and his friends not to.' This was a relief: it would not be ideal to consummate our marriage while strangers made an ungodly racket outside with metal pots and pans. 'Thank you,' I mouthed, and turned to Jean. 'Shall we say our farewells?' He nodded, and I shivered in delight at the look in his eyes.

Berthe and her husband had very kindly offered to let us use a room in their house for our wedding night. She walked there with us, opened the door, and showed us up the stairs. The room was under the eaves, with a four-poster oak bed, and looked out over a courtyard. Berthe had put candles on the bureau. She winked at us. 'Sleep well, *mes enfants.* Though I don't think you'll do much sleeping tonight.' I turned beet-red, and smiled. 'Thank you Berthe, and *à demain.*'

When we heard her footsteps going down the stair, we looked at one another. Jean lit the candles, and I put my bouquet of gardenias on the bureau. Their scent filled the air. Jean looked at me, and the tenderness in his eyes took my breath away. He traced the outline of my jaw with his finger, and very slowly and deliberately began to unbutton my dress. Very gently, he eased my dress from my shoulders, and it fell in a pool at my feet. 'God, you're lovely!' he said. His voice was hoarse, and I could feel his urgency.

When I put my hand on his chest, I could feel the mad beating of his heart.

I gazed into his eyes and, surprised at my own boldness, started to unfasten the buttons on his shirt. He ripped it off, swept me up into his arms and carried me to the bed. Outside, I could hear the soft sound of the rain falling against the roof, but inside there was only the play of light and shadow in the candle flames, as our bodies flowed together in a rhythm that it felt like something we'd always known, something infinitely magical and good and right. Jean was a revelation, and the unique combination of power and tenderness when he entered me took my breath away. I wondered if it was possible to die of a surfeit of bliss, but I knew that if I did die in his arms tonight, I would go to my grave happy. Berthe was right: we did not sleep much at all that night but the following morning I had never felt so awake, and so alive.

Holding hands, Jean and I walked down to the Convent. The rain had passed, and the weather was warm and sunny. We had arranged to have our things transported to the ship, and we wanted to make sure that Marthe and Marie were ready for the long voyage. Claudette and Clemence would come with us to France to help take care of the girls. Jean, while I was being fitted for my wedding dress, had taken care of the documents emancipating the remaining slaves at Les Chenes, and had spoken to a broker about putting the land on the market. Later, the funds would be put in trust for the girls. Fortunately, Jean had some income of his own, so we were able to pay for our passage, but we would have to be frugal until he established his legal practice and I was able to find a teaching position. With his hand in mine, in the Louisiana sun, I knew that together we could do anything.

It was evening when the boat pulled away from the pier. The entire Convent had turned out to bid us farewell. I could see the faces of Mother Jerome, Father Beaubois, Sister Fidelis, Berthe and her husband, all waving madly. Jean saw that my eyes were wet, and he put his arm around my shoulders. 'Are you sad to be leaving Louisiana, my darling?' he asked.

It was important for me to be honest, always. 'Yes,' I said. 'It will be wonderful to be in France with you, because France is, of course, our home country. But Louisiana has become home as well. Somehow I have a feeling that we will return one day.'

Standing at the rail, Jean and I waved until our friends were lost from sight, and the boat sailed off into the current of the great river, bearing us toward the Gulf and to France.

SUSAN CASTILLO STREET

Susan Castillo Street is Harriet Beecher Stowe Professor
Emerita, King's College London. She has published widely on
literatures of the colonial Americas, nineteenth-century
American literature, and the Southern Gothic; she is also a
published poet, with three collections, *The Gun-Runner's
Daughter* (Aldrich, 2018), *Abiding Chemistry* (Aldrich, 2015*),
and *The Candlewoman's Trade* (Diehard, 2003), a pamphlet,
Constellations, (Three Drops Press, 2016) and contributions to
major anthologies and journals. She lives between London and
the Sussex countryside.

Casket Girls

Discussion questions for book groups:

1. Both Sidonie and Immaculata dream of being heroes. What does heroism mean for each of them? Do they achieve their goal?

2. Although Sidonie and Joelle come from similar backgrounds, how do their aspirations and personalities differ?

3. How do Sidonie's views on religion and ethics evolve?

4. How is the natural world portrayed in *Casket Girls*, and how do the protagonists' views of Louisiana nature change?

5. Discuss the interaction between Sidonie and her students. What does she learn from the worldviews of Native American and enslaved women?

6. What prompts Sidonie to fall in love with Jean?

7. Compare and contrast the male characters in the book: Father Beaubois, Jean and Armand Ardoin, and the overseer, Bertrand.

8. Discuss power and powerlessness in the portrayal of enslaved people such as Palmyre, Imbangala, Octavia and Clotilde.

9. In many ways, the landscapes of Louisiana are haunted. By whom and what?

10. What impact does the past in Haiti have on the lives of Armand, Palmyre, Jean and Imbangala?

11. Imagine that you are writing the first chapter of a sequel to *Casket Girls*. Will Sidonie and Jean find happiness in France? Will they ever return to Louisiana?